UNLEASHED

V Plague Book One

Dirk Patton

Dirk Patton

Published by Voodoo Dog Publishing LLC

Printed in the United States of America

First Printing, 2013

ISBN-13: 978-1511500388

ISBN-10: 1511500387

Unleashed

Table of Contents

Also By Dirk Patton

The V Plague Series:

Unleashed: V Plague Book 1

Crucifixion: V Plague Book 2

Rolling Thunder: V Plague Book 3

Red Hammer: V Plague Book 4

Transmission: V Plague Book 5

Rules Of Engagement: A John Chase Short Story

Days Of Perdition: V Plague Book 6

Indestructible: V Plague Book 7

Recovery: V Plague Book 8

Precipice: V Plague Book 9

Anvil: V Plague Book 10

Merciless: V Plague Book 11

Fulcrum: V Plague Book 12

Hunter's Rain: A John Chase Novella

Unleashed

Exodus: V Plague Book 13

Scourge: V Plague Book 14

Fractured: V Plague Book 15

Brimstone: V Plague Book 16

Abaddon: V Plague Book 17

Cataclysm: V Plague Book 18

Legion: V Plague Book 19

The 36 Series

36: A Novel

The Void: A 36 Novel

Other Titles by Dirk Patton

The Awakening

Fool's Gold

Author's Note

Like many people these days, I'm a fan of apocalyptic fiction and am an avid reader and watcher of all things zombie or zombie-like. I used to work for a company that required my travel to the Atlanta area, and the hotel and swampy marsh described early in the book really exist just as described. In fact, I got the idea for this book while staying at the hotel when I got up one morning, looked out the window and saw a thick layer of mist lying on top of the water. Two locals, wearing waders and carrying long poles (I never found out what they were doing) were moving slowly through the thigh deep water looking for something, and their resemblance to shambling zombies was downright eerie.

I've read too many books and watched too many TV shows and movies where the writers, at least for my taste, spent way too much time padding their word counts with unnecessary descriptions, dialogue, and flashbacks. I wanted to tell a fast paced story and drop in nuggets of detail along the way, hopefully ending up with one of those books that you just have to see what happens next, over and over, until you look at the clock and it's way past your bedtime.

For those readers that are familiar with the Atlanta area, you will recognize some of the locations described, and you won't recognize others. I've taken a lot of liberties with different locations, changing them as necessary to make the story work. Anything that is not accurate is completely intentional.

Thank you for reading Unleashed, and if you enjoyed it, I would very much appreciate your positive review on Amazon.

Dirk Patton

You can visit my website at www.dirkpatton.com or like my Facebook page at www.facebook.com/RealDirkPatton or follow me on Amazon by visiting www.amazon.com/author/dirkpatton and clicking on "Follow".

Unleashed

1

The Boeing 737-800 banked slightly as it aligned for touchdown at Atlanta's Hartsfield Jackson International Airport. Slight turbulence caused a few bumps as we descended the last few hundred feet to the tarmac. The elderly woman beside me let out a slow sigh, like an inner tube deflating, as the landing gear thumped onto the runway.

My back and ass were sore from the four-hour flight from Phoenix to Atlanta with almost another hour in my seat before takeoff. I was in first class and had been the second person to board the plane. Part of me thought I should feel sorry for all the people jammed into coach, but I've logged enough hours in the air that I only feel relief that I now have enough miles under my belt that the airline always upgrades me.

As usual for Atlanta, we taxied so long that it felt as if the pilot was trying to drive the plane back to Arizona, but we finally made it to the gate. There was the normal scramble to stand up and be ready to go as soon as the Captain turned off the fasten seat belt sign and I quickly made my way down the jetway and started the long, weaving trek through the terminal.

Even though I was absorbed in reading all the emails that were popping up on my phone, it didn't take long to notice the increased security in the airport. Uniformed police were everywhere. Standing and watching the crowds. Walking in pairs. Working dogs along the crowded concourses. I was surprised when I boarded the airport subway train to see a uniformed officer in each car.

I fly in and out of Atlanta on business at least three times a month. I've never seen a cop in any of the train cars, let alone all of them. They looked alert and intense, not bored like a cop who gets assigned a security detail just because the politicians want things to look good for the public. I was glad to get off the train and exit to fresh air through baggage claim.

The curb was jammed with police vehicles of every stripe. Marked cars, vans and SUVs took up much of the space, but there were also a good amount of unmarked vehicles that were too new and shiny to belong to any agency that was not federal. Uniformed officers were very visible as well as a good contingent of unsmiling men wearing suits and small earpieces.

The usual crush of cabs and courtesy vans were continually being waved on, not allowed to stop. It seemed that no less than a dozen pairs of eyes were scrutinizing every traveler. Texting my wife to let her know I'd arrived safely, I made my way to the rental car center without any problems, checked a car out with minimal effort and got on the road to my hotel in Alpharetta.

Alpharetta is a suburb north of Atlanta, about forty-five miles from the airport. My company's corporate offices are located there, and it was my home away from home. Driving north from the airport there was again a very large and noticeable police presence.

Georgia State Police cruisers were sitting on the shoulder every three or four miles. Many of the overpasses, as I drove through downtown Atlanta, had a Trooper parked on them, standing at the railing watching the freeway traffic. Some were using binoculars to get a better look at vehicles or drivers that caught their attention. All looked like they were on high alert.

I thumbed on the rental SUV's radio and set it to scan for stations, hoping to find some news about what had triggered such a massive police presence. I've traveled a lot over the past decade or so, and this was comparable police activity to immediately after the attacks on the World Trade Centers on 9/11.

No news on the FM dial, I fiddled with the unfamiliar settings until I got the AM band and repeated the scan. Lots of talk. In fact, all talk except for a faint station that was playing mariachi music. The topics were about football, politics, or finance, anything except local news.

I shut the radio off and dialed my wife's cell phone back in Arizona, intending to ask her to look on the Internet for any news reports, but I kept getting a 'call failed' error from the phone. I finally gave up trying. I'd call her from the phone in my hotel room when I checked in.

The sun was low on the horizon when I parked at the hotel. It was a nothing special Hilton Garden Inn with the best features being that there was a Starbucks a couple of doors down, and it was walking distance to my company headquarters. Checking in I asked the desk clerk if he had heard any news that would explain all the police, but he hadn't and didn't seem at all interested. Handing my room key across he informed me about the breakfast that was served in the lobby each morning and jangled my nerves a bit with the news that the hotel's phones and Internet were down.

In my room, I dumped my bags on the floor and tried calling my wife again from my cell. Same 'call failed' message. I picked up the room phone and was momentarily excited to hear a dial tone, but when I pressed 9 for an outside line, I was only greeted with silence. I tried texting, but the message never sent, and I tried to access the Internet with my iPhone browser, but the connection timed out.

Experiencing some mounting anxiety, I clicked on the TV and sat on the edge of the couch cushion, lighting a cigarette as I waited for the TV to finish starting up. When it did, it tuned itself to the hotel's information channel. I quickly scanned, looking for any news. There was the standard assortment of pre-primetime shows for the first ten stations until I landed on CNN.

Someone was interviewing a soccer player about something I cared nothing about. I kept clicking and found MSNBC, equally devoid of any real news, then Headline News reporting on a market bombing in Iraq that had happened yesterday. Nothing. I tried my cell and room phone again with no better results.

I spent ten minutes surfing, looking for any information, then finally turned the TV off, grabbed my room key and car keys and headed downstairs. My office was only a couple of blocks away. I knew that we paid a lot of money for redundant and hardened data circuits that also carried our Voice Over IP telephone traffic. I was sure I would be able to make an outgoing call from the office.

Normally I would have walked, but I was a little spooked and didn't want to be far from my rental car, so I drove the short distance. I absently noted the swamp that filled the land bordered by my hotel and the street that led to the office. The sun was down by now, and there was a faint mist starting to form over the surface of the water. I'm not a superstitious man, and in my day was something on the bad side of badass, but I hit the lock button for the SUV's doors and felt better when they promptly thunked into place.

The parking lot at the office was empty but well-lit when I pulled in. It's large, stretching out from the building to a green belt on two sides, the swamp on the third. I parked as close to the doors as I could, not giving a crap about using a handicapped spot in an empty parking lot at night.

My key card tripped the electronic lock. I tugged open the heavy glass door, entering a marble-floored lobby. To my left was a receptionist area. When I picked up the handset off the massive phone bank sitting on the desk, there was no dial tone even though an extension light started glowing red. Not sure if there was something special that needed to be done to use this phone, I hung up, noted the extension light went out, then headed deeper into the building to find one that was not more complicated than a physics experiment.

I used my key card to access the executive conference room, the lights automatically coming on as I entered. A normal looking phone sat on a side table between a couple of leather chairs, and again no dial tone when I checked. I gently returned the handset to the cradle, not sure why I was careful to be quiet. Looking around the room, I spotted the large plasma display mounted to the wall, the remote control precisely placed in the center of the mahogany conference table that nearly filled the space.

My company subscribed to satellite TV service, and there were many more channels than what the hotel offered. Sinking into a plush leather conference chair, I spent the next hour surfing any news channel I could find. Nothing. Not even the normal news cycle. It seemed that every news outlet was pre-occupied with Hollywood gossip, pop culture puff pieces or interviews with minor celebrities. I don't watch enough TV to know if this was normal or something out of the ordinary, but it didn't make me feel any better.

After an hour, and multiple checks of my cell phone, the office phone, and the Internet, I gave up and decided to go back to the hotel and get some rest. I couldn't find any news to indicate there was anything strange going on in the world, and I passed my case of the willies off on being jet lagged and needing some rest.

I stopped at a convenience store and was only mildly surprised to see a sign on the door that read "Credit Card machine is down. Cash Only." I bought a six pack of beer, paid cash and headed back to the hotel.

Room service provided the burger and fries that I washed down with three beers before falling into bed and a deep sleep.

2

I don't know what woke me, but it was enough to bring me fully awake with creeping gooseflesh on my arms. The case of the willies from the evening before was back with a vengeance.

I lay there for a time, listening, but the hotel was quiet. It was too far from the Interstate to hear any late night truck traffic, plus I've found in the past that it is pretty well insulated and quiet as far as hotels go.

After a bit, I gave up on falling back asleep and rolled out of bed to check my cell. No calls, texts or emails, and now it showed no service. The room phone still had a dial tone, but nothing when I tried to get an outside line.

Turning the TV on, I dressed quickly in yesterday's travel clothes of jeans, polo shirt and running shoes. As I was tying the laces, the TV came up, and I got a glimpse of a harried news anchor with a look of horror on her face before the damn thing followed its startup programming and changed to the hotel information channel.

Cursing, I grabbed the remote and stabbed the channel button repeatedly with my thumb until I was back on the news station. When I saw the banner across the bottom of the screen, the remote fell out of my hand and clattered onto the glass coffee table.

"America Attacked – Millions Dead" the banner screamed. I read the words over and over as if they would say something different if I just read them enough times. They didn't. It took an effort of will to tear my eyes off the banner and look at the images on the screen and listen to the shaking voice.

Apparently, we were viewing New York City, but it looked more like hell on earth. The image was shaky and grainy from being taken at a great altitude, and as I listened it was explained that this was a feed from a military drone flying over New York City at fifty-five-thousand feet. Through the smoke and dust, all that was visible were ruined buildings that were on fire.

"- - again, at 11:33 PM Eastern time, a series of nuclear bombs were detonated in the greater New York City area. The information we have at this time is that there were nine separate detonations that all occurred within seconds of each other. We have received wildly varying accounts of the size of the bombs, but no formal information from the White House or the Pentagon at this time.

"New York appears to be mostly either destroyed or on fire. The population of the area attacked is greater than eight million and so far we haven't seen any signs of life. We're expecting a statement from the White House sometime this morning but we..."

The reporter paused, but the video feed of the destruction in New York continued to play on the screen.

After a few moments, "We're receiving unconfirmed reports of attacks on other cities on the Eastern Seaboard. These attacks are being reported as non-nuclear, but we don't have any other information at this time.

"The fires burning in New York are visible as far away as Philadelphia and Boston, and we're trying to get information on the direction of the radioactive fall...."

The screen went black for a moment then changed to the logo for the Emergency Broadcast System overlaid with a banner that read 'This Is Not A Test'. I grabbed the remote and pushed buttons, but every channel was displaying the same screen and over the TV speakers sounded the familiar high pitched tone unique to America's EBS.

I sat stunned, staring at the TV, not believing what I had just seen. This was the type of thing that only happened in the movies. Inactivity didn't last long before my need for information kicked in.

Remembering the clock radio on the nightstand, I dove across the bed and grabbed it, fumbling for the power button, then the AM band when only static was found on FM. Rolling the dial, I found some garbled stations, and then frantically reversed when I heard a strong voice that was static covered. It took some fine tuning before a male voice blared out of the tiny speaker.

"We have been attacked. The New York area is just gone after multiple nuclear blasts. There are also unconfirmed reports of nukes being detonated in DC and LA. The following cities have had some type of nerve agent released in them and should not be approached: Boston, Philadelphia, Washington DC, Baltimore, Charlotte, Miami, Atlanta, Memphis, Chicago, St Louis, Detroit, Minneapolis, Cleveland, Dallas, Houston, Denver, Los Angeles, San Francisco, Portland and Seattle.

"Reports are that the nerve agent was released from aerial sprayers attached to small planes that flew over each of these cities and their suburbs. What the nerve agent is we still don't know, but it seems to be dangerous whether inhaled or just touching the skin. Many witnesses have reported paralysis and convulsions within seconds.

"Communication across the country has been disrupted, seemingly as part of a pre-planned Homeland Security response. All telephones, data lines, TV and radio have been shut down, and I'm sure we'll be shut off as soon as we're found."

There was the sound of papers and objects being shuffled and it was obvious this was an amateur who was keeping his microphone open while he gathered his thoughts. There was some unintelligible conversation in the background then the voice resumed.

"This is Max. I'm back with you to tell the truth about the events that are unfolding in our great nation. Unconfirmed reports are now coming in from several places across the country of missile launches. These would be American ICBMs, and so far we've had reports from Kansas, South Dakota and Texas of missiles launching and appearing to head west.

"Now if this was the Russians, those missiles would be heading north to go over the pole, but they're heading west. That's not the Middle East either people. That's China. Or North Korea."

More muted conversation then Max came back on, "And another report of launches, this time from the Gulf of Mexico. Reported missile launches from far off shore. My guess would be submarine based missiles. They headed west also.

"The end of times is here my friends. Prepare for the anarchy that will reign in our world.

Don't approach cities, and if you're in a city, get out! We aren't the only country with missiles, and I don't believe for a moment that we can launch and no one else will.

"Take food and water with you. Get away from the cities. I only hope you exercised your second amendment right and have a gun to protect yourself and your loved ones."

There was a pause and the longest exchange yet of muffled background conversation. It seemed that Max had someone helping him gather information, but the only way they could relay it to him was face to face. After a few moments there was total silence, then the scrape of a match being struck and the inhalation of smoke.

"My friends," Max paused to exhale what sounded like a big hit off a joint, "I'm getting some more information, and I just don't know what to believe, but I'll pass it on, and you decide. Victims of the nerve agent are coming out of the paralysis and attacking anyone around them.

"Someone has suggested that maybe the nerve agent is triggering hyper-aggression, but my youngest boy thinks that the Zombies are finally here." Max tried a derisive laugh but didn't pull it off. It turned into more of a strangled cough.

"We have to move now before the Federals find us and shut us down. Keep listening to this frequency for the truth about what's happening. This is Max and God save us all."

There were a couple of snapping sounds then nothing but static. I peered at the radio dial but couldn't make out the frequency. I thought it was 650 AM and was digging through my backpack for reading glasses when the power went out and plunged the room into darkness.

3

I involuntarily held the breath that caught when the lights went out. It seemed the whole world was holding its breath. After a moment, I slowly let it out, then caught it again when I heard the faint sounds of a woman screaming. It was coming from outside, and I carefully made my way to the window. The sun was coming up, and there was light around the curtains, but it had a strange quality to it.

Opening the drapes, I looked down from my fifth-floor window onto the swamp I had driven around the night before. A dense layer of mist hung just above the surface of the water, but what caught my attention was downtown Atlanta, thirty-five miles to the south. Atlanta was burning.

Dense, black smoke billowed across much of the horizon, lit from within by what must have been thousands of fires as the city was consumed in flame. My mouth fell open as I stared at what looked like a Hieronymus Bosch painting of hell. How did it all happen so fast? Was civilization really that fragile?

I don't know how long I would have stood staring at the inferno, but another of the screams that had first brought me to the window pulled my attention away. In the swamp, wading through water to her waist was a woman who appeared to be completely nude. Behind her trudged three men.

As I watched, one of the men stepped into what had to be a deep hole and fell forward into the slime choked water. Instead of swimming he started thrashing violently until he sank from sight. His two companions never even turned their heads or tried to help him, just maintained their pursuit of the woman.

They were gaining on her as she struggled through the water. She turned her head to see how close they were and let out another scream. This was the one that got me moving. I burst out of my hotel room door and collided with an immensely fat man that was standing in the hallway.

I bounced off him like a tennis ball, spinning sideways but managing to maintain my footing. I started to apologize, but the words died in my mouth when he turned towards me, and I saw his face.

Morgue grey is the only description I could come up with for the color of his skin, at least under the weak, emergency lighting. His eyes were solid red orbs, no pupil or iris visible. Black blood dripped from both ears and nostrils, and his lips were skinned back, exposing bleeding gums. He took a lumbering step toward me, raising an arm in my general direction and making a sound that was halfway between a snarl and a wet gurgle.

The nerve agent was here! I didn't know if I could help him, but I knew I could help the woman in the swamp if I could just get past and to the fire stairs.

I slipped to the side, and the man cocked his head as if he was tracking the sound of my movement, then swiveled his bulk towards me.

"Hey, buddy. I need to get downstairs to help..." I didn't get to finish the sentence before his head snapped into direct alignment with me and he charged.

Maybe stampeded is a better word given his size, as he was at least four hundred pounds of beef on the hoof heading directly at me. A gurgling snarl was coming from his mouth as he built up speed. Well, not exactly speed as he was slow with an uncoordinated gait, but in the tight space, he didn't need to be a speedster.

I remembered Max's words, 'the nerve agent is causing hyper aggression', and that was sure what I was seeing. I dodged to the side, threw an elbow with all my two hundred and thirty pounds behind it to his kidney and slipped sideways as he slammed into the wall with a crash that rattled the doors around us.

Immediately, from several of the rooms, a clatter of fists banging on wood and the same snarl started. I looked around to make sure none of the doors were opening behind me, then turned back to the mountainous threat that had righted itself and was coming toward me, showing no sign of injury from either my elbow strike or the impact with the wall.

The way to the fire stairs was now clear, and I could have run, but I didn't like the idea of leaving this guy to shamble after me. Dancing to the side I leaned out and delivered a straight kick to the side of his left knee.

The already overstressed joint gave with a snap, and he collapsed to the floor, still snarling but showing no indication of pain. He tried to stand, and when the ruined knee couldn't support his bulk, he started pulling himself towards me on the carpet with his arms. Now I turned and ran.

I hit the fire door at speed, trusting momentum to carry me through any threats that waited on the other side, but the stairwell was empty. I raced down the stairs, some of my speed fueled by the creepy encounter I'd just had in the hall, some by the thought of the struggling woman I was trying to save.

I hit the ground floor exit door with a bang and crashed through. Thirty feet in front of me, the parking lot ended at a grassy border where the swamp began. The woman was another fifty feet out in the water, struggling, and started screaming for help when she saw me. The two men chasing her were closing the distance on their prey. I was too far away to tell if they were in the same condition as the fat man I'd just put down.

To my right in the parking lot were three more men who had been moving towards the woman's screams but had now changed direction towards me. They were close enough for me to see the solid red eyes and hear the same snarls and hisses coming from each of them. Oh shit!

Remembering how the fat man seemed to track me by sound, I froze in place, holding my breath, but they kept coming, snarling continuously. Then the woman in the swamp screamed for help again, and all three of them swiveled towards her and picked up speed.

They weren't what I'd call fast, but they could cover a good amount of ground in a relatively short time. Their pace was probably comparable to an average person taking a leisurely stroll. I could easily move faster than them.

I met the eyes of the woman, and even from a distance I could see the terror and fatigue on her face. She wasn't going to last much longer if I didn't do something. Looking around for any type of weapon, I spotted a sapling pine tree at the end of the building that had two large landscaping stakes driven into the ground supporting it. These are the thick wooden poles that are about seven feet long, with a sharpened point that looks like a pencil, driven into the ground and tied to a young tree for support.

As quietly as I could, I stepped onto the grass, moved to the tree and started working one of them loose from the ground. Apparently I made more noise than I thought because the man closest to me swiveled his head in my direction, then changed course directly for me. He was less than 10 feet away when the stake finally released from the ground. I ripped it away from the tree tie downs. Just like the fat man, his eyes were red orbs and blood trickled from his ears and nose. As I raised my weapon, his pace didn't falter, and the blank expression on his face didn't change. He just kept coming.

I planted my feet well apart for balance and swung the length of wood in a giant arc like I was trying to break open a piñata. It struck the side of his head and snapped off a good eighteen inches of its length from the impact. The man dropped like the proverbial sack of potatoes and lay still. I hoped he was down for the count.

The sounds of our scuffle had attracted the attention of one of the other men from the parking lot who was now heading directly for me. I'm a big guy at six-two and two hundred and thirty pounds, but this guy had, at least, three inches and fifty pounds on me. There was no way I wanted to get into a grappling contest with him.

Risking a glance, I noted the woman had stopped moving and was sobbing as her pursuers from the swamp and parking lot closed the distance. Time was running out quickly. With few options, I charged my attacker with the pole extended like a lance and buried the sharpened end into his stomach. There was a moment of resistance when it met his flesh. Then I could feel the sharp point push through the skin and bury in his abdomen. This guy was finished.

I pulled back, wanting to use it again and was caught unprepared when he grabbed it and yanked, pulling me with it. I barely recovered in time to avoid his clumsy attempt to wrap me up in a bear hug and backed away in shock. He stood there, gently swaying, with at least a foot of the stake buried in his guts. There was no indication that he felt any pain from a wound that should have put him down permanently. He started to turn to face me. I grabbed the wood and wrenched it out of his body before he could get another grip on it.

I stepped to the side, raised the stake over my head and using both hands drove the sharp point directly into his blood red right eye. If I had hoped that I could take him out with a thrust to the head, I was disappointed. The taper on the end was too shallow, and while it pierced his eye, it was stopped from reaching his brain by the eye socket. I felt the hard stop in my arms and quickly pulled away, stepped back and swung for the bleachers. The pole snapped again when it hit the side of his head, leaving me with a four-foot club with a nasty 10-inch splinter as thick as my thumb protruding from the end.

He was slowed down but not stopped. Quickly lunging forward, I buried the splinter in his left eye, my forward progress stopping when it hit the inside of the back of his skull. Pulling the club out of his head, I spun towards the swamp as he hit the ground with a meaty thump.

The woman was still standing in place, but she had stopped sobbing, apparently too terrified to even cry. The two men that had pursued her through the swamp were no more than ten feet behind her, and the remaining parking lot guy was about fifteen feet in front. She was in water to mid-thigh, and I could now tell that she wasn't completely naked.

She was wearing what looked like a gold sequined G-String, and nothing else. *Stripper*, flashed through my head, but she could just as easily have been dressed that way in the privacy of her own home when she had to run for her life. See how my mind works?

I had a moment to evaluate the situation. When she had gone quiet, her pursuers had stopped in place. More evidence for my theory that the blood red eyes indicated blindness, and they could only track us by sound. What I didn't know was how long they would stand still waiting for a sound before they started flailing about looking for their prey.

Up on my toes, I circled around behind parking lot guy, holding an index finger to my lips to tell the woman to stay quiet. In position behind him, club held in my right hand like a spear ready to be thrown, I hissed loud enough for him to hear but hopefully not alert the guys in the swamp.

He immediately snapped his head around and let out the start of a gurgling snarl. He never finished the turn or the sound because I buried the splinter in his eye the second I had a target. He dropped, snapping off most of it in his head as he went down on the asphalt.

"Run to me now!" I hissed at the woman, frantically making the universal 'come here' wave, bouncing up and down on the balls of my feet.

She threw a look over her shoulder and then seemed to gather her strength for a final surge through the thigh deep water. Pulling ahead of her pursuers, she gained speed as she reached water that was below her knees, high-stepping the last few yards onto the grass and sprinting to me.

The woman was exceptionally pretty, even soaking wet and streaked with muck from the swamp, but I didn't have time to admire her. I expected her to run and stop beside or behind me, not throw herself against me and wrap her arms around my neck. She looked to be in excellent physical condition and was tall for a woman, nearly as tall as me despite being barefoot, so the unexpected impact of her body nearly knocked me off my feet.

She was breathing like a locomotive, shaking like a leaf and doing her best to squeeze me in half but wasn't making a sound. The men in the swamp weren't so quiet. When she had surged forward and made a lot of noise splashing through the water, they had also started forward, snapping their jaws and snarling. I was getting a much better look at them now, both of them with the red eyes and blood dripping from ears and noses.

The guy on the left looked like a college student. Hair too long to have a real job, silver stud glinting in his right eyebrow, made all the more noticeable by the contrast to the red eyes. The other one was a Georgia State Trooper. Amazingly his Smokey Bear hat was still in place, and his weapon was still holstered, yet he gave no indication he was even aware he was armed as he approached us.

I still had a four-foot wooden club in my hand but didn't like my odds against these two. I wrapped my arms around the woman's waist, pressed my mouth to her ear and mumbled so only she could hear, "They hunt by sound. I'm going to move us. Don't make any noise. Quiet!"

I lifted her free of the ground and slowly began stepping sideways towards the open parking lot. By this time, they had reached the edge of the asphalt and both stumbled with the footing change then came to a stop. I had moved us maybe a dozen feet out of line with their advance, and when they stopped, I froze.

They stood in place, swaying slightly, heads tilted back and swiveling side to side. I could hear them sniffing the air, and it scared me even more than I already was. Hiding from something hunting you by sound was difficult, but manageable. Sound *and* smell? Exponentially more difficult. There was no breeze to worry about upwind or downwind, but that could change at any moment, blowing our scent directly to them.

Normally I would have enjoyed holding a G-String clad woman tight against me, but let me tell you this was anything but erotic. She was absolutely silent but still shaking. Whether cold from being in the water or out of sheer terror, at least she had calmed her breathing. Unfortunately, she still had me in a stranglehold and if our hunters charged us we were goners.

Carefully wrapping my right arm around her waist, I slowly exerted pressure to the side, peeling her off of me. She resisted at first, and then relaxed enough for me to guide her to a position beside and slightly behind that would allow me freedom of movement. My hand still resting on the small of her back as she moved, I started to step back with her and managed to kick what was probably the only empty beer can in the parking lot.

The can clattered across the pavement loud enough to, no pun intended, raise the dead. Both heads instantly snapped toward us, and they charged, arms extended forward and wide to sweep in any prey that they might have run past. I pushed her hard towards the larger open parking area, and side slipped the Trooper's grasp, his fingers brushing my sleeve.

His snarl rose an octave and he whirled in my direction, the college student turning towards the sound. I stepped in and rammed the now blunted stake into the bridge of the Trooper's nose with all my weight behind the blow. I might as well have been striking a tree for all the good it did. His head rocked back from the force, but he didn't even notice the nasty gash that opened on his face and the blood pouring down from his broken nose. He just kept snarling and advancing.

Backpedaling, trying to get room to fight, I tripped over my own feet and crashed to the ground. The stake slipped out of my hand and bounced across the pavement. For a moment they paused, heads tracking the direction of the clatter, but somehow they knew their prey was still right in front of them. They started forward again, looming over me. I was scrambling backward like a crab on its back when the woman started yelling.

"Hey, assholes! Over here! Come get me if you're man enough. Come on you fuckers. I'm right here!" I risked a glance in her direction. She was screaming at the top of her lungs and jumping up and down, waving her arms.

They stopped their advance on me, and I froze, holding my breath. I knew she was trying to distract them, and the courage she was showing was incredible. Their heads turned toward her, but they didn't move.

"Come on you dickless cocksuckers! I'm right here!" She screamed even louder, and they finally turned away from me and started a slow rush in her direction.

Looking for my club, I spotted it farther away than I thought it could have gone but also spotted a nicely rounded rock about the size of a small cantaloupe laying at the edge of the parking lot. Quietly scrambling to my feet, I scooped the rock up in both hands and charged the cop with it raised over my head. He heard my approach and turned in time for me to cave in the front of his skull. He crumpled to the ground at my feet without a sound.

The college student was still moving toward the woman's screams, and she was getting pretty creative in her names for him. Ripping the Trooper's pistol out of his belt holster, I rushed the college student. The weapon was a standard police issue Glock nine mm, and I quickly made sure a round was chambered. Coming up beside the last attacker I put the pistol's muzzle against the side of his head and pulled the trigger, blowing blood and brains across the parking lot. He dropped as silently as the Trooper had.

Breathing hard, I stood still and stared at the man I'd just killed. Was he a man, or had I killed some kind of zombie thingy? The little voice in my head was moments away from a hysterical giggle when I contemplated the idea of zombies, but I pushed it down. I stepped back to the Trooper and took the duty belt off the body, strapping it around my waist and holstering the Glock.

The belt had two magazine pouches, both with fully loaded spare mags, a pair of handcuffs strapped to it at the small of my back, and various rings and hooks that I had no idea what they were for. At the moment, all I cared about was the weapon and extra ammunition.

“Thank you,” the woman had come over to me while I was robbing the dead. “You saved my life.” She stood in front of me wearing next to nothing, covered in filth, and yet didn’t appear to be the least bit self-conscious.

“I think we’re even. That was pretty brave to draw them away like that.”

She looked away then back at me, “It was as much self-preservation as anything. They’ve been chasing me for over two hours. I couldn’t have survived much longer without your help. You’re the first normal person I’ve seen.”

I was shocked to hear that. “Where were you? What happened?”

“I dance at a club not too far from here, but you can probably guess that from looking at me,” she made a ‘look at this’ gesture with her hands in front of her nearly nude body. “I was on stage when all hell broke loose.”

4

Rachel Miles reached behind her back and undid the clasp that held up her gold sequined bikini top, slid it over her shoulders and as it dropped to the stage used her upper arms to press her breasts together to the hoots and howls of the crowd. She was a third of the way through her second song, on stage at the Toy Box gentleman's club north of Atlanta.

New York had been nuked hours ago, but the fat pig of a boss that owned the club refused to close early and had threatened to fire her if she didn't go on stage. The bar was half full of hardcore drinkers, but Rachel couldn't see any of them because of the bright lights focused on her performance.

Ashley Box was her stage name, and while she certainly had the looks and personality to make money in strip clubs, she detested the job. But where else was she going to make five hundred dollars a night without having to spread her legs? It paid the bills, her college tuition, and left plenty more for her to drive a decent car and maintain a small but nice apartment in a good area of Atlanta. One more year of med school and she'd be able to quit. She'd have her MD without the crushing mountain of student loan debt that most of her classmates were accumulating.

Rachel was staring at the lights, bent over to show her assets to the crowd, when the first sounds of a disturbance reached her over the pounding music. Accustomed to bar fights, and confident the bouncers, Rick and Jeff, both former Georgia offensive linemen, would make quick work of any troublemakers, she ignored the sounds and kept swaying her hips in time to the music. The six-inch stiletto heels she was wearing were killing her feet tonight, and she couldn't wait to finish this set. She only had one more, then could head home and get some studying done before collapsing into bed.

The song ended and the stage lights dimmed, allowing Rachel a view of the disturbance by the door that was growing in volume. She was shocked to see Sandy, a small blonde that danced in the club and supplemented her income giving blowjobs in the parking lot, hanging on to Jeff's thick neck and biting him. What the hell was going on? Rick, the other bouncer, grabbed her by the hair and ripped her off Jeff's back, flinging her against the wall. He turned to his friend who had collapsed onto the floor and appeared to be going into convulsions and didn't notice that Sandy bounced off the wall and got back to her feet like nothing had happened.

Her eyes were blood red, visible even from across the room, and her mouth, neck and chest were slick with Jeff's blood. With a scream, she leapt onto Rick's back as he bent over his injured friend, locked her arms around him and sank her teeth into his overdeveloped neck muscles. Rick howled in pain, lurched to his feet and reached over his head to grab the much smaller woman. He tore her loose, lifted her in the air upside down and drove her headfirst into the floor where she collapsed and didn't move again. Rachel clearly heard the snap when Sandy's neck broke.

"Crazy fucking bitch!" Rick roared, staring down at the body.

Rachel felt like she was in a waking nightmare, and things got worse when Jeff rose to his feet behind Rick. His eyes were the same blood red as Sandy's had been and he let loose with a bone-chilling snarl. Rick whirled when he heard the sound and tried to raise a hand to fend off the charging attack from Jeff, but it was too late. They both crashed to the floor, sending tables, chairs and a few customers scattering like leaves. Jeff clamped on to Rick's throat with his teeth and growling and hissing the whole time started ripping flesh. He finally tore open the carotid artery and was soaked in a jet of bright red arterial blood.

Rachel stood gaping in horror, her mind unable to comprehend what her eyes were seeing.

She remained frozen in place until a hand reached out from the edge of the stage and grabbed her left ankle, savagely pulling her leg out from under her. She fell on her ass in the middle of the stage, her ankle held in a painful vice like grip. Lying on her back she raised her head and started to scream, but it died in her throat when she saw her attacker was another of the dancers named Lisa.

Lisa's eyes were the same blood red color, but only the whites and her face was smeared with blood. She leapt over the chairs and the brass rail at the edge of the stage, snarling deep in her chest and pulling on Rachel's leg. Rachel tried to scoot away but the grip on her ankle was too strong, and she only succeeded in allowing Lisa to pull her closer. Rachel started kicking with her free leg, feeling the solid blows connecting, but having no effect on the grip on her ankle. Lisa pulled further up onto the stage, her upper body now pinning Rachel's left leg and her grip shifted to Rachel's thigh.

Now Rachel started to scream for help, pulling her right leg up and kicking in a stomping motion, once, twice then a third time. Suddenly the grip went slack, and Lisa stopped moving. Rachel continued to scream for a few moments then dared to look and had to turn her head to the side and vomit on the stage.

Her stomp kicks while wearing stiletto heels had gashed open Lisa's face to the bone in two long, ragged tears. The third kick had buried the entire six-inch spiked heel directly into Lisa's left eye. The shoe was stuck in the dead girl's skull.

Rachel reached down and unbuckled the shoe, slipping her foot out and using it to push the body off her left leg. She abandoned the other shoe as well, standing up and surveying the bar. There were only a few customers left that didn't have blood red eyes, and they were now far outnumbered by the gang that was led by Jeff, the bouncer. As she watched, two of the customers went down screaming under the weight of Jeff and two dancers.

She started to back towards the stage exit when Carl, the bartender, leapt over the bar with a shotgun in his hands. Rachel's first impulse was to run to him for protection, but she stopped and watched as he fired two deafening blasts into the body of a man charging him with a snarl. The shotgun blasts shredded clothing and flesh and knocked the man to the ground, but moments later he was back on his feet. Rachel turned and fled the stage, hearing three more blasts from Carl's shotgun.

Rachel raced through the dressing area, elbowing a shorter girl aside that leapt at her as she passed, then hit the emergency fire door at full stride and burst into the back parking lot. She was barefoot and wearing only a G-String, but had never been so happy to be outside in her life.

The fire door opened into the back parking lot. Rachel took a moment to get her bearings, flooded with relief when she saw a Georgia Highway Patrol cruiser with blue lights flashing screech to a stop in the parking lot. She started running towards the cop who was getting out of his car with a nightstick in hand.

Neither of them saw the two young men with long hair, dressed in jeans and polo shirts come out of the dark behind a pickup truck until they were already on the Trooper. He had time to swing the nightstick once, making a solid connection with one of the men's upper leg, but the blow had no effect, and they swarmed him and carried him to the ground. Both of them started biting and clawing, but he was able to fight them off and move to the far side of the cruiser where he stood swaying and shaking.

Rachel ran around the perimeter of the parking lot, keeping vehicles between her and the two young men. She reached the cop and grabbed his arm, feeling safer despite having watched him be attacked. The Trooper turned his head and looked at her, sweat pouring off his face.

He had bite marks on his forearms and hands, and deep fingernail scratches on his face.

He opened his mouth to say something, but all that came out was a gurgle. A moan followed, and the pain reflected in his eyes must have been agonizing. He started to crumple to his knees, only Rachel's support keeping him upright.

The two young men were circling the front of the cruiser and Rachel tugged the Trooper's arm, leading him around the back of the car. She was intent on keeping it between them and their attackers. They kept circling, gurgling and snarling, red eyes glowing from the huge neon sign mounted to the roof of the strip club.

On their second circuit of the cruiser, the Trooper stopped cold. Rachel lost her grip on his arm as she kept going a couple of steps. She turned and gasped to see blood dripping from his ears and nose. As she watched, his eyes widened and seemed to bulge forward out of his head as if under great pressure, then first one then the other turned completely red.

"Oh my God," Rachel breathed, and took another step away from the Trooper.

With a snarl he stepped toward her, arms raised to shoulder height and out at forty-five-degree angles. Perfect for sweeping any prey into his grip. Rachel turned and ran.

5

For the moment, the woman and I were the only living things in the parking lot other than a fat, glossy black crow sitting on the roof of a red Chevy. It cawed at us several times before flying away to the north, away from the inferno that was downtown Atlanta. The woman approached me slowly, carefully looking me up and down, her eyes nervously pausing on the weapon in my hand.

"When you fought them, were you bitten? Scratched?" Her voice was low and husky, raw from all the screaming she had been doing.

"What?" I asked. Everything was too surreal and now this crazy, naked woman wanted to know if I'd been bitten?

She took a cautious step forward, "Were you bitten?" She spoke slower this time, as if I were a child.

"No. They never touched me. Why?"

She came closer and continued her visual inspection. "I watched that one and his friend," she pointed at the young man I had shot in the head, "attack and bite the Trooper. Within one to two minutes he was just like them and trying to kill me."

I stood staring at her, breathing harder than I needed, but the adrenaline from the fight was still in my system.

I said, "They bit him? And he became like them? This is crazy. You're describing something like a zombie or a vampire."

She raised her chin and stared back at me defiantly, "I may look like a brainless bimbo at the moment, but I know what I saw. The Trooper was fine, normal until he was attacked. He was bitten and scratched and in less than two minutes I watched him change into one of them and start trying to kill me."

She crossed her arms under her breasts, and while I would have thought it difficult for an almost naked woman to look dignified, she managed to pull it off.

"OK, so I guess I believe you. Any idea what the hell is wrong with them? Why are they trying to kill us?"

She relaxed slightly and moved over to stand next to me, looking down at the body of the young man. "I was hoping you would know. All I know is New York got nuked last night. The owner of the club where I work wouldn't close, and a few hours ago these things started attacking people in the club."

I looked back over at the dead Trooper, then out across the swamp. A couple of hundred yards away there were four figures wading through the water in our direction. Uh Oh.

I scanned the parking lot and found no threats, but out on the perimeter road that came from my company's office building, there was a small group of figures walking towards us. I slowly raised my arm, Rachel turning to see whom I was waving at. They didn't acknowledge my greeting in any way. Oh, shit.

"We've got to get out of here. Now!" I said.

I took her hand in mine as if it was the most natural thing to do and broke into a trot across the parking lot to where my rental SUV was parked. Half way there I skidded to a stop and slapped my pants pockets with a feeling of dread. No keys. They were in my room on the fifth floor of the hotel. There was no way I could climb the stairs, get my keys and get back before the approaching threat cut off our escape.

"What's wrong?" She asked me, not letting go of my hand.

"No keys. They're up on the fifth floor in my room. I don't suppose you know how to hot-wire a car, do you?"

I didn't expect an affirmative answer, and I didn't get one. The look of horror on her face told me what I needed to know. We were on foot, multiple threats approaching from at least two directions, and she was already exhausted from fighting her way through the swamp. Exhausted or not, we didn't have a choice. We had to run.

6

We ran across the parking lot, her slightly behind and to my left, holding my hand. My right was my shooting hand, and I was keeping it free and available to draw the pistol if I needed it. Considering these things, alright I guess I was ready to call them Zombies even though they weren't actually reanimated dead, apparently hunted by sound and smell. I didn't want to have to fire off the weapon and attract every one of them within hearing distance. I suspected they used sound for finding their prey at a distance, then sound and smell when they closed in.

Cutting the corner on the parking lot we made it to the road with about a hundred yards of clearance from each group of Zombies – infected? - but turned left towards the ones in the swamp. The water would slow their progress and let us get by them. I settled into a fast jog, the woman staying with me and maintaining a death grip on my hand. I was impressed. As freaked out as she had to be, as I was, she was staying with me and not slowing me down or complaining.

We didn't make much noise, just the sound of my running shoes and her bare feet on the asphalt along with our heavier breathing, but the infected in the swamp detected us and changed direction to pursue. I glanced over my shoulder and saw the group, all male, behind us. They were almost speed walking, but not quite. They weren't moving that much slower than we were.

My instinct was to push harder and open up some distance, but I was worried about tiring. I had slept most of the night and was relatively refreshed and strong. I was pretty sure she had been up a long time, certainly all night, and had to be exhausted from her run through the swamp.

Ahead, the road curved slightly, then straightened as it approached a large intersection with shopping on each corner. Several cars were piled into each other in the intersection. I hoped we would find one of them drivable with the keys still in the ignition.

My hopes were dashed when figures appeared from behind the vehicles as we approached, and started coming towards us. Three large parking lots on the northeast, southeast and southwest corners were virtually empty of cars as none of the retail shops had been open when all of this happened. But there were groups of figures in each of the parking lots that all turned in our direction as we approached.

The northwest corner, across the intersection and to our right, was a massive parking lot for a Wal-Mart Super Center. Cars were scattered across the parking lot, some belonging to employees and some to shoppers that needed something in the middle of the night. There weren't any infected milling about that parking lot.

"There," I pointed with my right hand, making sure she knew where we were going.

"How?" She gasped a response.

"Be ready to run flat out. We're going through the ones ahead." I indicated the infected in the middle of the intersection, directly ahead of us.

There were four of them, three men and a woman if it matters, and they were bunched up at the trunk of a mid-sized Japanese sedan as they tried to locate us. I would have preferred to go around, but there were broad drainage ditches on either side of the road as it approached the intersection and I didn't want to get bogged down in mud or hurt by some unseen debris that lay hidden in the weeds. A sprained ankle or broken leg would be a death sentence.

Coming up on the intersection, I angled to the left, intending to keep the crashed cars between the infected and us. I also wanted a good look at the condition of the vehicles. The first one we came to was a ten-year-old Chevy Malibu, and I dismissed it outright when I saw the crumpled front end and puddle of anti-freeze on the pavement under the engine. It was crashed into the side of a twenty-five-year-old Ford F-250 pickup that had been jacked up and outfitted with oversized wheels and tires.

The truck was a four-door behemoth, and its damage from the accident was limited to the left side of the rear bumper. It looked in nearly pristine condition, despite its age, and I was counting on the owner having cared for the drive train as meticulously as he had the appearance. Only one problem. When I dashed up to the driver's side door, I could see there were no keys in the ignition.

The infected in the intersection had split up, the three men bumping and groping their way around a couple of cars, but the woman leapt onto the hood of first one car, then another. How she was doing this blind was beyond me, and she also seemed much more coordinated and agile than the men. She sprang to the roof of the Chevy that was crashed against the Ford truck, then with a loud snarl on into the bed of the truck. She was moving fast. Too fast and getting too close.

I drew the pistol which was ready to go and side stepped to get a better angle on her. That's when I saw her eyes. Blood red like the men I'd seen up close, but only the whites of her eyes were red. She still had irises and pupils and could obviously still see. This slowed me for a heartbeat, long enough for her to leap at us. I fired a single round that punched through her forehead and blew out the back of her skull. Her body went limp in mid-leap, falling to the ground at our feet.

I wanted to take a closer look at this one, but the men were fast approaching with snarls of their own, and the infected that had been following us down the road were now less than fifty yards away. I quickly glanced around, and my blood ran cold when I saw the number of infected converging on us from the surrounding parking lots. First things first. I raised my arm and fired three shots, and each of the men closest to us dropped dead to the pavement.

The one in the middle was a guy about my age, early forties, built like a tank and wearing jeans, muddy work boots, and a Ford hat. It didn't take Colombo to deduce he was likely the driver of the truck, and I dashed forward and felt in his pants pocket with my left hand, pistol in my right ready to fire if he so much as twitched. In his right front pocket was a wad of keys, and one of them was a big silver deal with Ford stamped prominently on it.

We were running out of time and had to take a chance. If we got in the truck and this wasn't the right Ford key, we'd be trapped, surrounded by infected. If we didn't get in the truck our only open path was the Wal-Mart, and while the parking lot was still empty, I didn't hold out much hope that the store wasn't infested. I didn't want to find out.

"In the truck!" I guided her towards the open driver's door and followed her into the cab. She scooted over to make room for me but stayed close, so we were touching when I sat behind the wheel and slammed the door closed. I inserted the key in the ignition, and it fit! I took a breath, held it, and turned the key. It didn't turn. Wrong Ford.

"Goddamn it! I'm sorry." I said, then the infected were at the doors, and I just had time to hit the electric lock button before hands started pounding on the windows and body of the truck.

A woman who looked no more than twenty leapt onto the hood and squatted directly in front of me, staring through the heavy windshield. Just like the female I'd killed, the whites of her eyes were blood red, but she still had irises and pupils. Looking into those eyes, I couldn't see any sign of humanity, just primal hunger and predatory intelligence.

I looked out the side window at a man who was hung up bumping against the outside rear view mirror. His eyes were the same solid red I'd seen back at the hotel parking lot. I wasn't sure why there was a difference, but I was sure that women had just become what I always thought they were. The most dangerous members of the human race.

The woman sitting next to me was shivering. It wasn't cold. The sun was well up. The cab of the truck was quickly growing hot and stifling. In normal times, I would never have presumed to try to comfort her, but these weren't normal times. I put my arm around her shoulders and pulled her to me and just held her while she went from shivering to outright sobs. The female infected squatting on the hood watched us like a cat watches a mouse hole.

When she got her emotions under control, the woman straightened up slightly without breaking contact with me. She wiped her eyes with a grimy hand and sniffed back the last of her tears. Around us were now at least fifty infected, the men bumping into the sides of the truck and hammering on it with their fists and forearms in what seemed to be frustration.

The women were what really scared me. Another woman had leapt onto the hood and squatted on the passenger side, staring at us through the windshield with her bloody eyes. Three more women had leapt into the bed of the truck and stared at us through the back window. At least ten more stood a few yards back from the truck, beyond the milling males, and just stared patiently.

"What do we do?" She sat up straight, and I slowly moved my arm away from her shoulders. I found myself moving slowly because of some instinct that told me not to startle the women sitting on the hood of the truck. If any of them had enough intelligence remaining to find a rock to smash the truck's windows, we were toast.

"Good question," I answered. "But I don't have a clue at the moment. It's going to get real hot in here real soon, and I don't think we'll survive the day without water."

I slowly turned my head and looked around the cab of the truck. Clean and organized. Nothing out of place. I carefully checked the glove box, which only held the owner's manual and a small flashlight. I slipped the flashlight into my pocket after making sure it worked.

Under the back seat was a small tool case with an assortment of sockets, Allen wrenches, and various other tools in it. I held the case in my lap, considering my options, then pulled out the largest screwdriver in the kit.

She looked at me but didn't question what I was doing as I leaned forward and inserted the tip of the screwdriver into the truck's ignition. When I leaned forward, the woman on the hood did as well until her face was almost touching the windshield. She curled her lips back in a snarl I could hear clearly through the heavy glass. Her teeth were stained red, and there was debris, I didn't care to think about the origin of, stuck between them.

Ignoring her, I pushed down on the screwdriver while twisting to the right and there was a sharp snap from the ignition. Unfortunately, that was all that happened. I didn't know what I was doing. I'd never stolen a car before, only seen episodes of COPs where some kid gets busted for grand theft, and he got the car running by 'punching' the ignition. I had to try something. I didn't want to die today.

7

The heat and humidity in the cab of the truck had become oppressive. Sweat poured off both of us, soaking into the upholstery and continually adding to the humidity. We had slept off and on throughout the day, startling awake whenever there was an aggressively loud impact on the truck from the crowd of infected. I didn't think we had long. We were both severely dehydrated and recently she had started to cry out when her legs were racked with spasms from muscle cramps.

The two women on the hood had not moved all day. Amazingly they had remained in the same squatting position despite the long hours and growing heat. They may have been infected, but they still had human skin, and both showed signs of severe sunburn.

Neither indicated that they felt any discomfort. I, on the other hand, had a left arm that was nearly blistered from the sun coming through the driver's side window. However, with four more hours of direct sun on the cab of the truck and surrounded by infected, this was the least of my worries.

"We're going to die in here, aren't we?" Her voice was a dry mumble, barely audible above the constant snarling and banging from the infected.

I thought about giving some upbeat answer, something to give her hope, but, in the end, decided she deserved honesty. "Yes, I think so. We likely don't have much longer in this heat."

She sighed deeply, the sound conveying her resignation to her fate.

"I don't even know your name," she said.

I smiled. Names had not been at the top of my priority list. "I'm John. John Chase."

"Very nice to meet you, Mr. John Chase. I'm Rachel Miles. And I never thanked you for saving my life earlier." Her voice gained a little strength as she talked, but she was still mumbling. Her face was shrouded with stringy, sweat soaked hair.

"I think you did, but you're welcome. Not sure I did you any favors." I looked out the windshield and met the eyes of the woman directly in front of me. She snarled, but otherwise didn't move.

Rachel was quiet for a long time. So long, in fact, I was thinking about checking to see if she'd passed out, then she started talking in a low monotone. She told me she was in Medical School and only a year away from graduating. She told me about growing up in North Carolina and moving to Atlanta after high school.

Her parents were both dead, and she had no siblings or other family. She talked about dancing in the strip club and sleeping two hours a night so she had time to study and attend class. Then she told me the story of how she and I met in a hotel parking lot with infected people trying to kill us.

I listened to her talk, undoing my pre-conceptions about a woman stripping for a living. She had a job that paid the bills so she could do something better with her life. That was more than most people could say these days. Then I wondered if there was anyone other than us left to worry about careers and having a better life.

I happened to glance at the ignition with the screwdriver hanging out of it while I had these thoughts and my heart leapt in my chest. From the back of the ignition switch, hanging below the dash and barely visible, were several wires. Apparently knocked loose when I broke the switch earlier, these had to be the wires that would start the truck. After all, what was an ignition switch other than a device that mechanically closed an electrical circuit so the engine would start and run?

I grabbed the tool kit off the floor where I had dropped it and dug through until I found a small pair of wire cutters. Rachel picked up on my excitement and sat up straighter, adrenaline momentarily overcoming dehydration and muscle cramps. I reached under the dash and carefully clipped all the wires, then stripped about an inch of insulation off each of the cut ends.

Methodically, I started touching wires together; blue to white/blue, green to white/green, red to white/red; the red to white/red finally lighting up the dash and the radio started playing a country music CD. I had found the equivalent of the 'key on' position of the switch.

Rachel grabbed my arm in excitement. A small cry escaped her lips. The two female infected on the hood of the truck could tell something was happening. They became agitated, bouncing up and down while snarling and slapping the windshield with their hands.

I firmly twisted the wires together and picked the blue and white/blue to try first for the starter. I touched them together, and nothing happened. I fumbled as I grasped the green and white/green wires, caught my breath and touched them. There was a spark, and I got a hell of a jolt of electricity that made me release them, but I was rewarded with a momentary whine from the truck's starter.

To her credit, Rachel kept her mouth shut. She could have easily been one of those people who have to offer an opinion or suggestion or criticism about everything, and I was mildly surprised that she remained silent. Obviously, at some point in her life, she had learned the lesson of keeping your mouth shut if you didn't have something constructive to offer.

The women on the hood became more agitated. It spread like wildfire to the crowd of infected that surrounded us. Dozens of pairs of fists started pounding on the glass and body of the truck. I looked out the windows and noticed for the first time that the crowd had grown sometime during the day to what I guessed was in excess of a hundred and fifty. Maybe all the noise the ones that originally cornered us made had attracted others and others and so on.

The truck lurched precariously. I looked to my right to see the entire passenger side lined with large males. They were hitting and pushing on the truck. There was enough flesh there that if by accident or design their efforts happened to coordinate they could flip us over. With a burst of fear, I returned my attention to the wiring. I tried not to let myself be distracted by the increasing range of motion of the truck as the infected rocked it side to side.

Firmly grasping the starter wires, I made sure I was only holding them on the plastic insulation and firmly touched them together. The starter whined for a couple of seconds then the big diesel engine rattled to life. The starter continued to whine and I quickly separated the wires that powered it. It went quiet, the diesel settling into a smooth but loud idle.

I bent the wires away from each other and sat against the back of the seat as one of the female infected on the hood threw herself against the windshield with a screaming snarl. The blood dripping from her nose made a smear on the glass that reminded me of a Rorschach ink blot test, but I didn't have time to look at it and figure out what I saw in the shape.

The horde of infected around us went into a fever pitch of snarling and slamming into the truck, and now both women on the hood were repeatedly slamming themselves into the windshield in an attempt to get to us. In front of us was a crashed VW and there was a small Toyota behind us with no room to steer around either one. I put my foot on the brake and shifted the Ford into reverse, the heavy duty transmission going into gear with a satisfyingly hard clunk.

I said, "Hold on," and hit the accelerator. The truck lurched backwards and crunched into the side of the Toyota. I kept feeding throttle. The oversized tires grabbed the pavement, and we pushed it back ten feet.

One of the female infected on the hood had lost her balance and fallen off when the truck suddenly moved, but the other held to the lip of the hood closest to the cab with one hand and pounded her fist on the windshield with the other. The one who had fallen off was on her feet and would have already leapt back on the hood, but the crowd that had been on either side of the truck had flowed into the empty space left when I had backed up, and she was temporarily blocked.

In the rearview, I could see several infected that had been between the back bumper and the Toyota that were now crushed. What would have been mortal wounds to a normal human, rendering them unable to move, seemed to have little effect on the infected other than to slow them down because of damaged hips and legs.

I shifted into drive, turned the wheel to point us around the crashed VW, and fed throttle to the big truck. We moved and immediately started feeling thuds from the suspension as the push bar on the front knocked infected down moments before we rolled over them. Large males held onto the mirrors on each side and the females in the bed began smashing their heads against the rear window. My adrenaline surged when I heard the rear window crack from one of their impacts. I started swerving back and forth across the road to throw them off balance.

Our speed quickly built to forty, and I kept swerving. This kept the females in back distracted, just trying to stay in the truck and the males on each side held on with a death grip. Their legs swung almost horizontally every time I cut the wheel. The female on the hood was now holding on with two hands and smashing her head into the windshield, but the thick glass was harder than the human skull, infected or not.

She cocked her head back and launched a massive head butt into the glass. I felt as much as heard the impact, and watched the feral light in her eyes die just before she went limp and slipped off the front of the hood and under the big tires.

"Holy shit," Rachel said. "Did you see that? She just bashed her own brains out trying to get to us."

I was concentrating on driving and keeping our unwelcome passengers occupied and didn't answer. The males on either side started smashing their heads into the side windows each time the momentum from a swerve brought them back against the truck. I risked a glance in the rear view mirror and did a double take.

The two females in the bed had found a way to brace themselves and were preparing to start attacking the rear window again. I turned my attention back to the road and slammed on the brakes, the big truck skittering across the asphalt in protest. The females in back slammed forward into the back window, but not as an attack. One of the males lost his grip and tumbled forward, coming to rest thirty feet down the road and immediately lurching to his feet and starting towards us.

I sat watching him and watching the two women in back in the mirror. The remaining male was on Rachel's side, and he started pounding on the window with his fists and smashing his head into the glass. Infected were hurrying towards us from surrounding parking lots. The horde that had previously surrounded us was in hot pursuit about 200 yards behind.

"What are you doing? Go!" Rachel's voice pitched up an octave on the last word, and she grabbed my right arm hard enough to hurt.

"Wait," I said and kept my concentration on the mirror.

The infected in front of us had almost reached the push bar when I floored the accelerator and stood on the brake pedal. Diesels aren't known for neck-snapping acceleration, and I needed a sudden surge forward for what I wanted to do. The big engine quickly built to a roar. As the rear tires started to break free, I let off the brake and kept my right foot hard down on the throttle.

The truck shot forward, battering the male in front out of the way, but the best reward was watching the females in the rear tumble backwards out of the bed over the tailgate. I had timed it perfectly. As they were standing up, the sudden acceleration was like pulling a rug out from under their feet.

In the mirror, I could see them hit the pavement, tumble, then gather themselves and start pursuing us. Not only were they more agile than the males, they were faster too, moving at a very fast run. Nothing short of a flat out sprint was going to out distance them. Maybe.

We were finally free of all of our riders except for one male that stubbornly clung to the passenger mirror. Rachel shied away from that side of the truck, pushing against me as he started trying to break the glass with his head again. Ahead of us an abandoned delivery van for the Atlanta Journal Constitution sat half in the traffic lane. I headed directly for it at 50 miles an hour.

The infected was still holding on when we reached the abandoned vehicle, and I steered us to neatly peel him off the side of our truck. There was a thud followed by a splash of blood onto the side window. Then he was gone.

I had managed to not lose the passenger side mirror in the maneuver, and looking in it I could see him lying in an unmoving heap in the road behind us. His head must have hit the back of the newspaper van at speed, and judging by the amount of blood on our window it had pretty much disintegrated like an overripe watermelon.

I steered us back to the middle of the road and reduced speed, making sure I would have enough reaction time in case we needed to avoid an unseen obstacle. Rachel leaned over to the side window and peered out to make sure we didn't have any other riders. My side was clear and when she sat back she looked at me and smiled.

"That was pretty quick thinking." She said.

I smiled back, hands shaking and stomach fluttering from the adrenaline that was still pumping through my system.

I said, "Climb into the back seat and make sure the bed is clear. I don't see anything in the mirror, but all I can see is the last couple of feet of the bed and the inside of the tailgate."

"All clear," she said a moment later, crawling back into the front seat and resuming her position, pressing against me. I didn't complain, and I didn't read anything into it. I had even stopped noticing she was basically naked. I was freaked out. She had to be at least as scared as I was. Physical contact with another human was still part of our animal instinct, and there was absolutely nothing erotic or sexual about it.

8

The big Ford's air conditioning worked well. Within a few minutes, we were both shivering from the cold air blasting out of the dash vents, but neither of us wanted to turn it off or down. We were dehydrated, hungry and exhausted. Adrenaline was keeping us going, but I knew we'd crash and burn as soon as it bled off.

As I piloted the truck down the road, slowing frequently to avoid wrecked and abandoned vehicles, infected continually appeared and shuffled towards us. It quickly became apparent that the rattle of the heavy duty diesel engine announced our presence and provoked a Pavlovian response from them.

More often than I liked, an infected appeared from behind an empty vehicle and stepped into our path. They were smashed down by the massive grill guard mounted to the front of the Ford, then pulped under the oversized off-road tires.

Finding the Ford was a blessing. Short of an armored car or a military vehicle, it was about the best transportation for our situation. With the added benefit of a beefy four-wheel drive system, we weren't restricted to pavement.

I glanced at the dash and noted the fuel tank was over three-quarters full. I also noticed a switch on the dash marked 'fuel' and realized the truck had dual tanks. I flipped the switch to change tanks and the gauge quickly swung all the way past the full indicator. God Bless rednecks!

"Where are we going?" Rachel leaned forward and adjusted the AC vent that was blowing directly on her.

Her question hit me like a slap across the face. Katie! My wife was in Arizona. I'd been so focused on the crisis at hand, I'd forgotten about what she must be going through. Guilt at temporarily forgetting about her washed over me, sapping most of my strength, my shoulders slumping.

"What?" Rachel asked, looking around in a panic, thinking my reaction was due to some new threat.

"My wife. Katie. She's in Arizona. Alone." I squared my shoulders and started thinking.

Katie was a farm girl, raised in Michigan by a Marine, who survived Pearl Harbor and the fighting in the Pacific. She'd been the only girl, and the baby, in a family with three boys. She could fight and shoot with the best of them, but had she had the chance to arm herself and fight?

"I'm going to Arizona." I announced without giving it a second's thought. "I'm going to find some food, water, and weapons. Then I'm going to get my wife."

Rachel was quiet, staring ahead through the windshield for a time before she spoke, "If you'll have me, I'll help you. I've got no one, and from the looks of Atlanta, I don't even have a home anymore."

If I'd been thinking even half way clearly, I would have been amazed at how quickly we had adjusted to a world that had just fallen apart around us.

9

We drove a couple of miles south before finding a major road that turned to the west and looked like it would provide us access to the expressway that ran through the area. The road I was looking for was GA 400, an eight-lane toll road that serviced the northern suburbs of Atlanta.

But what I needed was a map. I knew the geography of the US pretty well, but I didn't know the routes to get out of the Atlanta area without getting lost in suburban and rural areas.

We drove and pushed through more wrecks, regularly bouncing infected off the front of the truck as we made our way towards the expressway. The road we were on swept up a rise. As we gained elevation, I could see the signs for toll road entrances to go north and south.

I slowed as we approached the northbound onramp, not knowing which way to go, but hesitant to go any closer to the inferno that Atlanta had become. Idling past the entrance we crested the overpass and I brought us to a gentle stop.

The northbound lanes were partially clogged with crashed and abandoned cars but were passable if one drove slowly enough. Southbound was completely empty for as far as I could see.

Infected males shambled on the pavement, turning to face us as they heard the sound of the idling diesel engine. More of them crawled on the pavement and in the grassy median, apparently too damaged to walk, but not damaged enough to be down for the count.

I looked south, to my left, and the scene was repeated. Raising my eyes, I could see the thick, oily, black smoke boiling up from Atlanta. Even in the daylight, it glowed within from the fires burning in the city. Rachel gasped and grabbed my arm, pointing ahead across the overpass.

Not a mile ahead of us was a gas station with attached convenience mart. I didn't see anything more unusual than abandoned cars and shambling infected.

"What do you see?" I asked, eyes searching.

"The power's on at the gas station. Look at the sign."

She was right. A vintage Union 76, giant orange ball sign was rotating away as if everything was normal. I made a decision without consciously thinking about it and stepped on the accelerator.

As we approached, I noted the empty and abandoned vehicles at the pumps, several of them with gas nozzles still inserted in their fuel tanks. I also noted the half dozen or so infected that turned at our approach and started shambling towards us. They were all male, and moving slower than the females I'd seen, but that didn't make them one bit less dangerous.

They met me in the road, fifty yards shy of the gas station. I used the truck to dispatch the largest concentration in one crushing, grinding and bloody impact. Two remained on their feet and turned to follow us as I whipped into the station's parking lot. A green handled fuel nozzle, green for diesel, was visible sticking out of the tank of an abandoned VW Jetta. No opportunity like the present.

"I'm getting out to get that nozzle out of the car," I said to Rachel, pointing at the VW. "When I have it clear, push the car out of the way so I can top off our tanks. I don't know when we'll be able to find fuel again."

We screeched to a halt behind the VW, and I eased us forward until our front bumper crunched into the car. Throwing the transmission in park, I took a quick look around and jumped out of the truck, pistol in hand. Rachel slid behind the wheel and dropped the big truck's transmission into drive, ready to push.

Tearing the nozzle from the VW, I stepped back and she hit the throttle. The Ford's tires grabbed the concrete of the gas station driveway and with a protesting squeal of rubber and crumpling metal, shoved the small car forward.

The pump was still activated from the VW owner's presumably interrupted fueling, so as soon as I inserted the nozzle into the Ford's fuel tank and squeezed the lever, fuel started flowing. Rachel rolled her window down.

"Two coming up behind you," she warned, sounding as calm as if she was talking to me about the weather.

These two were the survivors from the group I'd bashed in the street and were now only about ten yards away. Both of them were making that snarling, gurgling sound that set my hair on end. I stepped away from the pumps, raised the pistol and dropped both of them with two quick head shots. Glancing around, I counted at least twenty more infected converging on the noise I was making, the closest more than two hundred yards out. Fortunately, I still didn't see any fast moving females.

"Stay with the truck," I shouted to Rachel and ran across the concrete apron to the convenience mart doors.

I stopped at the closed glass door and peered in. Everything looked so normal. The lights were on; the shelves were stocked, and there wasn't any sign of disturbance. Running out of time, I yanked the door open and stepped in, pistol at the ready, whistling loudly to draw out any infected. I gave it five seconds and when there was no answering snarl I lunged for the counter and grabbed a fistful of plastic shopping bags.

Shoving the pistol in my waistband, I ran to the glass door fronted coolers and filled several bags with bottles of cold water. Next, I scooped up armfuls of candy bars, protein bars, canned food; anything that looked like it was edible and would travel well.

Arms loaded, I dashed for the door, praying I wouldn't meet an infected in such a defenseless position. Just before I pushed out I glanced at the counter and stopped short when I saw the road atlas display. Reversing course, I was juggling heavy shopping bags to reach for one of the thick map books when Rachel started honking the truck's horn.

I looked out the front door and saw a female infected staring back at me. She pushed on the door, which fortunately only opened out. When it didn't move, she started banging on it with her fists; face pushed to the glass and lips peeled back in a snarl.

I looked over her and saw the converging crowd was now less than forty yards from the gas pumps and closing ground fast. Grabbing the atlas, I juggled the bags back into a stable position and ran directly at the door. I'm a big guy, and the female infected looked like she had been a high school or college-aged girl, and soaking wet couldn't have weighed more than 100 pounds.

I hit the door in full stride, blasting through and sending her tumbling back and away from the point of impact. My new map flew out of my hand and went skittering across the parking lot.

Seeing me coming, Rachel leaned across the seat and popped open the passenger door. I ran, skidding, to the side of the truck and dumped my looted goods into the cab. I heard the snarl and slap of feet behind me and reached for my pistol, but my hand was tangled in the plastic shopping bags. Leaping back, a bag full of canned goods came with me, swinging from my right wrist, the tough plastic refusing to break.

The infected was right there, running at me, leaping, eyes wide, lips skinned back from bloody teeth, a snarling scream coming up from her throat. Not even thinking, just reacting, I stepped to the side and swung the heavy bag of cans. I swung hard. The bag hit her squarely in the face and exploded open, cans of chili and soup flying in every direction.

The impact stopped the infected in mid-leap, and she crashed to the ground, immediately jumping back to her feet and turning to attack. Hand free of the weight of the bag I pulled my pistol and shot her in the forehead, stepping over her body as it was falling. I had to get the nozzle out of the truck's tank and the cap back on so we didn't lose precious fuel as we drove away.

A male infected met me by the pump, and I dispatched him with another well-placed shot, yanked the nozzle out of the tank and let it drop to the ground as I fumbled the fuel cap back on. I had glanced at the pump's readout and was surprised that the truck had held almost fifteen gallons in the partially empty tank.

Quick and dirty math told me I probably had two, fifty-gallon tanks. I was betting the truck would get around fifteen miles per gallon, so we should be good for close to fifteen hundred miles before we ran out of fuel. That wouldn't get us to Arizona, but it was sure as hell a good start.

Rachel had scooted over and closed and locked the passenger door, and I was starting to step up into the cab when my left leg was yanked out from under me. I hit the ground hard, breath whistling out of my lungs. Lying there, I was momentarily paralyzed as my body refused to respond. A crawling infected, he must have been under the VW and worked his way back, gripped my right foot and started pulling himself up my legs, teeth snapping the whole time.

His head had just reached my feet, and he bit down on my right foot. The shoe saved me for the moment; then my body started responding again. I took a deep breath, yanked the pistol out of my pants, took careful aim at my attacker's head and pulled the trigger. Nothing. Either a misfire or the weapon had failed to lock open when it ran out of ammunition.

I started kicking the infected in the forehead with the heel of my left foot and manually cycled the automatic pistol's slide, but it locked open, empty. A snarl above me heralded the arrival of another infected, ready to fall on me and have a feast. I kept kicking, trying to scoot away from them both, but the damn thing had a hold on my foot like a Terrier on a rat. It wasn't letting go.

Looking up, I prepared to fend off the latest dinner guest. Hoping I would be able to crack his skull using the empty weapon like a club, I was startled when a shadow leapt over me from the cab of the truck.

Rachel landed on both feet, astride my upper body and swung the tire iron with both hands. If Hollywood was still in business, I had the perfect Wonder Woman for them.

The tire iron connected with a sickening crunch and the infected dropped like a puppet with cut strings, bloody head bouncing on the concrete a few inches from mine, dead red eyes staring at me. Rachel spun, dispatched the male chomping on my shoe in the same fashion and grabbed my shirt, screaming at me to get in the truck.

Scrambling to my feet, I followed her bare ass into the cab, slamming the door behind me. Before I could even hit the lock button, fists started pounding on the window trying to get to the prey that was escaping. I dropped the tranny into reverse, hit the throttle and roared backwards a few yards, then into drive and swung around the VW, crushed a few infected in the process and turned back east onto the road with a skittering of tires.

I headed to the toll road ramps, bounced over the median, and turned onto the southbound off ramp heading north against the direction of travel for those lanes. I hadn't seen another vehicle moving since the evening before and driving against traffic seemed a better idea than driving closer to Atlanta.

My breathing finally slowed down as we settled into a steady forty miles per hour on the toll road. Rachel took a couple of deep breaths also. I could feel her body shaking as the adrenaline drained off. After a mile or so she picked through the bags on the floor, pulling out a bottle of water for each of us.

"I don't suppose it would be too much to ask for you to get me a shirt the next time we stop, would it?" She asked with a perfectly straight face, handing me a bottle of water.

10

The water revived us as we drove, and we devoured several of the protein bars I had liberated from the gas station market. Even with all of the sugar and protein, I was exhausted and started to get concerned about finding a secure place to spend the night.

We had driven north on GA400 for a few miles before heading west on surface streets. We didn't have a plan other than getting away from the inferno that was Atlanta. We soon found ourselves in a residential neighborhood with neatly maintained lawns and tree-shaded streets.

Some of the houses we passed had obviously been abandoned in a hurry, garages standing open and empty. Others looked buttoned up tightly. Some of these were occupied, blinds twitching open as the sound of the truck's big diesel rattled down the quiet streets.

I slowed as we approached a four-way intersection where two police cruisers completely blocked the road, roof lights flashing. No one was visible, and one of the cruiser's doors was standing open. Easing to a stop fifty yards short of the intersection, I scanned the area looking for any threat.

Despite not seeing any danger, the short hairs on the back of my neck were standing on end. I rolled my window down as I scanned the neighborhood, but all I could hear was the idling of the diesel. Not wanting to turn off the engine, I eased the transmission into reverse and backed into an empty driveway, as the street was too narrow to make a U-turn with the big truck.

The sound of roaring engines reached me as I was shifting back into drive and two sedans, both Toyotas I think, screeched out of adjacent driveways and slid to a stop in front of me. I was blocked in, a closed garage door only feet from my rear bumper. I didn't hesitate to floor the throttle.

The diesel engine roared, and the rear tires screamed in protest as the truck lurched forward and crunched into the sedan on my left. Time seemed to slow down, and I saw the white oval of a face behind the wheel of the car as the big Ford bulled it aside. From the corner of my eye I registered movement to my right and then bullets were smacking into the cab of the truck.

"Down," I screamed to Rachel as the path in front of us opened with a rending of sheet metal.

Rachel dove to the floor and rolled herself into a ball in the passenger side foot well. The truck was accelerating away from the ambush, but moments later a bullet punched through the rear window of the truck, then the windshield, traveling a path where her head had just been.

I took the first side street I came to, the truck threatening to roll up on two wheels as I wrenched it through the turn without letting off the throttle. A final bullet pinged off the back; then we were clear. Expecting pursuit, I kept on the speed with an eye on the mirrors, but nothing appeared behind us. A couple of miles and several turns later I felt it was safe to slow down.

"What the fuck was that?" Rachel asked as she climbed back onto the seat.

"That was the human race at its best," I answered, taking another turn to get us heading west once again. "World's always been full of assholes, and I'm guessing these guys either wanted the truck, you, or both."

Rachel didn't have a response to that, and we were quiet for a bit as I kept pushing us towards the west. The neighborhoods were all the same, a mix of obviously abandoned houses and others that were occupied by people hunkering down.

We hadn't seen any infected in some time, and I stayed on high alert for any more ambushes. We were poorly armed and in no way able to fight off a concerted attack. I knew many of the houses probably had guns and ammunition in them but was hesitant to stop.

Reaching Georgia Highway 20, I continued our path west, dodging abandoned car accidents and the occasional roving band of infected. We saw no more people on the streets, but the farther west we went, the more infected we encountered. The males slowly shambled after us, but the females charged us at a frightening speed. I didn't think we would last long on foot trying to outrun them.

It was now fully dark and after the third time a screaming infected female ran into the side of the truck, scaring the shit out of both of us, we decided it was time to find a secure place to stop for the night.

"There was a service station with roll up doors about two miles back," Rachel said, placing her hand lightly on my arm. She was exhausted and spooked; the light touch a plea to get off the road.

"Let's see what it looks like," I said and cranked the truck through a U-turn.

The service station looked like it had once been a chain gas station but was now an independent automotive repair shop. I drove past, slowing slightly, and didn't see any obvious danger. U-turning again, I wheeled into the parking lot and backed the truck to the single service bay.

Loosening the Glock in the holster to make sure it would draw smoothly if needed, I grabbed the tire iron and stepped down out of the cab.

"Slide over and be ready to back into the bay when I get the door open." I said, slamming the truck door before Rachel had a chance to respond.

I watched for a second to make sure she got behind the wheel, then stepped behind the truck and tried the door. Mercifully it was unlocked, and I was able to raise it with a squeal of poorly lubricated metal.

Moving out of the way, I slapped the side of the truck as an all clear, and Rachel quickly backed into the garage. Turning to step in behind her, my only warning that I was being attacked was the slap of feet on pavement.

I spun around in time to meet an infected female that launched herself at me from a full run. She wasn't a big woman, but 110 pounds hit me square in the chest and knocked me flat on my ass.

The tire iron flew out of my hand, clanging across the garage bay. I got my hands in front of me and locked on her shoulders, holding the snapping teeth at bay, and with a mighty grunt, I shoved her away. She flew a few feet and hit the front bumper of the truck with a sickening thud, scrambling back to a crouch faster than she should have been able to.

Fumbling for the pistol and raising it, I snapped off a shot as she launched herself like a missile. I was happy to see the long-dormant skills hadn't atrophied too much, as the hollow point round punched through her face and continued on to blow out the back of her head.

Frozen for half a second, I stared at the twitching corpse then swiveled to scan the driveway. I didn't see any additional threats, but then I hadn't seen the female that had just nearly killed me. Standing, I kicked the corpse out of the garage and jerked the door down, slapping a locking pin home to secure us inside.

"How do I shut the engine off?" Rachel asked out the open driver side window. "We don't need to asphyxiate ourselves after surviving this long."

Opening the door, I reached across her bare legs and disconnected the two wires that kept the engine running. The diesel clattered to a stop and silence descended in the garage, the ticking of the cooling engine the only sound.

I rolled the truck window up, locked the door and told Rachel to stay put. The next several minutes were spent checking the entire garage and office area and making sure all the entrances were secure. Satisfied at last, I returned to the truck and motioned Rachel out.

Stepping stiffly from the cab, she looked down at the puddle of blood on the floor from the infected I had shot. Then her gaze moved to the front driver side tire, which was completely flat. A hole the size of a half dollar was visible in the sidewall.

Unlike in the movies where you see the hero shoot someone in the head and everything behind that person gets splattered in only blood and brains, in real life there's also a bullet that exits the back of the head and can still cause damage. The shot I was so proud of had blasted through the infected woman's skull and torn into the sidewall of the tire.

My body cried for sleep, but I wasn't going to rest without making sure our transportation was ready to go. Finding a floor jack I raised the truck and got the tire changed. I searched the garage, but they apparently didn't sell tires, so we were stuck going forward without a spare. I still put the ruined tire and wheel into the back of the truck in case we could find a replacement tire as we traveled.

Next, I inspected the truck for damage. The gleaming push bar on the front bumper was now scuffed and scratched from battering our way out of the ambush, but it was still solid. There were numerous bullet holes in the truck's sheet metal and glass, as well as the cracked rear window from the infected female that had tried to head-butt her way in. I reinforced the glass as best I could with duct tape.

Raising the hood, I checked over the engine. Hoses and belts were good; oil and coolant were fine as well. Closing the hood, I looked to the back of the garage bay and noticed a roll of heavy gauge wire mesh. Having seen how quickly our windows were failing, I dragged the wire over to the truck, then went in search of tools.

I had finished covering the back window with the wire mesh, cut to size and attached around the edge of the glass with sheet metal screws into the truck's body when Rachel returned. She was barefoot and wearing a set of mechanic's coveralls that would have been large on me. She had wet hair and a clean face.

"Think that will stop them?" She asked, combing her fingers through her hair.

"It will, at least, slow them down," I answered, driving the first screw for one of the side windows. "You look better."

"I feel better. I'm just glad the water is still on."

Rachel watched me work for a few moments, then stepped up beside me and started helping. Working together, we had all of the truck's glass covered in less than an hour. Stepping back, I appraised our handiwork. It wasn't pretty, but I doubted the glass by itself would survive another day.

We spent another half hour gathering jugs of motor oil, anti-freeze, brake fluid; anything we thought the truck might need. I found a couple of cans of pressurized tire inflator/sealer and threw them in with the haul, then got it all stowed securely in the bed of the pick-up.

We filled every bottle we could find with water from the small sink in the bathroom off the garage office and secured it in the back seat. Two boxes full of tools I selected went into the bed and were strapped down tightly.

Finally, I searched the entire building for weapons but found nothing except a rusting filet knife. Never knowing what use it could be put to, I tossed it into the truck and headed to the bathroom to clean up as best I could.

Exhausted, but cleaner, I returned to the truck to find Rachel curled up on the back seat fast asleep. Carefully, so I didn't wake her, I crawled into the front and lay across the seat on my back. I fell asleep in seconds, the pistol resting on my stomach with my right hand on top of it.

11

"Max here again with the truth about what's happening. Information is sketchy, but I'll tell you what I know and what I think I know.

"First, don't approach cities. The cities that were attacked are death traps. The effects of the nerve agent that was released are deadly to both those exposed to it as well as those who were not initially infected. The exposed are coming out of comas in a hyper-aggressive state and will attack anyone not already exposed. I don't know how or why this is happening, but I've got dozens of reports of people being attacked and ripped to shreds by their friends, family or neighbors.

"I've also personally seen women that have been exposed, infected I guess, so aggressive that I can only compare them to a lioness. They are fast, don't seem to feel pain, and are nearly unstoppable. The infected men I've seen are just as dangerous, but slower and much less coordinated. I can't explain it, but I'm sure there's some scientist somewhere that can.

"As far as I know the infected aren't contagious, but I think it's a safe bet that if they have any of the nerve agent on their skin or clothing, you would be infected by coming into contact with them. Reports are that the infection is spreading.

"The government continues to remain absent, and reports are that the entire command structure of the US Government has retreated to hardened bunkers and is communicating with the military via secure satellite links. Civilian communications of all sorts remain offline.

"There is severe civil unrest in the cities that were not attacked. Rioting, looting, fires burning out of control. Avoid the cities at all costs. It's only going to get worse.

"More missiles have been launched, some going north which can only mean Russian targets, but most going west. There have been no reports of retaliation, and so far I've had no luck in reaching anyone outside the continental US to find out what's happening in the rest of the world.

"We've had to move twice in the last twelve hours. Once to avoid military forces that were tracking our signal, and again to escape a large group of infected. We're ready to move again before the military triangulates our signal, and we get a visit from one of the drones they so love to use.

"Again, avoid the cities. Avoid the infected at all costs, and don't trust the authorities. I don't know why they've abandoned us, but at this point, they can't be trusted. Until my next broadcast, be safe."

The signal cut off before Max finished speaking the word "safe", and was replaced with the sound of static.

I had awakened to a hot and humid Georgia morning and turned on the truck's radio to see if there was anything broadcasting. As before, there was only static as I scrolled through both the FM and AM bands, so I had left the radio on, tuned to the frequency on which I'd first heard Max. When I returned from the bathroom, I was rewarded with his update.

Rachel was still in the back seat, silent and unmoving, and I thought she was still sleeping until she spoke.

"Why would the government cut us off like this? Shouldn't they be doing everything they can to help us?"

I thought about it before answering, "I don't have any idea. It doesn't make any sense to me either."

She turned over and looked at me for a few minutes before climbing out of the backseat and disappearing into the bathroom. She returned a few minutes later and hopped up on the lowered tailgate next to me.

"I don't suppose we have a toothbrush or any toothpaste." She said.

"I'll put it on the list." I said, trying to make it sound light-hearted but failing miserably.

Rachel looked over at me through tangled hair, "So what's the plan?"

I let out a big sigh before answering. By nature, I was a person who analyzed situations and made decisions quickly. The US Army had recognized this trait early and honed it to a fine skill. College and work after the army had polished it, but at the moment, I felt like I was in a daze and thinking at about half of my normal rate.

Trying to get my brain in gear, I started to lay out our situation and options.

"We're cut off from any form of government help or protection. In fact, I haven't even seen a cop since this all started. Infected are roaming the streets and will attack as soon as they see us, but I think the bigger danger may be from other people.

"This just started, and already we've had to escape an attempted ambush. Fortunately, those guys were amateurs or we might have been in some trouble. We might not be so lucky next time.

"I'm heading for Arizona, to get to my wife. I don't know what it's like there, but if anyone can hold out it will be her. That's at least seventeen-hundred miles through what sounds like will be hostile territory. No comfortable hotels or restaurants along the way.

"I guess the first question is what are you doing?"

I looked at her and reached into my shirt pocket for a pack of cigarettes that wasn't there. Another item for the list the next time I looted a store.

Rachel shook her head, the tangled hair swirling around and hiding her face.

"I don't have anywhere better to go, and sure don't want to be on my own, so I guess I'm with you." She answered while staring between her swinging feet at the stained garage floor, reaffirming her prior commitment to go with me.

I was relieved. She had already shown a good head for crisis situations, not to mention saving my life at the first gas station we'd stopped at.

"Good. First thing we need is more supplies. These protein bars aren't going to last long. Just as important, we need weapons. We're going to have to defend ourselves, and a tire iron and nearly empty pistol aren't going to cut it. And, I need to find a map."

Talking was helping, and I was starting to think again; starting to plan how we would make it across the majority of the United States.

"Why a map? We just follow the freeways, right?" She asked.

"If the freeways are open and safe, that would be great, but I have a feeling that there's going to be a lot of bad guys ready to ambush anything moving on the Interstate system. Also, freeways go through big cities. We need to go around them. I know how to get to Arizona, but I don't know how to avoid all the dangers between here and there." I answered.

She thought about that for a moment then nodded her head in agreement. "You're right. OK, so what's first?"

"Weapons, then food, medical supplies, then a map. In that order." I didn't even hesitate with my answer.

12

I started the truck, twisted the right wires together to keep it running and stepped out of the cab so Rachel could slide behind the wheel. In place, she put her foot on the brake and held it there while shifting the big transmission into drive, so the truck was ready to go the instant I raised the garage door.

The roll up door had a row of grimy windows set into it at head height, so I was able to look out into the parking lot and surrounding area for any threats. Several infected males were slowly lumbering down the street, apparently aimless in their travels. They were far enough away to not be an immediate concern.

I was more worried about the females. The one that had attacked me the night before had been so damn fast and strong it was scary. My only advantage had been that I outweighed her by a good 100 pounds, and not for the first time I was thankful that as I settled into corporate life, I had kept myself in shape.

Two hours a day in the gym had been a pain, but I was still one strong son of a bitch. All that said, I didn't want to get in a foot race with one of the females.

I scanned the area again, moving to change my viewing angle, but still saw nothing other than the males. No vehicles moving, no other uninfected people moving, no animals, and thankfully no infected females.

Glancing back at Rachel, we made eye contact, and I nodded that the area was clear. She nodded back to indicate she was ready. Glock in my right hand I released the door's locking pin with my left and pulled, shoving it all the way open.

I stepped out of the bay, assuming a two-handed shooting stance with the Glock at low ready, which means the weapon was at a forty-five degree down angle from my body with both arms straight out in front of me. It would take a fraction of a second to raise the pistol and engage a target if we were threatened.

The note of the diesel engine rose as Rachel fed it some fuel and the truck rolled out of the garage and stopped when it was completely clear. I started moving quickly for the cab but spun around when I heard running feet behind me. The pistol swiveled with me and rose as I spun. My eyes searched for and found a target, but I was caught off guard by what I saw.

Running towards me, with a guttural scream, was a little girl that couldn't have been more than ten years old. The front of her shirt was covered with blood and her eyes glowed red in the sunlight. I hesitated pulling the trigger. Any adult attacking me would have already been shot, but I wasn't prepared for a child.

Recovering from my hesitation, I realized it was too late to shoot. Stepping to the side as she launched herself into the air, I clubbed the back of her head with the pistol butt as she flashed past and landed in a heap of flailing limbs by the rear tire of the truck.

I hit her hard. Not a tap. Hard. Hard enough to have brought down a grown man. She couldn't have weighed more than sixty pounds, but she sprang back to her feet like all I had done was tickle her.

"Fuck this," I muttered to myself and side stepped so the truck was no longer behind her in my line of fire.

She snarled and raised her arms, hands held like claws, but I fired before she could charge. The body dropped to the pavement and lay still.

Spinning, I sighted in on the males that had been on the street, but they were still more than twenty yards away and moving just slightly faster than a slow lumber. Grabbing the handle, I yanked the door open and slid behind the wheel of the truck as Rachel moved out of my way.

Dropping the truck into drive, I accelerated straight for the approaching infected males and ran down two of them. The massive push bar on the front knocked them to the ground; then they felt like minor speed bumps as the big off road tires bounced over the bodies.

At the street, I turned right and continued our westerly direction of travel. After a bit, I realized that Rachel was watching me, and I turned to meet her gaze.

"Are you OK?" She asked.

"Just fine," I answered after a bit. "I always wanted to shoot a little girl in the head."

After a moment, Rachel placed her hand on my right arm and left it there. We drove that way for a while, neither of us saying anything.

13

We kept working our way west, keeping our speed down enough to avoid accidents and the lumbering males, but fast enough that all the females could do was run at us as we quickly outpaced them. I was not comforted to see that when they started chasing us, they didn't give up until we were out of sight.

This didn't bode well if we ever found ourselves on foot. We'd be quickly run to ground unless we could find secure shelter or fight them off.

We had yet to see any uninfected people since the attempted ambush the day before. This changed as we approached a four-lane state highway that ran roughly north and south.

A small group of five men stood around an ancient Ford Taurus in a convenience store parking lot, staring at us as we approached. They looked like blue collar workers and were armed with a variety of hunting rifles and shotguns.

I felt Rachel tense up next to me as we approached, but she didn't say anything. The men didn't try to flag us down and didn't make any threatening moves with their weapons, but I'm not a great believer in the goodness or charity of the human race, so I accelerated slightly as we drew abreast of them and kept going.

"You didn't trust them?" Rachel asked when we crested a rise in the road and could no longer see them behind us.

"Let's just put it this way. We're in no position to help them, and at the moment, we don't need their help. Probably better for all to keep our distance.

"People are going to be getting hungry very quickly, and they're already scared. That's a dangerous combination. Add to that the fact that civil authority has evaporated, and there's not much that would prevent a group like that from trying to kill me and take you and the truck." I answered.

Rachel thought about that for a moment before answering, "You have a pretty dim view of society."

"I can't remember who said it, but the quote is something like 'Society is only a thin veneer that masks the animal that man really is', or something like that. I've seen for myself what people do when there's no authority in charge."

Rachel started to answer but stopped herself and pointed at a side road we had just passed. "Would an outfitters shop have what we need?"

By way of answer, I hit the brakes and slowed the truck enough to make a U-Turn in the middle of the road. For once in my life, I wouldn't have minded a cop showing up to give me a ticket for the illegal maneuver.

I drove back to the side street and turned the direction Rachel had pointed. A block down on our left was a small cinder block building with a chain link fence protecting the rear parking lot.

The sign on the front advertised that it was an outfitter for hunting and shooting. Underneath, in slightly smaller lettering that looked like an afterthought, the sign said the store was a one stop shop for all my tactical needs.

I grinned from ear to ear. This was like a present being dropped in my lap. A moment later the grin disappeared when I turned the corner to get the truck off the main road. The shop's steel security door was torn out of its frame and lay on the sidewalk.

The inside of the store was dark, and I couldn't tell if there were a hundred infected waiting inside for me or if it was empty. Oh well, only one way to find out.

Parking the truck by the door I left the motor running. I was torn, as the diesel engine was so loud it would mask the sound of threats, but having the truck ready to go might save our lives. I opted to take the risk and deal with the engine noise.

Carefully scanning in all directions, I couldn't detect any threats. I told Rachel to slide behind the wheel, lock the doors, put the truck in drive and keep her foot on the brake. In an emergency, I could dive into the bed of the truck, and she could have us moving instantly.

Pistol in a two-handed combat grip, I stepped around the back of the truck and flattened my back against the cinder block wall next to the open doorway. I wasn't wild about silhouetting myself for anyone lying in wait, but we needed the type of supplies that I hoped were in the store.

I leaned my head forward and tried to see through the door, but the daylight penetrated a few feet at best, the rest of the store invisible to my day adjusted vision. Taking a deep breath, I moved, stepping sideways through the door and out of the light as quickly as I could.

Pistol up and ready to fire, I scanned my surroundings as best I could in the dark, my hands keeping the pistol perfectly synchronized with my line of sight as I'd been taught so many years ago.

A bumping, shuffling sound caught my attention from deeper in the gloom and I focused on the direction it was coming from. My eyes were adjusting to the dark interior, and I realized it wasn't pitch black in the store. I could see what looked like a body on the floor a few yards away; then it stood up, and the stray light caught its eyes, which flashed a bright yellow.

I was caught off guard, expecting an infected to stand up. Instead, a large German Shepherd stood there; tail held tightly between its back legs and head lowered below shoulder level. He stared at me and me at him. A long moment later he let out a low whine and slowly sat down.

Now I'm a sucker for dogs. Trusting that the dog would be more agitated if there were any threats in the store, I cautiously approached him. He tracked me with those yellow eyes the whole time, head and ears up, but he didn't try to move away or exhibit any aggressive behavior.

When I got close, I started talking to him in a low, even voice. I kept approaching until I was a foot in front of him with my hand held out for him to sniff the back. He gave me a sniff, then a lick on my hand and another low whine. His tongue and nose were as dry and rough as sandpaper.

I raised my hand and placed it on top of his head, gently scratching between his ears, then working down to his collar. A leash that I couldn't see in the gloom connected his collar to an eyebolt set into a steel framed display case.

Trusting my new friend, I squatted down with my face just inches in front of his and unhooked the leash. He immediately stood up and shook, then nuzzled my hand and moved to press his flank against my leg.

The dog was seriously dehydrated, probably having gone a couple of days without water. I'd take care of that shortly. He was going with me if he would get in the truck.

Stepping behind the display counter, I started searching the store. From next to the register I grabbed a fistful of plastic bags and started filling them with everything I could find that might be useful. I was excited to find a handheld GPS and stuffed that into a bag with lots of extra batteries. A lantern, portable cook stove, a mess kit for camping, socks, boots (I took a guess on Rachel's sizes), clothing, and much more.

The store had been ransacked, but so far it looked like the looters had been after weapons and ammunition only. Those were the two things I hadn't found any of yet. Still grabbing items, I came across some canvas duffel bags and shoved all of my filled plastic shopping bags into them.

When I had two large duffels so full I could barely zip them, I set them by the end of the counter and snapped on a small flashlight I'd found. The display cases that apparently had held firearms were all smashed and empty. The shelves behind them that were stickered for ammunition were also bare.

I started looking for a back room or office, doubting that the owner had his entire inventory out on display. A door behind a rack of boony hats was marked PRIVATE and was still intact. Grabbing one of the hats and putting it on my head, I opened the door and walked into the arms of an infected male who had been trapped in the office.

The dog let out a growl and launched off the ground, clamping his powerful jaws on the man's forearm. The weight of the dog dragged the arm down and unbalanced the infected. This bought me the opportunity to push away, shove the pistol into the soft tissue under its chin and pull the trigger. The muffled shot blew out the top of its head and the body dropped to the floor, the dog releasing his bite and sitting down as if he were guarding the body.

I scanned the office with the small flashlight and spotted what I'd hoped to see. A vault was set into the side wall of the room. The door was closed, and I held my breath as I tugged on the handle. I sighed with relief when it came open, battery powered lights snapping on to illuminate the inside.

The vault wasn't large, probably no more than eight by ten feet, but as I had hoped, there were weapons and ammunition stored inside. I looked over my shoulder at the infected I'd just killed, probably the store owner, and thanked him.

Ten minutes later, freshly armed, I stepped out of the vault with a duffel bag full of ammo. It must have weighed well over 100 pounds, which sounds like a lot of ammo, but I know from experience just how fast you can burn through bullets in a firefight. I had cleaned out the vault, and it was time to go.

Back in the main store area, I adjusted the sling of the M4 rifle I'd just acquired. I grabbed the two waiting duffels with my left hand, ammo duffel with my right, and headed for the door. The dog stayed by my side, and I was glad to see his tail had come up slightly as he had grown more comfortable with me.

We stepped through the door into the daylight, and I was momentarily blinded. I knew better. Should have stood inside the doorway looking out for a few moments to give my eyes a chance to adjust, but my mental clock was screaming at me that we'd been in one place too long. The dog growled deep in his chest when a voice with a thick Georgia accent told me to stop right where I was.

14

I froze in place, one step outside the doorway, and turned towards the voice. It was the group of men we'd passed earlier. I mentally kicked myself for being dumb enough to stop so soon after seeing them.

The man that had spoken was a big, hard looking guy with an equally large belly. He was dressed in well-worn jeans, a checked work shirt and work boots with dried mud on them. He looked like he hadn't shaved for a week and greasy hair stuck out from underneath a ball cap that was so dirty I couldn't tell what it originally advertised. The others were similarly dressed, and my guess was they were co-workers.

He held a long-barreled shotgun pointed between me and the dog who had stopped a few feet in front and to my left. A quick glance around spotted three of the other four guys that I had seen with him. One of them was behind me with a bolt action rifle pointed at my back, one was behind the talker keeping an eye out for infected, and the third was in front of the truck with a scoped rifle pointed directly at Rachel as she sat behind the steering wheel. Where the hell was the other guy?

"So what we got here?" The talker asked with a big grin that revealed tobacco stained teeth. "Looks like a looter. What you boys think?"

The guy behind me spoke up, "Looks like an asshole to me, Danny." I heard him spit; followed by a wet splash when what I figured was a stream of tobacco juice hit the sidewalk.

"So whyn't you go on and put them bags down, Mr. Looter. And that fancy rifle while you're at it. We'll just hold on to everything until the rightful owner claims it." He was grinning, but the smile didn't make it to his eyes. He had eyes like a pig, small and dark, the pupil and iris so close in color that you couldn't see anything except dark.

I slowly flexed my knees and half squatted, lowering the more than two hundred pounds of duffel bags to the ground, never taking my eyes off the leader.

"You sure you want to do this?" I asked in a low voice as I straightened back up.

The grin didn't falter, "Evan, you get that fancy rifle off his back for me. I think it's time to upgrade from this scatter gun."

I prepared myself but didn't tense as Evan stepped up behind me. I felt him grab the rifle barrel and tug, and I turned slightly and let him pull the sling over my head. He now had a rifle in each hand and couldn't use either one.

As I had turned and ducked for Evan to pull the rifle off my shoulder, I had slipped my hand under my shirt and onto the butt of the pistol I'd picked up in the outfitter store vault. An FNX45, loaded with sixteen rounds of .45 caliber hollow point was in my hand and ready to go.

I leaned to the other side and brought the pistol up and put three rounds into Danny, two to the chest and one to the head. He dropped like a sack of bricks. The other three froze, but I didn't.

Three more rounds dropped the lookout, but the other two had started moving again. The guy in front of the truck shifted his aim to me but before he could fire the engine roared and the truck shot forward with a screech of tires. He bounced off the push bar and flew backwards, landing on the pavement with a sickening crunch of breaking bones a second before the three-ton Ford rolled over him and crushed his skull.

The dog attacked at the same time. He hit Evan just above the waist and drove him to the ground on his back, both rifles flying out of his hands and clattering away. Evan started screaming as he fought the dog, but I silenced him by stepping up and planting the toe of my shoe into his balls as hard as I could.

All the fight and screaming went out of him instantly, and he curled into a ball with a pathetic moan. The dog backed off a foot but stood over him with hackles raised and teeth bared. I was really starting to like this pooch.

A squeal of tires caught my attention, and I ran to the corner of the building to see the rusty Taurus disappear down the road. Mystery of the last guy solved. He'd stayed with the car.

I motioned Rachel to unlock the truck, and I loaded the three duffel bags into the back seat. "Lock it back up. Gotta grab a couple more things."

Back in the vault, I picked up two more M4 rifles I had set out as well as a box full of empty thirty round magazines. I took one more look around but didn't spot anything else.

The dog was still guarding Evan when I got back outside. I heard the door locks thunk open as I approached the truck and I quickly stowed the rifles and magazines in the back seat.

"We've got company coming," Rachel said, pointing down the street at a couple of dozen males shambling towards us.

I whistled for the dog, and he looked up at me. I gestured at the back seat and in a flash of fur he bounded across the sidewalk and into the truck. I slammed the door and turned and looked at Evan.

He wasn't moving, and the infected males would be on him in less than a minute. I had a momentary thought that I should do something to help him, but dismissed it as quickly as it came to me. Hopping behind the wheel, I closed and locked the doors and drove away without another thought.

15

We drove for another half hour then stopped when we found an open park that was deserted. We were in a parking lot that was surrounded by soccer fields on all sides, giving us at least two hundred yards of open space to the nearest tree line. Two roads led in and out of the park, providing reasonable escape routes if we needed them, but I was confident we could just drive across the fields if necessary.

Heavy clouds were building to the north as the afternoon wore on, black and swollen on the bottom, and I expected a big storm within the next few hours. I'd experienced the kind of summer storms that can blast through Atlanta and I wanted to keep our stop short and find some shelter for the night.

The first order of business was to water Dog. Not 'the dog', just Dog. I didn't know his name but decided to name him after the dog John Wayne had in my favorite movie, Big Jake. So Dog it was.

I dug through the duffel bags until I found the mess kit I'd looted from the outfitter. A shallow aluminum bowl worked great, and I only gave Dog a little water at a time, allowing his stomach a chance to absorb rather than cramp and make him throw the water up.

Rachel watched me in silence, and I realized she hadn't said anything since we'd left the outfitters. "What's on your mind?" I asked, scratching Dog between the ears as I poured a little more water into his bowl.

She watched me another minute before asking, "Who the hell are you? You killed two of those men in less than two seconds, you left one to be killed by the infected and here you are petting a dog like nothing has happened." She stared at me closely with not exactly fear in her eyes, but concern over the psychopath she'd hooked up with.

I sighed and gave Dog some more water that he greedily lapped up. "I'm just a businessman that happened to be here and not at home when the shit hit the fan."

"Bullshit!" She turned sideways in the seat to fully face me and crossed her arms over her chest. "Businessmen don't know how to kill two men with a handgun faster than I can blink, then go on about their day like nothing happened. Businessmen don't even look like you for Christ's sake. I haven't seen arms like yours anywhere other than on TV or in magazines. Now tell me the truth. I need to trust you, and right now I don't."

I faced forward and sat for a minute, staring out the windshield at the gathering clouds. Dog, satiated for the moment, stuck his head between the two front seats and put his chin on the armrest between them. He could feel the tension in the truck but didn't seem inclined to take sides, rather kept shifting his expressive eyes, looking back and forth between Rachel and me.

Rachel reached out and put a hand on his head while she stared me down. Finally, I pulled out my wallet and handed her a business card. She took it and looked at it for a bit.

"You're a program manager for Tatushima?" She asked, the doubt clear in her voice.

"Yes, I am," I answered. "But I've not always been a program manager. Army Special Forces, Green Beret, and then a tactical assault trainer for the DEA before I got into a more boring line of work."

She handed me the card back, and I replaced it in my wallet before returning the wallet to my pocket. I looked at her and shrugged my shoulders.

"Don't know what to tell you. At best, those guys would have taken everything we had and left us standing there with no way to defend ourselves. At worst, well… I think you can imagine what the worst would have been.

"Guys like that were kept in control, mostly, by the police and the threat of jail if they let their urges get the best of them. This is their big opportunity to finally behave the way they want to, not the way society tells them they have to.

"I didn't start it. I didn't go looking for trouble with them. All I did was finish it. Permanently. Unfortunately, I expect we'll run into more people like them than we will good people. I've spent a lot of time in places in the world that were coming apart at the seams, and there are always assholes like these guys that see opportunity to prey on the weak. I don't like bullies much, and that's all they are."

This was probably the most I'd said to Rachel at one time since I had rescued her the previous morning. I expected her to take some time to digest what I'd just said and then try to argue with me and tell me why I was wrong.

"OK then. Thank you for telling me. Now we'd better find some place to shelter for the night before that storm gets here. I really don't want to spend the night…"

We both jumped, and Dog leapt to his feet and started growling when the whole truck rocked from the impact of two infected females slamming into the right rear door. We'd been so absorbed in our conversation that none of us had seen them coming.

Looking around, I spotted several more running towards us across the empty fields. At least 20 males were shambling along behind them.

"Time to go," I said, putting the truck in gear and hitting the throttle. We quickly pulled away, but one of the females that had slammed into the truck had a grip on the mesh covering Rachel's side window and was pulling on it, trying to rip it off the truck and get inside.

"Get on the floor," I shouted at Rachel, who instantly complied.

Hitting a button on the driver's door, the passenger window buzzed down, and suddenly the cab was filled with the roar of the diesel and the snarls of the infected woman. Raising the .45, I fired a single shot that took the top of her head off, the body dropping away. A heartbeat later there was a hard bump as a rear tire bounced over her. I rolled the window up, and Rachel climbed back into her seat looking shaken.

"What the hell?" Rachel asked. "Where did they come from? There weren't any around when we pulled in."

I slowed at the end of the access road to the park and turned back onto the main road. Immediately ahead, about a quarter of a mile, was an overpass and large signs indicating we were approaching I-575.

The visible portion of the freeway was jammed with cars as were the adjacent surface streets and on ramps. Hundreds, if not thousands, of people wandered amongst the stalled cars. As we got closer, I recognized the uncoordinated walk of the infected and jammed on the brakes.

"That's where they came from," I said, staring in horror as the crowd seemed to notice us all at once. Males started slowly turning and shambling our way, but too many females to count started sprinting down the road directly at us.

"Oh shit," Rachel muttered, a hand over her mouth.

"Oh shit is right," I said and hit the throttle, wrenching the truck through a tire-screeching U-turn.

Heading back the way we had just come from, we quickly encountered the females that had raced across the park and followed us out onto the road. They ran straight at us with no fear.

As we reached the front of the pack, I backed off the throttle and dropped our speed to just under thirty. Even the heavy, welded push bar on the front of the truck could only take so many impacts from all the human bodies running at us. The first two were bulled aside by the truck with stomach clenching thuds, but the third female was young and looked to be in excellent shape.

With a leap, she cleared the front of the truck and slammed into the wire mesh covered windshield. The wire did its job and absorbed the impact. If not for it, we'd most likely have had the female in our laps, as she'd have crashed right through the already compromised glass.

I kept driving, mowing down females as we went, then we were clear of the pack. But we still had our passenger who had a death grip on the wire mesh. I tried slamming on the brakes at forty miles an hour, but all this did was get a yelp from Dog when he was thrown against the backs of the front seats. The female still clung like a barnacle.

"Shoot her!" Rachel's voice was up a couple of octaves, and I could hear the stress in it.

"I don't want to put another hole in the windshield," I said as I tried swerving the big truck from side to side to shake the infected loose. The maneuvers had about as much effect as when I slammed on the brakes. Dog, with no seatbelt, was definitely getting the worst of it.

Spotting a large, empty parking lot, I made a sharp turn. Roaring into the lot, I spun the wheel and jammed on the brakes, the truck coming to a stop in a cloud of tire smoke after sliding sideways for twenty feet. The female was thrown off balance, staying on the truck with the grip of only one hand.

In a flash I had my door open and jumped out, raising my pistol to acquire my target. I was shocked to see that the female had already regained her balance and had her feet planted, ready to spring. Without hesitating, I fired, and the heavy hollow point slug nearly decapitated the body. She flopped dead onto the hood, and I had to walk around and drag the body off the truck.

"Fuck these things are fast!" I said to myself as I hurried back to the driver's side of the cab.

Back in the relative safety of the truck I checked the area and saw no immediate danger. A quick search of the duffel bags yielded the GPS I'd found as well as an old school road map. I handed Rachel the GPS and some batteries and asked her to get it running while I checked the map. I also reminded her to keep watch, so we didn't get surprised again.

The map was hard to see, and I reached up to turn on the reading light before I realized how dark it had gotten. The clouds had made it to us; the low bellies swollen with rain. As I watched, the first drops struck the windshield, slowly at first then quickly becoming a torrential downpour.

The noise of the rain on the metal roof of the truck was almost deafening, but nothing compared to the bone-jarring blast of sound from lightning that cracked right over our heads. The thunder had blasted at the same time as we saw the brilliant flash, so it had to be very close.

Dog started whining, and Rachel turned to comfort him as another bolt of lightning lit the world around us. In the strobe effect, I could see shambling and running figures coming towards us. Damn it; I just needed two minutes to look at a map.

Stomping on the throttle, we roared out of the parking lot and turned north away from the main road that seemed to have a good population of infected. We were quickly in residential neighborhoods, most of the houses smaller ranch style homes that had been built in the 70s and 80s as Atlanta continued to sprawl and the northern suburbs boomed.

The rain was relentless, now driven at an angle by the rising wind. Water was coming in around my duct tape reinforcement of the windshield, so the glass was wet inside and out. Visibility wasn't much more than to the end of the hood.

We passed another park, barely visible in the rain, then back into another neighborhood of single story homes, these slightly newer and mostly built of the red brick that is so common in construction in the Atlanta area. We didn't see a light, movement or an infected anywhere and I started to think we should shelter in one of the homes for the night.

The problem was that we had no way of knowing if a house was occupied by people hiding out, full of infected, or sitting empty. I had no desire to shoot it out with a homeowner who was just defending his home. Neither did I want to open a front door and have to deal with the infected lady of the house.

The storm made my decision for me. The rain increased in volume, and the wind picked up, rocking the three-ton truck like it was a Tonka Toy. Lightning continued to flash overhead, and we watched a tree explode on a ridgeline directly in front of us when it was struck.

"OK, enough," I said. "See any good possibilities?"

Rachel peered through the storm as I drove, then suddenly sat up and pointed, "There! The one with the garage door up."

I spotted the house she pointed out. It was a small brick one story with an attached two car garage. The house was dark and the front door closed, but the garage was open and empty. I was willing to take the odds that this house had been abandoned in a hurry.

I turned into the driveway and continued into the garage. There were no hiding places to check or worry about so I jumped out and released the garage door from the automatic opener track then pulled it down. The truck was still running, quickly filling the garage with stinking diesel exhaust fumes. I rushed to disconnect the wires and shut the engine off.

The fury of the storm lashing the aluminum garage door was so loud I could hardly tell the truck was no longer running. I made a mental note to find an electrical switch to wire into the truck, so we didn't have to twist two wires together every time we wanted to start it.

It was dark in the garage, but I brought out my looted flashlight and pulled the pistol.

"Dog," I called, and he jumped to the front seat then down to the garage floor through the door I'd left open.

Rachel stepped out of the truck, Glock in hand. I looked at her, and she glared back at me. "Don't say a word, Mr. Bad Ass. I've saved your life twice now, and I'm getting a little tired of being left behind in the truck."

I looked at Dog, who seemed to be smiling at me, shook my head and moved to the door into the house. Dog came up beside me and gave it a good sniff then stood still looking at me, waiting for me to do something. I didn't know how he'd react if there were either people or infected on the other side of the door, but I didn't think in either case he'd be as calm as he was.

16

Clicking the safety off on the pistol, I quietly turned the knob and eased the door open. All was quiet, or, at least, any sounds within the house were masked by the raging storm outside. As the door swung open, I paid attention to Dog, trusting him to be an early warning if the house was inhabited.

He just stood quietly at the open door, nose twitching. I stepped into the hallway and Dog stayed by my side. Rachel brought up the rear, padding silently in her bare feet. We quickly checked the entire house and found it empty. With that out of the way, I made sure all the doors were securely locked, and all the windows were covered. I didn't want any visitors.

The house looked like it had been home to a couple. There were three bedrooms, two of them musty smelling and being used for storage. The master was a shambles with drawers pulled out of the dressers and left lying on the floor amidst heaps of clothing. It looked like someone had packed and left in a hurry.

The kitchen was small and not particularly clean, but the cupboard was well stocked with canned foods. The range was gas burning, and I was happy to hear the hiss of natural gas when I turned the knob. The burner didn't ignite because the range used an electric starter and the power was off, but a simple match would solve that problem, and we'd have a hot meal.

Rachel checked the water, and it was still on, and it even got hot as she let it run. Must be a gas hot water heater with a pilot light.

"First shower!" She grinned across the room at me.

I grinned back. "I'll make dinner while you clean up. Keep your pistol close and leave the bathroom door open. If you hear me shout..."

"Got it," she answered, still smiling. Apparently not even the end of the world could dampen her spirits when a hot shower was available. Rachel went down the hall to the bathroom and moments later I heard the shower start up.

The storm still raged outside as I started pulling cans out of the pantry. A large can of chunky beef stew went into a bowl on the floor, and Dog devoured it in less than a minute, licked the bowl spotlessly clean and went over and laid down in the corner with a contented sigh.

I found a large skillet and after getting the stovetop lit, put it on the burner and started adding the contents of several cans. I wouldn't win any culinary awards, but as I added two cans of Spam, a can of baked beans and another of corn, I thought the aroma coming from the pan was one of the best I'd ever smelled.

Giving everything a stir, I searched some more cabinets and found a couple loaves of sourdough bread. Cutting the tops off each, I hollowed out the insides and put them on plates, the bread from inside the loaves on the side. Each one made a perfect bread bowl.

The shower had been off for a few minutes, and I was about to go looking for Rachel when she walked into the kitchen.

"That smells fantastic," she said, coming over to the stove to look in the skillet. Rachel had found clean clothes in the master bedroom closet that almost fit. She had on a pair of cotton shorts that were short enough to not leave much to the imagination and a thin T-Shirt that was stretched almost impossibly tight over her breasts.

"And it's ready. Hope you're hungry," I answered, trying to keep my eyes from drifting to the hard nipples stressing the thin fabric of the shirt, or the long legs left bare by the short shorts.

I scooped generous portions of the skillet contents into the bread bowls and carried them to the table while Rachel found water glasses and filled them at the sink for us. A quick search of drawers yielded a couple of spoons, and we settled down at the table.

The kitchen was almost dark due to the heavy clouds outside and the closed blinds at all the windows, but I didn't care to show a light that might be seen by either survivors or infected. We both dug in, too hungry to spend any time talking. From across the room, Dog watched us, his chin on his front paws. When my food was half gone, I was able to slow myself down and enjoy eating the meal.

"So I was thinking about why those infected showed up at the park when we stopped this afternoon," I said, then shoveled another spoonful into my mouth.

Rachel paused with a spoon halfway to her mouth and looked at me with raised eyebrows. I chewed, swallowed and continued.

"I think it was the sound of the truck idling. I think mechanical sounds are going to draw these things like a moth to a flame. I've got to find a switch I can wire into the truck so we can shut it off and start it easily when we stop."

"How many of them do you think are out there?" Rachel asked, getting up to refill our water.

I thought for a minute before answering, "I don't have a clue. So far we've seen far more infected than we have survivors. I'm shocked the nerve gas was so effective and spread so fast. Based on what we've seen so far it seems like most of the population have been infected."

That thought hit both of us like a slap in the face. Suddenly my food didn't taste good anymore. I put the remains on the floor for Dog, who gladly polished it off for me. When he was done, I picked the plate up and washed it in the sink. Not that it mattered, but old habits die hard.

I made another tour of the house, checking windows and doors to make sure we were secure. The worst of the storm had passed, but it was still raining and now completely dark outside. I put a piece of duct tape over my flashlight lens and poked a small hole in it so only a tiny beam of light could make it out.

Using the muted flashlight, I carefully covered the master bedroom windows with blankets, taping the edges to the wall with more duct tape to prevent any light from escaping. The battery-powered LED lantern I had looted had a night light setting, and I turned it on in the bedroom for Rachel then went to the living room and covered those windows as well, taping the blankets as I had in the master bedroom. I'd be sleeping on the couch tonight. There was only one bed in the house, and I'd already decided to give it to Rachel.

Next, I retrieved a 12-gauge shotgun I'd found in the outfitter store vault and showed Rachel how to load it, rack the slide and where the safety button was. After having her rack a few shells through the gun and reload it, she was about as familiar with a shotgun as she was going to be until we were somewhere safe that I could teach her how to aim, control and fire the weapon.

I showered with my pistol in the shower with me, safe inside a plastic zip sandwich bag I'd found in the kitchen. The hot water felt wonderful and released a lot of the tension I was carrying in my shoulders and upper back.

Dried off, I dressed in the khaki camouflage cargo pants I'd found at the outfitter and a matching camo T-Shirt. I tried on the steel toed hunting boots, which fit well, and left them sitting open and ready at the edge of the couch.

With a fully loaded rifle on the floor next to me and a loaded pistol in my waistband, I laid back on the couch. I closed my eyes, but the voice of a long gone instructor popped into my head, 'Check everything, check it again, then check to make sure you checked it right, numbnuts.'

I smiled at the memory of Sergeant Willis, swung my feet to the floor and made another round of the house with Dog padding along at my side. All the doors and windows were locked tight. The blankets in the bedroom were still tightly covering the window, and Rachel was breathing heavily as she slept, cocooned in a light blanket with only her face exposed.

I turned off the lantern's night light to save the batteries and headed back to the living room, feeling my way in the dark. Passing one of the other bedrooms, I stepped in and up to the window that looked to the street in front of the house. Carefully moving the curtains an inch open, I looked out at the rain-soaked front yard.

The clouds were breaking up, and a small amount of moonlight lit the street. I stood there watching for a few minutes but didn't see anything. I was about to close the gap in the curtains and go to bed when movement across the street caught my eye. My pulse picked up until I identified the fat raccoon that waddled into view. He stopped and sniffed the air, then slowly made his way up the street. I closed the curtains tight and went to bed.

17

I snapped awake when Dog growled deep in his chest. My hand automatically grasped the butt of the pistol in my waistband. I drew the weapon and swung my feet to the floor silently, watching Dog and trying to figure out what had him agitated. He was staring intently at the front window of the living room. I couldn't hear anything, and didn't have any idea what time it was other than early as it was still dark.

I stood up carefully and made my way to the bedroom next to the living room, eased my way up to the curtains and a millimeter at a time opened them enough to see out the window. All the clouds had moved out, and there was enough moonlight for me to see what must have been hundreds of infected stumbling down the street, all headed to the north.

They filled the road, flowing around abandoned cars and spilling up onto the lawns of the houses that lined it. Both males and females moved together, the females appearing much more coordinated in their movements. Occasionally children could be seen in the crowd, and just like the adults the males were slow and uncoordinated, the females moving with almost animal-like fluidity and grace.

I closed the curtains as slowly and carefully as I had opened them and quietly backed away from the window. Deciding it was best to wake Rachel in case we were discovered, I made my way out to the hall and down to the master bedroom where she was sleeping.

She hadn't moved since I'd done my last check of the house before going to sleep, still wrapped up in the blanket and snoring softly. I knelt onto one knee, leaned over her and put a hand over her mouth to prevent her from crying out in case I startled her.

Her eyes instantly flew open wide with panic, and she started struggling. I wrapped my other arm around her, using the blanket to help control her movements and put my lips against her ear.

"It's OK; it's me. There's infected outside. We can't make any noise," I mumbled in her ear.

She stopped struggling, but her body remained tense. Slowly I released her then removed my hand from her mouth, ready to clamp it back in place if she started to speak. When it was obvious she was under control; I stepped back, and she sat up and shed the blanket. I motioned for her to follow me, using my taped flashlight to give her enough light to see.

Rachel stood up, crossed her arms across her breasts and followed me to the other bedroom. Again, I very cautiously opened the curtains enough to look out and was dismayed to see that the number of infected had grown. What had been a steady stream just a few minutes before had now grown to a tightly packed mass of human bodies flooding through the neighborhood.

I moved aside, and Rachel looked out the opening. She caught her breath but made no other sound. After a moment, she moved back, and I carefully put the curtains back in place. Fumbling in the dark, I reached out for her, felt her arm and followed it down until I took her hand in mine. I led her through the darkened house out to the living room where Dog still stared at the front windows with his ears at full alert.

Pulling Rachel to me I put my lips back to her ear and mumbled, “Let’s get dressed and ready to move, just in case. I got hunting clothes and boots for you from the outfitter. I’m going to turn my flashlight on so we can see. Don’t make a sound.”

Rachel nodded, and I didn’t so much see it as feel her hair move against my face. I turned on the flashlight and aimed the beam at the floor. The light seemed brilliant after the tomb-like darkness, but I kept it on the dark colored carpet, which absorbed much of the light and didn't create any reflections.

I pointed at the duffel bag next to the coffee table, and Rachel slowly dug through it until she found pants, shirt, socks and the pair of boots I'd guessed at on size. She held the clothes up to herself and nodded when they looked like a pretty good fit. I was surprised when she didn't hesitate to strip naked right there in front of me, then remembered her state of dress when I'd found her.

A few minutes later she was dressed in the new clothes and both of us had our boots on. I retied her laces, showing her how to knot them so they didn't come loose at an inconvenient time.

I dug through the other duffel and pulled out canvas web belts and holsters. Handing one to Rachel, I put the other one on and holstered my pistol on my right hip. Rachel watched what I did and copied me. Next came tactical equipment vests for each of us.

Taking a seat on the couch, I motioned for Rachel to join me. I then spread my blanket on top of the coffee table and placed the case of thirty round magazines on it. From the duffel bag full of ammo, I retrieved several boxes of 5.56 mm.

Indicating for Rachel to watch what I did, I took a magazine and carefully and quietly started loading it. After a bit, Rachel picked one up and helped. As each magazine was finished, I found a pouch for it on my vest until it was completely full. Then we started filling up Rachel's vest. When we were done, each of us was carrying fifteen magazines for a total of four hundred and fifty rounds each.

Finding and filling the spare magazines for my .45 and Rachel's nine mm pistol gave each of us another hundred rounds of spare pistol ammunition on our bodies. I had Rachel stand up slowly and adjusted her vest so it fit properly and didn't rattle when she moved. Anything that wouldn't adjust got duct taped and silenced.

Finally, I slung one of the M4 rifles over her head and adjusted the sling for a good fit for her size. With hand gestures and mumbled explanations, I showed her how to insert a magazine, charge the weapon, turn it off and on safe, change magazines and aim. In response to my question of whether she'd ever fired a rifle before, she shook her head.

I rummaged to the bottom of another duffel and pulled out two backpacks that had built in water bladders and drinking tubes. Showing these to Rachel, I mimed that I wanted her to take them to the kitchen and fill them with water. I wanted to check on the infected while she did that.

Moving slowly so I didn't bang into anything and make a sound, I crept up to the bedroom window and peeked through the curtains. The sky was lightening. Visibility had improved greatly, but I didn't need the extra light to see that there was still a sea of bodies moving up the street.

I couldn't even hazard a guess as to how many there were. They were moving so slow and were packed so tightly together that I had to concentrate to pick out individuals. Closing the curtains, I went back to the living room where Rachel was carefully placing the backpacks on the coffee table.

We spent some time distributing spare clothing and food into the packs. I put all the remaining three hundred rounds of nine mm ammo in Rachel's, loading mine up with .45 and 5.56. I debated shotgun ammo but decided to stick with the rifle rather than the 12 gauge. If we lost the truck, we'd lose the shotgun with it.

Preparations made, we settled onto the couch. I had a map and my flashlight, and Rachel scooted next to me to get a look. I traced my finger across the page, following I-575 until I came to the interchange where we'd turned around yesterday. Tracing backwards, I spotted where I thought we were, or, at least, the right neighborhood.

A few minutes of searching found an overpass that crossed I-575 a few miles to the northwest of us. This looked on the map to just be a bridge over the interstate without any entrance or exit ramps. My assumption was that this would not be jammed by people fleeing the city.

I memorized as much of the route as I could and worked on mapping our way farther west. A large lake lay beyond the 575 that we would have to make our way around, then we'd have to deal with I-75, which ran up to Tennessee to the north and back to downtown Atlanta to the south. I expected 75 to be completely impassable.

Looking for a route around the lake, I didn't like our options. Going south to skirt the water would take us a good distance back toward Atlanta. If we went north and around, it looked like there was only one small highway that cut through some rugged country.

I whispered my concerns into Rachel's ear and traced the routes on the map with my finger to demonstrate. She peered intently at the map for a few minutes, then using her index finger traced a route due north from our location up into the north Georgia hills. We'd still have to cross 575, but the route she was proposing would take us through some sparsely populated areas.

I nodded my agreement, irritated with myself that I was so focused on westerly travel that I had overlooked the obvious. I was concerned for my wife, and all I wanted to do was to get to Arizona and make sure she was safe. She's tough as nails and probably smarter than I am, but there's a reason men ruled the world until very recent history, and the world was quickly devolving back to that mode. At least she was well armed and knew how to shoot.

Putting Katie out of my mind, as much as I could, I spent some time studying the map and fixing roads and travel directions in my head. Not that Rachel couldn't read the map for me while I was driving, but it was always better to have an idea of which way we were going and how we were going to get there.

I looked up when Rachel lightly touched my arm and followed her gaze to where Dog was lying in the middle of the living room floor. He had been alert and tense from the moment he had wakened me, eyes fixed on the front windows, but now he was lying down and even though his ears were straight up his eyes were closed.

I watched him for a minute then looked at Rachel and motioned to the bedroom. She followed me and we peeked out the curtained windows at what looked like was going to be a crystal clear day. What made it even better was that no infected were in sight.

Mailboxes were broken over, bushes and lawns trampled into mud, smears of something I assumed was blood were on all the parked cars, but that was the only sign of the infected. I let out the breath I hadn't realized I was holding and heard Rachel do the same.

"What the hell was that?" She asked in a very quiet voice.

"I don't know. At first, I thought maybe they'd heard something in that direction, but I think the females would have been out in front of the pack if that was the case."

We stood looking out the window for a few more moments until I carefully put the curtains back in place.

"The bad thing is they were all heading the same direction we just decided to go, and I don't think we'd survive an encounter with a group that large. Even in the truck. They could batter their way in or even turn us over if they have any ability to work together."

Rachel stared back at me, and I could see in her eyes that she didn't know what to say to that.

"Maybe we should go back to the westerly route and find a way around the lake," I suggested.

She was thoughtful for a moment then nodded her head slowly as if in partial agreement. "We don't seem to have much choice. The last thing I want is to run into that crowd, or any others for that matter."

The street we were on ran roughly southwest to northeast, and if I was looking at the correct street on the map, it continued to curve north of us until it was an eastbound road. Assuming the crowd- herd??- followed the path of least resistance the road would take them away from our immediate direction of travel. Not far enough that I was comfortable going due north, but it looked like we could make our way northwest then over the 575.

After getting across the interstate, I decided we would take the route around the north end of the lake. That way looked much less populated, and I was nervous about getting cornered and overwhelmed by a mass of infected.

Rachel leaned back on the couch, breathed deeply then let out a long, slow sigh. “How long can this last?” She asked.

I looked away from the map, “What do you mean?”

“I mean, how long can this last? The infected people. Humans can’t go long without water. A couple of weeks maybe without food, but no more than three days without water when they’re out there wandering around all day in the heat.”

“They’re probably drinking and eating, but I can’t imagine what they’re eating. Well, at least the males. They don't seem coordinated enough to scavenge for food. The females seem quite capable."

Rachel continued to stare straight ahead at a dark plasma TV screen. "I'm trying to wrap my head around this. I can certainly understand biotoxins, even bacterial or viral infections that would cause hyper-aggression, but any I'm aware of burn the host out in a few hours to a day. There's not any sign so far of that happening here."

"That you're aware of."

Rachel looked at me and smiled a sad smile, "What I mean is, you'd think there was hope that the infected people would have already started dying off. But we've not seen any sign of that. The scary thought here is that everyone that is infected – and I'm not sure that's an entirely accurate term – is finding water and food and will continue to remain a threat to the rest of us.

"I'm also confused about the crowd or herd behavior we just saw. That's not consistent with any disease, or toxin I can think of that would cause the aggressive behavior. These people should be just as aggressive towards each other as they are towards us." She turned her head and looked me in the eye.

"I understand what you're saying, but does it matter?"

"It does if we can find a way to counteract their aggression towards us."

"You have an idea?"

Rachel let out a short, sardonic laugh, "Yeah. I'm a fourth-year med student paying the bills by shaking my tits and ass in men's faces. If I was a seasoned researcher with a lab and the right equipment, then maybe..."

I thought about what she said but couldn't think of anything to say in response. After a bit, I headed to the kitchen to make us some food before we got back on the road.

18

The truck started easily on the first try, the diesel engine loud in the closed garage. All our gear and Dog was already loaded in the back seat, and Rachel was behind the wheel ready to go when I raised the door. Moments later we were out of the garage, down the driveway and headed southwest on the street in front of the house.

I intended to go south a short distance before starting to work our way northwest through the neighborhoods. My hope was to completely avoid the herd that had passed in front of the house. A block south I made a right, keeping the speed down which also kept the volume of the engine down. I had fallen in love with the big Ford truck, but at times, I wished for a nice, quiet gasoline engine.

We slowly made it through the surrounding neighborhoods, turning off to keep heading in a generally northwest direction. By now my memorization of our route had failed, and Rachel was navigating for me with the map spread across her lap. Dog was sitting on the rear floor with his head resting on the center console between us, appearing to be alertly watching the road ahead.

We passed through neighborhood after neighborhood with no sign of any life, survivor or infected. There was also no sign of any animal life other than birds. Ghost town came to mind as we passed nothing but houses that were dark and silent. I idly wondered if any of them held survivors like Rachel and me.

We turned onto a narrower street that was completely shaded by a long row of oaks and elms, and I hit the brakes when three figures walked into the road a few houses in front of us. In the deep shade of the tree cover, I couldn't tell if they were infected or not, but they seemed to move with a degree of coordination that the infected could not achieve.

None of the three appeared armed, nor did they make any aggressive or threatening moves. They just stood in the road a hundred yards in front of us. I scanned the street, looking for anything out of place that would indicate an impending ambush, but everything looked as normal as it could under the circumstances.

"What do you think?" I asked Rachel while continuing to scan. "Go around, or see what they want?"

Rachel consulted the map before answering, "To go around we have to backtrack almost a mile then follow a frontage road along the 575. I don't think that's a good option."

OK, then. Forward, I decided. Before stepping on the throttle, I laid the 12 gauge across my lap, resting the pistol grip on the console in front of Dog's nose and clicked the safety to the 'fire' position. Slowly I accelerated to ten miles an hour and rolled down the street towards the figures.

At fifty yards I could tell these were kids. At twenty yards I could tell they weren't infected as they were nervously shuffling their feet and looking around like they were afraid of being attacked. At ten yards I braked to a halt and could tell they were teenagers, a boy, and two girls.

The boy was overweight with an acne-ravaged face and long greasy hair that hung into his eyes. The two girls were painfully thin; both dressed in black with hair dyed the color of black shoe polish. One of them had piercings in her nose, lip, eyebrow and the full perimeter of each ear. The other had none other than a large jewel glinting on her right cheek.

"Well, looks like the Addams Family survived," I said.

Rachel looked at me like I was nuts, then tried to suppress a grin.

Rolling my window down, I motioned them to my side of the truck and put my hand on the shotgun's pistol grip, finger alongside the trigger guard. They exchanged glances, then the girl with the single jewel in her cheek approached. The other two moved closer together in the middle of the road.

"Hi," I said when she stopped a few feet from my window.

She looked back at me, and the eyes seemed too intelligent for the outfit. Oh well. I've certainly got no business judging anyone.

"Hi," She said.

"What are you doing out here?" Rachel raised her voice and asked.

"We thought you were our parents," She said. "My dad has a truck that sounds just like this, and when we heard it, we thought you were them."

"When's the last time you saw your parents?" I asked.

She thought about that for a minute before answering, "Two days ago. The news on the TV was scary, and they went out to the store to get supplies. Then the phones and TV stopped working, and they haven't come home."

I let out a sigh. How do you tell a kid that her parents were probably either infected or had been killed by infected? I looked to Rachel for help, but she just shook her head and shrugged her shoulders. I turned back to the girl I had mentally labeled as Jewell.

"The news isn't good. Thousands of people have been infected, and they're attacking anyone that's not infected. Your parents may not be able to make it home anytime soon." It was the best I could come up with.

"We've seen the infected," She said. "I killed two of them that attacked my brother in the back yard."

Rachel put her hand on my arm, and I turned my head slightly towards her. Not so far that I couldn't still see Jewell and her siblings, but far enough to hear her low whisper.

"Should we take them with us?"

I thought about that for a minute before turning fully back to the open window.

"What's your name?"

"Gwen, and that's Stacy and Kevin." She motioned to the two kids in front of us I'd dubbed McFly and Morticia. When she moved her arm, her jacket flapped, and I could see the butt of a 1911 .45 pistol in her waistband. She reached for the jacket, but her hand was too close to the pistol for comfort.

"Don't touch that pistol, Gwen. I'm a nice enough guy, but you don't want to try anything foolish."

She blushed but held my gaze. "I'm not going to try anything. I just didn't want you to see it and get the wrong idea."

"OK," I answered, making up my mind about Rachel's whispered question. "We're heading west, getting away from Atlanta. We have room, and we have food and water if you three want to come with us."

Gwen stood quietly as if sizing us up. I could see the wheels turning behind her eyes. I thought she was going to say yes.

"Fuck no, Gwen. No way. We wait right here just like Mom and Dad told us to. They'll be back."

This was Kevin, and I was reminded how much better kids' hearing is than mine. I was struggling to hear Gwen over the idle of the truck, and he'd heard me almost thirty feet away with the clattering engine between us.

Gwen's eyes shut down, and she looked over at her brother and sister before turning back to me, "We'll stay here. Our parents will be home soon."

"Are you sure that's a good idea? We saw a herd of thousands of infected move through a neighborhood just to the east early this morning."

She nodded but didn't say anything else.

"Do you need anything?" Rachel called out. "Food, water... anything?"

Gwen stole another glance at her siblings then turned back to us with a glint of hope in her eye. "Food. We haven't eaten in two days. That's OK for Kevin, but Stacy and I need to eat."

"Hey fuck you, Gwen." Kevin shouted, raising both middle fingers to give her the double bird. Even during the apocalypse siblings will fight with each other.

"OK, Gwen. Step back in front of the truck. I'm going to get out and unload some food for you. Now before I do that, remember what I said about not doing anything foolish."

I looked at her, hoping she had enough life experience to understand the message I was sending. Kids or not, if any of them drew a weapon, I wouldn't hesitate. A kid with a gun can kill you just as fast and just as dead as a trained soldier.

She nodded her head and moved back in front of the truck. I shifted the transmission into park and handed the shotgun to Rachel. "Safety is off, and there's a round in the chamber. Open your door and stand on the running board. If any of them pulls a gun while I'm unloading their supplies, you shoot them. Understand?"

Rachel stared at the shotgun in her hands like she didn't understand why she was holding it.

"Understand?" I asked, hardening my voice.

Rachel snapped out of it and after checking to make sure the area was clear, opened her door and stepped onto the running board, shotgun at the ready. The three kids stepped back when they saw the weapon.

"I'm just making sure we're ready if any infected show up. Stay right there and we'll get some food out for you," Rachel called.

The kids were calmed by a woman's voice and stopped moving away. I did a check of the area and stepped out and opened the back door of the truck. Dog hopped out and trotted to the closest tree while I gathered half of the canned and boxed food we had taken from the house we'd spent the night in.

The food was in a bunch of plastic grocery bags we'd found under the kitchen sink, and I quickly had two heavy bundles swinging from my hands. I walked a few feet in front of the truck and placed the bags on the ground. All three kids had their eyes glued to the food.

I let out a deep sigh and glanced back at Rachel. As if knowing what was on my mind, she gave me a quick nod then turned her attention back to keeping watch on the kids as well as looking for approaching infected.

"Do you guys want to come with us?" I asked. "It's pretty bad out there and- well, your parents- I'm just saying you might be safer with us. We could leave a note at your house for your folks."

All three started shaking their heads, and Gwen spoke up, "No. We'll wait. They'll be home soon. Thanks for the food."

I nodded my head and returned to the truck cab, closing the back door after Dog hopped in and resumed his spot. I got in and closed my door, Rachel doing the same on her side after making sure the shotgun was on safe.

As soon as we were back in the truck, Gwen dashed forward and grabbed the grocery bags. Food in hand, the three of them ran to a small, white house. They disappeared inside and the door closed.

I sat there for a minute looking at the house and was glad to see they had done a good job of covering windows from the inside. The house appeared empty. As long as they were careful and quiet, maybe the infected wouldn't find them.

"Think they'll make it?" Rachel asked quietly.

I shook my head, then answered when I realized she was looking at the house and not me.

"For a while. Until the food runs out, or they run out of water and have to go out and scavenge."

"We shouldn't leave them," she said, a note of distress in her voice.

"Unless we force them, they're not going to come with us."

I put the big truck in gear and slowly accelerated down the street. We kept heading northwest, finally coming to the road that led to the overpass that would hopefully get us safely over the 575. It was a narrow four-lane road with a center turn lane, lined with small businesses- mainly fast food joints, liquor stores, convenience stores, and auto repair shops.

As we approached the 575, the number of abandoned vehicles increased and we were frequently forced to steer through parking lots to get around. More and more infected were also present, the shambling males that tried to catch us and the much swifter females that sprinted at us. More than one female bounced off the side or front of the truck, but I kept the speed up enough that they were unable to hold on for a ride.

We finally made it onto the overpass with a respectable sized herd following. Despite their presence, I braked to a halt at the apex of the bridge, maneuvering the truck close enough to the guardrail to allow us a good view of the 575.

Both directions of the interstate were hopelessly jammed with cars. Some had apparently been involved in accidents and abandoned by their owners, but most were just stuck in gridlock and were now sitting empty. Flowing through the maze of steel and glass were thousands of infected, looking like a river flowing around rocks.

We were noticed immediately as we sat there idling, infected from every direction turning to make their way towards us. Several females, apparently frustrated with the pace, leapt up onto car hoods and roofs and raced towards us using the stalled vehicles like stepping stones. In my mirror, I could see the leading edge of the herd following us and decided we'd sat in one place long enough.

The road we were on ran west for a bit through sparsely populated countryside, then swung to the north, and we began to see more homes and businesses. Along with more buildings came more infected. We pushed on, and I raised our speed slightly, eager to move beyond Atlanta's sprawl and out into the country. My hope was that the farther we moved away from the city, the less infected we would encounter.

As we continued, this seemed to be the case. The road swung to the northwest and other than a narrow stretch of asphalt that ran to the south with a sign for a marina, there was nothing but the blacktop cutting through forest. The pavement was smooth and well maintained with wide, grassy shoulders and the terrain began rolling as we drove.

Relaxing slightly, I asked Rachel to double check her map for our next turn and pushed our speed up close to sixty. It was a beautiful day, the sun shining brightly as the afternoon wore on and for the first time since arriving in Atlanta my spirits started to lift. We drove through a series of dips in the road as we gained altitude, then climbed the biggest hill yet. Cresting the rise, it took me a moment to realize what I was seeing and another to react and jam on the brakes.

The tires screamed in protest and left smoking black marks on the pavement as I held the brakes down. We finally stopped, but not before we plowed into the back of a herd of infected so large that I couldn't see the far edge.

19

"Oh, shit," I heard Rachel say under her breath as thousands of heads snapped around in our direction and hands started beating on the truck. I could only see males, and for as clumsy and slow as they are, they were quickly surrounding us and pressing in. We would rapidly be enveloped in such a large mass, and I was afraid the truck wouldn't be able to move.

Throwing the transmission in reverse, I stomped on the throttle and the big diesel roared as we surged backwards. We had slid a few feet into the herd when we stopped, and I kept the throttle down and crashed through and over bodies until we reached clear pavement.

With thirty yards of open space now in front of us, I spun the wheel and turned us sideways in the road, stopping with the back bumper against the berm that rose up from the edge of the shoulder. I grabbed the gear selector to put the truck in drive.

I tugged, but the lever didn't move. Staring dumbly at the little red needle that indicated the gear, I pulled harder with no luck. I hammered the lever with the palm of my hand, trying to move it to P or D, but it wasn't budging. The truck was stuck in reverse, and we were backed against a berm of rocky soil. Didn't look like it was going anywhere.

"Get us out of here!" The stress in Rachel's voice snapped my attention to the herd of infected that were lumbering towards us, now only twenty yards away.

I made one last desperate attempt to move the gear selector, but it was stuck fast in reverse. Probably a two-dollar pin in the transmission linkage, but it didn't matter what the cause was.

Popping my door open I jumped down to the pavement, glad that I'd had the foresight to have Rachel and I load all our magazines into the tactical vests we were wearing. While Rachel scrambled across the seat and out my open door, I grabbed our backpacks, shrugging into mine before helping Rachel with hers. I grabbed the shotgun out of the front seat, slammed the door, and we started running just as the faster males reached the far side of the truck.

I didn't know where we were going, just knew that we had to get away from the herd before any females spotted us. Loaded like we were, there was no way we could outrun them.

Setting a steady, fast jogging pace that would put distance between the herd and us, we headed back to the east. I ran with my rifle slung across my back and the shotgun held ready across my chest. The Mossberg was loaded with buckshot alternating with slugs, and any infected I engaged would go down with one shot. The kinetic energy of either shell, delivered at close range, would be enough to stop anything smaller than a grizzly bear, and the bear would think twice about continuing an attack.

We opened some distance from the herd, Rachel slowing when we had a good hundred-yard buffer.

"Don't slow down," I said without breaking stride. "There's got to be females in that herd, and we need to get as far away as fast as possible."

As if my warning had been prophetic, there was a scream from behind us that made the hair on my arms stand on end. I glanced over my shoulder to see two females sprinting after us. They must have been farther up in the herd when we first made contact, and it took them this long to force their way through the crush of bodies and break out into the open where their speed made them such dangerous hunters.

"Keep going," I shouted to Rachel as I faced backwards and raised the shotgun.

The lead female was about twenty-five yards away when I fired the first round of buckshot. The mass of BB sized pellets slammed into her chest and very nearly stopped her cold in her tracks. She stumbled then fell to the pavement without a sound.

I racked the shotgun slide, ejecting the spent shell, which hit the asphalt with a hollow plastic sound. The next shell fed into the chamber, and this one was a slug. I fired at the second female that was racing towards me and no more than twenty yards away.

The slug tore into her left shoulder, causing damage that would have put any normal person down and most likely out for good. Her body jerked to the left with the impact. When she turned back, I could see that her left arm was being held to her shoulder by only a few tendons and strings of flesh. The slug had completely destroyed the bone and muscle at the socket, but other than momentarily slowing from the impact, she ignored the wound and continued on.

I racked the slide again, firing at no more than five yards. This shell was buckshot and the full force of the blast erased her face. Most of her head disintegrated but her body continued with forward momentum until it came to rest on the pavement at my feet.

I noted the lesson about severe injuries not being enough to stop an infected, scanned for more females, then turned and ran after Rachel. I moved at a fast pace, quickly passing and urging her to run faster to match my speed.

Rachel looked like she was in good shape, but I didn't know if that was dancing muscle with poor cardio conditioning to back it up. So far she was staying with me, but we hadn't run a quarter of a mile yet, and adrenaline will carry you a good distance before poor conditioning becomes evident.

Ahead of us, several males stumbled out of the woods, most of them losing their balance and falling onto the pavement before climbing to their feet and coming towards the sound we were making as we ran down the middle of the road.

"Behind me," I said to Rachel as we approached the group. They were spread out just enough to effectively cover the road from shoulder to shoulder, and I didn't want to take us into the woods.

Rachel fell in close behind me as we neared the first infected, a scrawny man wearing nothing but filthy white underwear. Without breaking stride, I smashed the shotgun barrel into the side of his head, knocking him to the side and to his knees. The group started to collapse in on us as I hit two more infected with the shotgun. We were almost clear when I heard a clatter and cry from Rachel.

Stopping and spinning around I saw her on the ground. One of the infected I had knocked down had grabbed her ankle and was trying to pull her to him with grunts and hisses as she kicked at his head with her free foot. She couldn't get a good angle, and the kicks were bouncing off with apparently no effect.

I fired the shotgun at an infected coming at me with his arms raised like a kid pretending to be a Halloween ghost. His head dissolved in a spray of blood and bone from the heavy slug and I snapped a kick into the chest of another infected that was shambling at me. He fell backwards. I stepped over the infected that had grabbed Rachel, pulled my pistol and fired a single shot into his head.

The grip on Rachel's ankle immediately loosened and she kicked free and scrambled to her feet. We stood back to back at the center of a group of eight males. I had wanted to move quickly and conserve ammo, but the scream of an approaching female spurred me to action. Raising the pistol, I fired five shots, and five bodies hit the ground like sacks of wet sand.

"Move!" I shouted to Rachel, and we ran east again.

Another scream from behind lent wings to our feet and Rachel began to pull away from me, long hair flying behind her in the wind. I made a mental note to have her tie her hair up in a bun so an infected couldn't get a handful of it and drag her to the ground, then I had to spin around to fight when another female screamed right behind me.

The female had been closer than I thought and as I turned I was hit in the chest by a body that knocked me flat on my back, whooshing all my breath out of my lungs. I landed with the shotgun across my chest. I was able to get it up and between me and the snapping teeth of the female infected that was on top. I pushed for all I was worth, and she flipped backwards off of me.

I scrabbled around on the ground, trying to get my breath and my feet back under me. I had only risen to a knee when the female launched at me again. Twisting to the side, I clubbed her with the shotgun and knocked her to the ground in a tangle of limbs. As she struggled to get back on her feet, Rachel stepped behind her and shot her in the back of the head with her pistol. The body flopped to the ground and twitched once, then lay still.

Behind us the herd was closing the distance, now down to less than fifty yards. More males were coming out of the woods. Behind the leading edge of the herd, I could hear multiple screams from females as they worked their way towards us. Picking myself up, I started running again, following Rachel, who didn't need to be told this time.

We ran for what felt like an hour but was probably closer to ten minutes. The herd still followed but was dropping farther and farther behind. The occasional male was still coming out of the woods, but we were able to either dodge them or knock them aside and keep up our pace.

We crested a rise, and I called a brief halt to survey our situation. Behind us, a good half a mile, was the leading edge of the herd that was in pursuit. Between the herd and us were a few dozen lumbering males that had stumbled out of the woods.

What concerned me most were the figures out in front of the herd that were sprinting towards us. I couldn't make out details at the distance, but they had to be female infected, and I counted at least twenty of them before I turned and started running again.

Twenty or more females would run us to ground and overwhelm us if we were caught in the open. I'm good with a gun, but I don't know anyone that's good enough to fend off that many attackers on the open road. We needed somewhere to not only make a defense but also, hopefully, hide from the herd so that we didn't become trapped.

Ahead I could see a road that cut through the woods at a ninety-degree angle and a small blue sign with white lettering. I wasn't close enough to read it, but remembered passing it earlier. It marked the entrance to a marina on a large lake. The same lake I had seen on the map that we were trying to get around.

I pointed at the road, and Rachel nodded her head in agreement or understanding. I didn't care which one at the moment. As we approached the intersection, the shoulder widened out into a level, grassy field. Cutting the corner off the intersection, we charged into the field.

I was slowing, but not as much as Rachel, who was starting to drop behind. Between weapons, ammo and packs I had at least a hundred pounds distributed across my body, and Rachel probably had close to seventy. I used to train with this kind of weight, but it had been a lot of years.

We cleared the field and pounded back onto the pavement just as a chorus of screams broke out behind us. I risked a glance over my shoulder and saw a group of females that had cleared the rise in the road and was in hot pursuit.

I dug deep and pushed harder, taking advantage of the slight downhill slope of the road as it dropped down to the lake. Rachel matched my pace but she was breathing like a steam engine, and I knew she didn't have many reserves left.

Several infected and three shotgun blasts later we pounded around a curve in the road, and I dropped the Mossberg on the pavement. It was empty, and I needed to shed some weight. I brought the rifle around to my front, made sure the safety was off and ran for all I was worth.

Screams behind us sounded much closer than I would have thought possible, but I didn't want to lose speed by looking back. Ahead we could see the road ending in a large marina, over a hundred boats moored on the blue lake.

More screams and I knew we'd have to fight. The females were closing and would be on us before we made the water.

"Find a boat and get it started," I yelled to Rachel as I started to slow.

"What are you doing?" She looked over her shoulder at me, terror in her eyes.

"Buying us time. Now go. I'll be right behind you."

I skidded to a stop, turned and dropped to my right knee as I brought the rifle up. There were nine females in close pursuit, danger close as we used to say, a larger group perhaps another two hundred yards behind them.

Just like I'd been trained so many years ago, I kept both eyes open, brought the rifle up and acquired my first target, at which I immediately fired. The closest female dropped to the pavement, a neat red hole in her forehead. I acquired my next target and fired, noting in my mind that it was down as I was already acquiring my next target.

I fired a total of eleven rounds to bring down nine infected with head shots, with the last one dropping close enough to me that I could smell the stench coming off its body. Damn fine shooting if I say so myself. I glanced over my shoulder and saw Rachel approach a large white cabin cruiser, pull her pistol and shoot an infected before boarding. We needed more time.

Scanning the area around me, I made note of several males dressed in dirty coveralls that were approaching from my left. I had time to deal with them a little later. Right now I had more females coming in fast.

Picking targets, I started putting them down, occasionally having to use a second shot to do the job. Hey, you try hitting something the size of a human head that is running at you full speed. It's not as easy as it looks in the movies.

I had dropped another dozen females when I had to change magazines. Old training paid off, and I swapped mags in under a second and resumed firing. I was stopping a lot of infected, but I wasn't holding my own. The females were too many and too fast for one shooter to hold off indefinitely.

Slowly, the distance shrank until I was getting nervous. I hadn't forgotten the males approaching from my left, but I couldn't take my attention off the females. I sent five more rounds downrange then heard the sweetest sound I could imagine. A boat horn.

I shot the three closest females, leapt to my feet and started running. The pavement sloped more steeply here, ending at a chain link gate that controlled access to a wooden dock. Fortunately, it was standing open. The dock was over two hundred yards long with arms spaced periodically at right angles to create slips for what must have been three hundred boats of all sizes.

I skidded as I approached the gate, grabbing the chain link and slamming it shut behind me. It swung out towards the pavement, so less than two seconds later when the first female slammed against the fencing, it rattled but held.

She screamed and tried to force her arms through the chain link to reach me. Quickly, more females began crashing against the gate and fence, their combined voices nearly deafening.

I trotted towards the boat Rachel had boarded. The boat was in the first slip closest to the central dock and would have to be backed out and motored down a side channel for a good distance before reaching the open lake. A sharp ninety-degree turn at the end meant we'd have to take it slow and pass close to the dock and several other boats when we made the turn.

Rachel was visible on the flying bridge of the boat, which sat well above all of the surrounding ones. She'd found us a large cabin cruiser, and I could hear the low, throaty rumble of the engine as I pounded down the dock.

Rachel was yelling, but I couldn't understand what she was trying to tell me. She resorted to pointing, and I looked over my shoulder to see one of the females finish scaling the fence and drop to the dock. Soon the others were following, and I picked up my speed.

They were only forty yards or so behind me as I reached the boat and there was no way I could get it untied, board and sail to safety without all of them swarming aboard. I raced to the bow line, releasing it from a heavy cleat bolted to the dock, then rushed to release the stern.

"I'll hold them. Pick me up at the end of the dock." I yelled to Rachel.

I didn't wait to see what she was doing. Dropping back onto my knee, I raised the rifle and acquired my first target.

In the half second between acquisition and firing, I saw what had probably been a pretty suburban soccer mom with long blonde hair. A fraction of a second later my bullet shattered her skull, and her body tumbled to a stop.

The dock was a better place tactically than the open road. Here the infected were funneled onto a surface no more than six feet wide, which made the whole job of killing them much more efficient. Acquire – Fire – Acquire – Fire.

I burned through thirty rounds, and now the flood of infected was hampered by the growing pile of bodies. They had to slow to climb the pile and when they did they made themselves an easier target.

Females were still arriving and climbing the fence, but I was keeping them a steady twenty yards away. Unfortunately, I didn't have unlimited ammunition. Swapping mags, I risked a glance over my shoulder and saw that Rachel had cleared the end of the side dock and was slowly approaching the end of the channel that led to the lake. Firing four more shots that brought down four infected, I stood up and ran for the end of the dock.

The screams behind me rose in volume, perhaps in frustration at their escaping prey. I ran hard, probably harder than I have ever run in my life. I could see the big boat negotiate the final turn then surge forward.

I ran past the final side dock, and now only blue lake water surrounded the wooden planks I ran on. I was less than 10 feet from the end when a scream sounded right behind me and a body crashed into my back, knocking both of us flat before we skidded over the edge and into the water.

20

The female clung to my pack as we sank, the hundred plus pounds of gear I wore dragging us down. After what seemed an eternity, first my toes and then my knees settled onto the muddy bottom of the lake. I was thrashing, trying to break the grip the infected had on me, but she clung tight.

Gathering my legs, I pushed against the lake bottom and arched backwards hoping to crush her into the mud and break free. Instead of flipping over backwards we smashed into something solid that loosened her grip slightly. It took me a moment, but when I realized it was one of the giant wooden pilings that supported the dock, I used all the strength in my legs to keep ramming us backwards into the post.

My lungs were on fire and felt ready to burst when she finally released me. I thrashed away and pushed for the surface, needing air more than I was worried about her.

Swimming with heavy packs and weapons strapped to your body may sound impossible. Not only can it be done, but the military trains all its Special Forces operators how to do it. However, having been trained years ago and executing on that training now were two different things. I didn't think I would make it and was preparing to dump the pack when my face broke the surface, and I was able to draw a deep breath.

I had come up under the dock and quickly grabbed on to a brace so I could more easily keep my head above water. The infected that had gone into the water with me bobbed to the surface a moment later, face down and not moving. I didn't believe my smashing her into the piling had killed her, rather thought she had drowned.

Right above my head were dozens of infected females, milling around. Waiting. The occasional scream pierced the air, but it didn't seem like they had spotted me. The rumble of the boat motor grew as Rachel approached the end of the dock, but she veered away as one of the females launched herself at the boat. The infected came up short and hit the water with a splash. She thrashed violently for almost a minute before going still and bobbing on the surface.

They couldn't swim! And I realized that they didn't recognize the danger of the water as more of them leapt off the end of the dock in an attempt to reach Rachel, who now had the boat sitting forty feet out on the lake. I waved from my hiding place, but she couldn't see me.

Taking a few deep breaths, I went under the water and started swimming out. The boat wasn't far, but you don't move fast with a ton of gear on your body, and I was forced to surface for air about halfway. A chorus of screams greeted me and was almost instantly followed by splashes all around as they tried to catch me.

Rachel spotted me now, and I saw her disappear off the flying bridge, a moment later appearing at the stern of the boat, rope in hand. I struggled through the water, fending off a female that landed close enough to get a fingertip grip on my pack. I had to hit her twice, and the loss of concentration caused me to sink. I fought my way back to the surface and kept struggling towards the boat as more splashes sounded behind me.

Already tired from the run to the lake, I was weakening when a rope smacked onto the surface of the water a couple of feet in front of me. With renewed energy I swam to it, grabbed on and started pulling hand over hand towards the boat. Minutes later I was holding on to a small platform with a ladder that was bolted to the boat's stern to allow easy access for swimmers.

Resting for a few minutes, I looked up into Rachel's smiling face and grinned like a goofy teenager, happy to be alive. Holding tight to the ladder, I got my feet under me and with what felt like Herculean effort, slowly climbed out of the water and into the boat. Rachel greeted me with a hug then helped me out of my gear before I dropped to the deck, exhausted.

"I thought I'd lost you."

"Thought I'd lost me too there for a bit," I answered, wiping water out of my eyes. "Thanks for the rope. Not sure I would have made it without it."

Rachel held my hand for a moment then turned her attention to the dock. The infected had stopped leaping into the water and now stood staring at us, screaming in frustration. A dozen bodies floated between the dock and us.

"Did they figure out they can't swim, or did they just give up?" Rachel asked.

"I don't know. Maybe there's still enough working brain in there for them to understand they can't survive in the water after seeing their companions die. Thank God they can't swim, or I'd have been toast."

A thought hit me as I stood back up, "Did you clear the boat?"

The look on Rachel's face answered my question before she could speak.

"Stay here, gun in hand. I'll be back," I said, drawing my pistol and checking the magazine to make sure it was fully loaded.

The boat was bigger than I had expected. I estimated it was fifty feet long, and it was a luxury cruiser with three staterooms, four heads, a galley, a large seating area called a salon and multiple other compartments that were a mix of storage space and various nautical uses that I couldn't identify. Checking everything thoroughly took nearly fifteen minutes. Fortunately, we were alone.

I made my way up to the flying bridge and motioned Rachel to join me. "Do you know anything about boats?" I asked her when she arrived.

"Some. I used to date a guy that had one, and we would go out almost every weekend in the summer. He always handled the boat, but I paid attention. What about you?"

"I know the pointy end is the front, and they're surrounded by water," I answered with a grin. "So I guess that makes you the captain, especially since you got it out of dock without sinking it."

"You didn't notice the scrapes along the side," Rachel smiled and stepped up to the controls. Moments later the engine revved, and she spun the wheel to set us on a course for the middle of the lake.

"Can we get out a ways from shore and drop anchor and stay there for a while?" I asked.

"Shouldn't be a problem." Rachel reached forward and fiddled with a couple of electronic displays. "Looks like we've got about seventy feet of water under us right now."

We were maybe half a mile from the dock with shoreline on each side about a quarter of a mile away. In front of us the lake looked to continue for miles, and from what I remembered of how it was drawn on the map, there was a myriad of small coves as the main lake twisted and turned.

Rachel cut the engine after using reverse to bring us to a stop in the water, then flipped a switch on the console that was protected by a plastic cover to prevent accidental activation. I jumped as a loud rattling sound and splash came from the front of the boat, relaxing when Rachel laughed at me.

"It's the anchor. Nothing you need to shoot."

I gave her a look that she ignored in favor of watching the heavy rope that was spooling out of a recessed compartment on the deck at the very front of the boat. When it stopped unwinding, she lifted the plastic cover and set the switch to the middle position.

"Anchor's down and locked. We'll pivot around it at the end of the line if there's any wind or current in the lake, but we'll stay put in this area," she said.

Looking around the flying bridge, I found the pair of binoculars I expected to be there. Raising them to my eyes, I focused on the dock we had escaped from. It was swarming with infected for its entire length, and the paved area was packed with swaying bodies.

"It looks like that entire herd followed us," I said, still scanning the distant shore.

"We have to be more careful," Rachel said. "If we hadn't been close to the marina we wouldn't have escaped.

"Agreed. We got very lucky. We've been very lucky up to now. I just didn't expect to run into another herd. Why the hell are they doing that? Where are they going?" My questions were really more rhetorical, but Rachel felt the need to talk about it.

"I don't know. Maybe something in the way their brains are affected has caused the herding instinct to become dominant. Humans are by nature tribal animals, not herd, so it doesn't make a lot of sense," she answered. "I'm also surprised that we're not finding uninfected people. This has spread so fast it's almost beyond belief. Especially when you try to explain why neither of us has been infected. Are we immune, or just very lucky?"

I lowered the binoculars and looked at her. “Good questions, but we don’t know enough to even start guessing.”

Making a final scan of the two closest shorelines, I put the binoculars back in their spot. “I’m going to take these wet clothes off and get my gear dried out. Do you mind checking the galley to see if there’s any food and water on board?”

“Will do, and I’ll bet a boat like this has a laundry on it. I’ll see if I can find it and we’ll get your clothes drying.”

I moved down to the deck where my pack was lying in a spreading puddle of water that was seeping out of it. Moving the pack to the edge of the deck so it would drain overboard into the lake, I sat on a thickly padded bench and pulled my waterlogged boots off.

Opening them up to the sun, I pulled off my vest and harness, then stripped down to my underwear. The hot Georgia sun felt good on my skin as I worked to unpack and spread everything out.

“Found it,” Rachel announced as she walked out onto deck. She gathered up the clothes I had taken off as well as the wet clothes from my pack and headed back inside.

I spent almost an hour stripping, cleaning and oiling weapons. Loaded magazines were emptied, dried, lightly oiled and reloaded. Fortunately, modern ammo can easily survive a casual dunking in water, and I wasn't particularly worried that any of it would fail to fire when needed.

The sun was setting as I was loading the last magazine and Rachel slid open the glass door that accessed the salon and called out that dinner was ready.

21

Whatever Rachel had put together for dinner smelled wonderful as I entered the cabin. I sat down at a small table that folded out of the way when not in use. That's when it hit me.

"Oh, shit!" I exclaimed, leaping to my feet and nearly upsetting the table in the process.

Rachel froze in place with a look of barely contained panic on her face, "What?" she whispered.

"Dog," I said, my gut churning. "We left him in the truck."

The look on her face morphed from fear to shock, then sadness. "But... how?"

"He was in the back seat when we bailed out of the truck. Son of a Bitch!"

I headed back to the open deck and started arranging the items I needed. Rachel followed, still holding a bowl of food she had been bringing to the table before my outburst.

"What are you doing?"

"I'm going to get him. He'll die in that truck, and I'm not going to let that happen." I started filling pockets and pouches on my vest with full magazines and spare ammunition, mentally cataloging what I thought I'd need for a quick raid to rescue Dog.

"Are you crazy?" There was a note of hysteria in Rachel's voice. "You can't fight through all those infected, save Dog and make it back here. You'll get killed, and I'll be on my own."

I finished packing the vest and started checking the loads in my pistol and rifle. "Rachel, this is exactly the kind of shit I trained for and pulled off for nearly half my life. It's getting dark; it's not far, and I'll be in and out before any of the infected even know I'm around."

She reached out and put a hand on my arm. I looked up and saw a tear rolling down her cheek. "What if you don't come back? I'll be on my own. I'm afraid..." she said in a low, emotion-choked voice.

I holstered my pistol and straightened up. "Me too. I've never been scared of anything in my life, but honestly this whole thing scares the living shit out of me."

Her lower lip started trembling, and I pulled her into a hug before she completely lost it.

"Rachel, you're smart and strong. You survived where most people didn't before we even met. But there's no point in even thinking about that because I'm coming back with Dog. Now, can you help me finish getting ready?"

Rachel squeezed me hard then pushed away and wiped the tears off her face, sniffed and tried to put on a smile that only half made it.

"What do you need?"

"I want to swim to shore. Starting this engine will excite all the infected, and I don't want them stirred up and waiting for me. Can you search the boat and see if there's any snorkeling gear? You know; flippers, goggles, breathing tube, whatever you can find. I could also use a couple of waterproof bags, and if there aren't any flippers then some kind of flotation device. I'm going to be weighed down pretty heavy with weapons and ammo."

Now I was a Green Beret, not a Navy SEAL. Yes, the Army trains us to operate in water, swim with gear on our backs and boots on our feet. But I'm not 20 anymore, and besides, I hadn't lived in the water the way SEALs do.

Rachel went into the cabin to start searching for my requested items while I finalized my equipment load. A few minutes later she returned with a big grin on her face and an armful of gear that she dumped on the deck.

I sorted through it and was pleased to find a set of swim fins, goggles, a couple of large rubberized canvas bags with rubber zip seals and a red buoy with a white diagonal stripe on it. Apparently the boat's owner had been a diver since the color scheme on the buoy is the international symbol used to warn other boaters that there are divers in the water.

Unlacing my boots, I placed them and my socks in one of the waterproof bags, sealing it tight. There were two sturdy nylon ropes attached to the bag and I slipped my arms through and wore it like a backpack. I shoved my feet into the flippers, less than thrilled with the too tight fit. But, beggars can't be choosers.

Swinging my legs over the stern of the boat, I put my finned feet onto the small swim platform. Leaning down, I dunked the goggles in the water to wet the inside of the lens and prevent them from fogging up on the swim to shore.

I debated using the buoy for flotation but decided it would be more of a hassle than it was worth. I was as lightly loaded as possible for the situation I was headed into. I had on a pair of black quick drying compression shorts with matching sleeveless shirt, my vest with all my spare mags and ammo, combat knife, pistol and rifle. I slipped the goggles over my head and adjusted them. I have a big head, and they were too small, but again when you're a beggar...

It was almost fully dark when I was ready to go. To the west, the sky was a deep shade of purple that would fade to black very quickly, but there was enough light for me to see the heavy bank of clouds that looked to be heading our way. All the better. Easier to operate under the cover of a storm if it made it into our area.

I turned to Rachel, who stood on the deck watching my preparations. She had a look of worry that reminded me so much of my wife that, for a moment, my heart ached that I wasn't in Arizona to take care of her.

"Leave the emotion behind, soldier. Emotion distracts us. Emotion gets us killed." The voice of my favorite instructor, from the land warfare school at Fort Bragg, was so loud in my head I almost looked to see if he was standing behind Rachel.

Suppressing the feelings that were running through me I gave Rachel my best, brave smile. "I'll be back. With Dog. But if I'm not back in twenty-four hours, you need to move on without me. Understand?"

Rachel nodded, stepped forward and leaned over the rail to kiss me on the cheek. "Come back. I'll be waiting."

Unleashed

I squeezed her hand, turned and slipped into the dark water of the lake.

22

The dock was still swarming with infected. Either side, the shoreline was heavily forested except for occasional breaks where large homes had been built and lush green lawns ran all the way to the water's edge. In my survey with the binoculars, before the sun went down, I had noted that all the lawns close to the dock had also been choked with slowly swaying bodies.

But there were less and less milling on the grass of the houses along the shoreline to the west of the dock. This was also the right direction to come ashore as close to the truck as possible.

I had chosen a particularly large mansion that also sported its own dock and boathouse for my landing site. I had a good third of a mile swim ahead of me, but the lake was calm and the water temperature pleasant. I started kicking, careful to keep my feet below the surface at all times so as not to make any splashing sounds that would alert the infected to my approach.

One-third of a mile doesn't sound like much, but when you're not accustomed to swimming that far with over forty pounds of weapons, ammo and gear on your body it takes a bit of time. Forty-five minutes later I made it to the boathouse without incident. I stood in chest-deep water, silently surveying the area for any sound or movement. I gave it ten minutes before moving into shallower water.

Moving carefully to maintain noise discipline, I approached the boathouse from the lake side. The boathouse was large, nothing more than a floating building anchored to the shore and open underneath so all I had to do was duck under the wall and surface inside next to a speedboat.

Again I stood perfectly still, only this time in waist deep water, and listened for any threat in the pitch black in the boathouse. After a few minutes of silence, I carefully moved between the speed boat and its access ramp, slowly pulling myself and my gear out of the water. I immediately went to one knee and raised my rifle to scan for threats.

When nothing materialized, I removed the swim fins and swapped them in the waterproof bag for my socks and boots. The goggles joined the fins in the bag and a couple of minutes later, feet dry, I was ready to go.

Silently stepping to a small window that faced a lawn and massive home with white clapboard siding, I paused to survey the area and again saw no sign of infected. I moved to the door and froze when it emitted a loud squeal as it swung open. It sucks getting old. Twenty years ago I would have anticipated this and been prepared.

Leaving the door a few inches ajar, I searched a small work bench in the boathouse, finally finding a rusting can of WD40. A few squirts on each hinge and I went back to the window to watch while the chemical lubricants had time to do their job.

Five minutes later I was able to swing the door open with only the faintest of sounds, closed it gently behind me and headed up the lawn. I moved at a fast walk, rifle to my shoulder at the ready, and angled across the hundred yards of green grass toward the right side of the house.

Approaching the house, I quickly changed direction and put my back against the wall when I heard the sound of a shoe scraping against the ground from around the corner. I had my rifle at the ready, then thought better of firing off a shot unless I had no other choice.

M4s are loud, and I didn't feel like alerting every infected around the lake that I was available for dinner. Lowering the rifle and letting it hang from its sling, I silently drew a Ka-Bar fighting knife with an eight-inch blade and moved to the corner of the house.

Peeking around, I saw an infected male stumbling about on a large patio area. He was dressed in what I suspected were once natty boating clothes but were now a muddy and bloody mess. I took my time to scan the area for any more infected. When I felt it was clear, I stepped around the corner and moved quickly behind the male, driving the Ka-Bar into the soft spot at the base of the skull where the spine meets the head.

He dropped like a puppet with its strings cut, my knife pulling out of his skull with a wet, sucking sound. I bent and wiped the blade clean on his clothing before re-sheathing, then brought my rifle back to the ready and moved across the patio and into the woods that had been neatly cut back from the lawn.

It was dark in the woods. Back in the day, I would have had night vision to help, but unfortunately, the gun shop I had raided either hadn't had any or they had already been taken. I had to move slowly to maintain noise discipline as well as not stumble upon an infected that just happened to be standing there. I didn't expect to meet any in the woods, but at the same time, I wasn't going to take any chances.

It took me an hour to navigate the woods at my slow and cautious pace. My face and arms were scratched from vines and small branches I couldn't see in the dark, and it felt like a family of mosquitoes had taken up residence on every inch of exposed skin. Ignoring the discomfort, I stopped when the woods ended at the road where we had abandoned the truck. To my left, the road disappeared over a rise, and if my navigation was good, that would be where I would find the truck.

I waited, hidden in the brush, watching and listening. Even though I knew the world had changed, it didn't hit me completely until that moment. I was on the edge of a major city with probably the busiest airport in the world, and the night was primeval quiet.

There was the sound of crickets, owls, and other nocturnal animals, but there wasn't a single modern human noise to be heard. No big diesel truck slowing on the freeway. No rap music, blasting way too loud from a car that probably cost less than the stereo system in it. No sounds of airplanes. Nothing. Just the quiet that had been here hundreds of years ago before the first European settlers showed up.

Refocusing on the road, I took my time scanning the pavement and the opposite tree line. I didn't see anything moving and didn't hear anything that I hadn't already noted. After a full fifteen minutes of watching, I decided to move.

Drawing my knife, I stepped out of the woods and started walking along a narrow strip of mown grass that separated the tree line from the edge of the asphalt. My steps were nearly silent to my own ears, so I knew the sound wasn't carrying more than a few feet. My rifle was tight to my shoulder, ready for use, as I approached the top of the rise.

Slowing my pace I eventually dropped to first my knees, then my belly to crawl the last few feet to the crest so that I didn't create a silhouette on top of the rise. I had to worry about more than just the infected.

A couple of hundred yards down the road the truck sat sideways on the pavement, gleaming faintly in the moonlight. I was relieved to note that the doors were closed. At least the infected hadn't had easy access to make a meal out of Dog. Unfortunately, there were more than fifty of them, both males and females, surrounding the truck and in the open bed.

Different plans swirled through my head and were quickly discarded. I couldn't take on this many infected single handed. If they had all been males, perhaps, but even then I would have to use the rifle and the sound would draw every infected within a half mile radius. I needed to find a way to draw them all away from the truck, so I could make a mad dash and rescue Dog.

I was concentrating so hard that I almost failed to note the sounds of shuffling footsteps behind me. Spinning around, I saw a large male only a few feet away. Damn it! Either I was slipping in my old age, or he was one stealthy son of a bitch. I launched off the ground, leading with the Ka-Bar as he lurched towards me, mouth open as he started to let out a gurgling snarl.

Coming off the ground, I drove upwards with my legs; the blade held straight out in my right hand like a spear. The tip met the soft tissue under his chin, and I kept shoving until it punched through his mouth and up into his brain.

It was like turning off a light switch. A strong, animated opponent suddenly went as limp as a sack of rice and collapsed. He fell on top of me, pushing me to the ground and covering me with his blood.

Cursing silently, I shoved the corpse away and pulled the knife out of his head. I wiped the blade on his clothes, but couldn't do anything about the sticky blood that coated my hand, arm and chest. It would have to wait until I got back to the lake and swam back out to the boat.

Crouching, I scanned the area, and it appeared clear. It had seemed clear earlier, but this big fucker had surprised me and almost ruined my evening. Making a mental note to keep scanning my immediate surroundings very frequently, I turned my attention back to the truck.

It didn't look like any of the infected had noted the brief scuffle. Good. Now, how to distract them long enough to silently run two hundred yards, get Dog out of the truck then disappear into the woods without unwanted company.

An idea took shape. I tried and found about a dozen holes in it, but couldn't come up with anything better. I began digging through the other waterproof bag while frequently scanning my surroundings. Inside were three reactive targets that I had grabbed when I was looting the sporting goods store.

Reactive targets, also called exploding targets, are a binary explosive. They are plastic containers about the size of a squat pickle jar that contain ammonium nitrate and powdered aluminum in separate packets.

When the two substances are mixed, and the container is struck with a high-velocity rifle slug, they react very violently and create a very loud blast and lots of smoke. They don't burn, so no worries about setting the forest on fire. My problem was how to shoot them with my rifle to get them to detonate without giving away my location to the infected.

Remembering something I'd been taught in the Army, I started scouting along the roadside. It took nearly half an hour, but I finally found what I was looking for. I had collected two, two-liter plastic bottles, Pepsi and Mountain Dew if it matters, and one large Arrowhead plastic water bottle.

An instructor I'd known at Fort Bragg had called these Hillbilly Silencers. Put the muzzle of your weapon into the mouth of the bottle, tape it on good and tight, and you had a one use, poor man's sound suppressor that would reduce the report of the rifle firing by almost eighty percent.

The downside was that each bottle only worked for one shot as it would get pretty well torn up by the bullet and the gasses expanding out of the muzzle of the weapon. If you needed a second or third quiet shot, you had to take the time to remove the remains of the current bottle and tape a new one on in its place.

My hope was that the bottle would reduce the report of my rifle enough for the sound to not carry the two hundred yards to the infected. Or at least, to not carry well enough for them to identify my position.

Pulling the plastic tabs on each of the containers that kept the two ingredients separated during shipping and storage, I shook them to get them ready, then placed each one back in the waterproof bag. Shouldering it, I crept back into the woods.

My plan was to work my way past the infected and place the targets on the side of the road about 100 yards beyond the truck. I would then return to my current position and put a round into the targets, hoping the resulting explosion and smoke would draw all the infected away from the truck. There were several holes in that plan.

First; I had to make my way silently through three hundred yards of forest, place the targets, and then retrace my path without alerting the infected.

Second; assuming I successfully placed the targets and made it back, I then had three tries to make a three hundred yard shot in the dark. Granted, the target containers were fluorescent orange, but they weren't significantly larger than my fist in profile. I would have three opportunities at best before I ran out of plastic bottles.

Third; I was counting on the Hillbilly Silencers to muffle the report of my rifle enough to not draw infected to my position.

Fourth; the infected had to be attracted to the explosion in sufficient numbers to allow me relatively free access to the truck.

Oh, and the Fifth; I had to get to the truck, get Dog out, and disappear without being spotted. I was confident I could easily outdistance the males, but if several females got on my trail, they could run me to ground very quickly. And they were damn strong.

There were probably about a dozen more problems with my plan that ran through my head as I worked through the brush. I put them aside so I could concentrate on noise discipline and scanning for any infected that might be loitering in the trees.

Twenty minutes later I had covered the two hundred yards and was parallel with the truck. In the faint moonlight I counted fifty infected around and on the truck, then quit counting and guessed the number was close to seventy.

About fifteen of them were females. More than enough to form a hunting pack, run me down and rip me to shreds. I was glad to note that the wire mesh I had covered all the truck's glass with was still intact. Other than scared, hungry and dehydrated, Dog should be OK.

Moving slower because of my proximity to the infected, I kept on, taking another twenty minutes to go the final hundred yards. Stopping on a small hump in the terrain, I belly crawled to the shoulder of the road and placed the targets on the edge of the asphalt. Every movement was slow and deliberate, bringing sweat out as I concentrated on not making any noise.

The mosquitoes that had found me in the forest had stayed with me, and the only positive news was that malaria and yellow fever didn't exist in Georgia. Regardless, I'd look like a pincushion and itch like a flea infested dog for a few days.

Targets in place, I retreated to the trees and paused to check them out. Each container was fluorescent orange and glowed in the weak moonlight. I had placed them one on top of another, making a short tower, trying to give myself a larger target. I also hoped the concussive force from one target exploding would cause a sympathetic detonation in the other two for a really spectacular BOOM, but I had no idea if that would work.

An hour later I was back on the rise where I had started, staring down the road. Clouds were scudding across the moon, and there was almost no light. I couldn't spot the targets. The sky looked like it would clear off soon, so I sat back, drank some water, waited and watched.

While I waited, I spent a few minutes repositioning the dead infected male that had almost made a meal of me earlier. Once I had the body lying across the road, at the highest point of the rise, I lay down behind it and set my rifle on its back. It made a perfect shooting rest.

Some time later a raccoon ambled out of the trees a few yards away. He stopped, looked at me, stood on his hind legs to sniff the air then quickly vanished back into the forest. I'm sure he could smell the infected, but didn't know if the smell of them or my infected blood soaked shirt was what had sent him scurrying off. I didn't waste too much time thinking about it as the clouds finally moved on and the moon came back out with what seemed like more intensity than before.

I had already prepped the rifle with the Pepsi bottle and had the Mountain Dew and Arrowhead bottles sitting there ready to go. The Pepsi bottle was held in place with a couple of wraps of duct tape, yes it's indispensable even in the apocalypse, and I had already wrapped a length of tape around the mouths of the two spare bottles to get them ready to be used.

Rolling onto my belly, I laid the rifle back on top of the body and scanned with its low power combat scope for the targets. I was getting concerned when I couldn't find them but finally spotted the bright orange plastic. I took a deep breath and slowly let it out through my nose.

This would be one hell of a shot. Three hundred yards on a target less than eleven inches tall and five inches wide. Easy shot with a rifle set up with a bipod and high power scope, but I didn't have either. I was relying on years of shooting that started with targeting coyotes in the West Texas desert when I was only twelve years old.

I spared a glance at the truck, but there was nothing new there. Same swarm of infected paying attention only to the meal inside the cab that they couldn't get to. Looking around, I checked the area behind me and found it clear of threats. Back to the rifle, I pulled the stock tight to my shoulder, pressed my cheek into place and acquired the target.

I held high, knowing that the 5.56 mm round would drop about an inch of vertical height for every hundred yards of horizontal distance traveled. At three hundred yards that made for a three-inch drop, so I aimed at the top target. It was a calm night with no wind, so I had no excuses to not get a hit.

Another deep breath, then I breathed out slowly and squeezed the trigger as my exhale stopped. The rifle made a strange popping noise that sounded like a combination of a bongo drum and snare drum, but not much louder than if I had clapped my hands together. The bottom and most of the sides of the Pepsi bottle blew out. The targets didn't detonate. Shit.

A quick check of the infected around the truck and I saw a couple of females that seemed to be looking around, but the Hillbilly Silencer had apparently done the trick. The problem was, I had no idea where my bullet went. Didn't know if I was high, low, left or right.

As quietly as I could, I stripped the Pepsi bottle off and replaced it with the Mountain Dew bottle and smoothed down the tape to hold it in place. I re-sighted on the target, held slightly higher this time and aimed a couple of degrees off to the left. Again; deep breath, exhale, fire.

No hit, and this time the bottle didn't work as well. Thinner plastic? Who knows. I checked the infected at the truck, and there were now several females standing away from the pack looking in my general direction. They obviously weren't sure I was there, or they would already be charging, but I was on borrowed time.

Third bottle on the rifle. Aim high and right, deep breath, exhale, fire. Nothing. I ripped the bottle off the end of the rifle as I watched half a dozen females start moving in my direction. Not running yet, but moving too fast for my comfort.

Fuck it. I stripped off my shirt and wound it tightly around the muzzle of the rifle. It wouldn't work as well as the bottles, but the fabric would suppress the muzzle flash and knock down a good amount of the report. Aim center mass on the target, adjust up a couple of degrees, deep breath, exhale and fire.

23

BOOM!

The detonation was far louder than I expected. I felt the concussion in my chest, and a huge cloud of white smoke marked where the targets had been. I ripped my attention away from the smoke to check on the infected. It looked like the diversion was working.

The pack had abandoned the truck and was moving towards the smoke cloud. All but two females, that is, who were still moving towards me. They must have either seen my movement as I fired or heard enough of the rifle report to keep their attention.

The pack had cleared the truck by a good ten yards when I yanked the singed shirt off the end of the barrel, slung the rifle, grabbed my pack and headed to get Dog. The two females spotted me as soon as I stood up and broke into a run directly at me. I kept the rifle slung, afraid to use it and alert the rest of the pack to my location. Instead, I drew the Ka-Bar and moved to meet them.

One of the females looked to have been in her late teens to early twenties and was in good shape. She was completely nude as she ran towards me and even in the heat of battle my mind wondered what she had been doing at the moment she got infected. The other was older, probably in her forties and grossly out of shape. She was still coming fast, but the younger one quickly outpaced her.

I met her about half way to the truck, her at a flat out run, me slowing to a trot so I could move laterally. She leapt at me, and I spun out of her grasp, completing the spin and jamming the knife into her lower back, directly into a kidney. Now, a normal human with an eight-inch knife wound to the kidney would go down and stay down, but she wasn't normal. She twisted around and almost pulled the knife from my grasp.

I spared a glance at the fat one who was still twenty yards away but closing fast. I needed to end this quickly before I had two of them on me and we drew the attention of the rest of the pack. Stepping inside the younger infected's reach, I slammed the hilt of the knife into her forehead with enough force to snap her head back and knock her to the ground.

Using my own momentum, I followed her down, right knee landing on her chest. I both heard and felt her breastbone and ribs snap when I came down with all of my weight. Reversing the knife in my grip, I stabbed into her eye and sank the blade to the hilt. Just like earlier, all animation left her body instantly.

Jumping back to my feet, I turned as the older female arrived with a snarl. I sidestepped and swept her legs so that she fell face first to the pavement. I was on her back in a second and drove the knife into the soft spot at the base of the skull. Another instant kill.

I cleaned the blade on the back of her shirt and checked on the pack. Several figures, most likely female, were already at the cloud of smoke that was still hanging in the air, the bulk of the pack still moving in that direction. They seemed to be completely focused on the diversion, and the truck was clear for the moment.

Running, I covered the last fifty yards as fast as I could, bending over to make sure there weren't any surprises under the truck before I stepped up close to it. Grabbing the driver's side handle, I yanked the door open and immediately heard a loud growl from deep within the darkness inside the cab.

"Dog," I mumbled in a low voice. "It's ok. Let's go."

Before I got the last words out of my mouth, he was standing on the driver's seat, tail wagging so hard that his whole body quivered. I couldn't help but take the time to rub his head with both hands, surprised at the sense of relief I felt that he was OK.

Stepping away, I checked on the pack's status and Dog jumped to the ground and quickly trotted to the back of the truck where he lifted his leg and peed on the rear tire. Immediate need taken care of, he trotted back to me and pressed his head against my hip.

The pack was still distracted and moving away. I headed directly for the tree line, Dog at my side. We made it out of the open and into the shelter of the forest without being spotted. I relaxed half a notch, thinking we were clear of the imminent danger and could quietly make our way to the lake. That mistake almost cost me my life, and very likely would have if not for Dog.

He let out a low growl just as a female screamed and lunged at me from no more than five feet away. Dog leapt and met her in the air, knocking her down. He fell on her and started tearing at her throat. I was immobilized for half a second then stepped forward and rammed the knife home in the infected's ear. Dog stopped attacking as soon as the corpse went limp.

Screams from the direction the pack had gone told me that we had been heard. Time to go. I set off deeper into the woods at an oblique angle from the road, making more noise than I cared to, but speed mattered right now.

After what I estimated to be fifty yards I changed direction, ran another thirty and stopped. Behind us were screams and the sounds of bodies crashing through the underbrush, but it all sounded like it was moving parallel to us, not toward us.

I looked down at Dog. His ears were at full alert as he stared in the direction of the screams, but he wasn't acting like we were about to be attacked. Maybe we'd managed to elude them in the woods. Quietly, we started moving towards the lake again.

Behind us, there weren't sounds of pursuit and the screams slowly died out. I only hoped that meant the infected were not on our trail, not that they'd found us and were sneaking through the woods to attack.

I didn't have any idea if the infected were capable of a level of reasoning that included knowing to stealthily track prey before attacking. For that matter, was it even reasoning or was it instinct? Again, I caught myself over analyzing things. I didn't care why they might do something; I just cared if they could or couldn't do something.

We kept moving, slow and quiet. There was an occasional scream in the woods behind us, but nothing that sounded like pursuit. Slowly we pushed our way through the heavy undergrowth, not encountering any infected.

Dog stayed two paces in front of me, ears at full mast and tail tucked tightly along his back legs. Every few seconds he would glance back to make sure I was still close to him, then would go back to scanning the dark forest in front of us.

More than an hour later we stopped at the edge of the neatly mown lawn I had crossed earlier in the evening. There weren't any infected visible in the open area, and we hadn't heard any noise from the ones behind us in over half an hour. Glancing down at Dog I noted that he was alert but not on guard, so took that as a sign that I wasn't missing anything. We crept out of the woods and picked up the pace as we crossed the open lawn, heading for the back of the house and the slope down to the lake.

There weren't any clouds left in the sky and the moon gave us plenty of light to make our way without worrying about tripping over anything or running into an infected that was just standing there waiting. We paused by the body of the infected I'd killed when passing this way earlier, Dog giving it a perfunctory sniff before turning away.

Checking around the corner of the house, I was pleased to see the path to the boathouse was open and clear. Dog and I dashed down the slope, my eyes raised to the lake. As we neared the dock, I slowed, then skidded to a stop, staring out at the water. The boat I had left Rachel on a few hours ago was gone.

24

I didn't have time to stand there and worry about why Rachel had moved the boat. Behind me, there was a chorus of screams that could only mean a small pack of females had spotted us. Glancing back as I pounded down the wooden dock I saw five females coming down the lawn at a full sprint.

Crashing through the boathouse door with Dog on my heels, I grabbed the key for the speedboat that was hanging from a peg. A smiling yellow rubber ducky was on the key chain, there so the key would float if it were dropped in the water.

I barely broke stride as I grabbed the key before leaping into the boat. Dog hesitated for a moment before following me in and taking up station between the two bucket seats. It was dark in the boathouse, and I couldn't see the ignition. Spending precious time, I dug a flashlight out of my pocket and clicked it on. I was now able to see the ignition, but I had just destroyed my night vision.

Inserting and twisting the key, the two giant Mercury motors on the back of the boat rumbled to life, masking the screams of the approaching females. I scrambled to throw off the lines that tied the boat in place and dropped into the driver's seat, hand already on the throttles. I looked up and cursed.

The boathouse had a pair of wooden doors that swung open in the middle to allow access to the lake, and they were closed. They looked to be rather sturdy, and I didn't like the odds of crashing through them with the boat.

Dog growled as the sound of running feet on the dock reached his ears a moment before it did mine. Pulling my pistol, I sighted on the latch mounted in the center of the doors, my target lit by the flashlight in my left hand that was doing double duty as a brace for my shooting hand. The doors were only twenty-five or thirty feet away, an easy shot, and I put six rounds into the brass latching mechanism.

A .45 hollow point round is a big, heavy bullet that will transfer a lot of energy when it strikes a target. The rounds I fired did as I expected. The latch shattered, then blew completely free of the surrounding wood. One of the doors began to slowly swing open.

The time it took me to shoot out the latch gave the females the time they needed to reach the boathouse, and as I shifted my aim point to the walk door the first one burst through with a nerve-shattering scream. I had her spotted with the small flashlight and immediately pulled the trigger. Her face distorted for a fraction of a second, then the whole back of her head blew out and covered the female behind her with blood and brains.

The second female jumped over her, and I fired twice. One round in the center of her chest slowed her, and a follow-up shot to the head put her down. Now there were two bodies piled in the open door and the next female had to slow to climb over them. She made an easy target and quickly joined her sisters. The fourth died as soon as she showed her head and with the doorway momentarily clear, I shoved both throttles to their stops and the engines bellowed with power.

The stern of the boat dropped into the water as the props instantly spun up to full speed and the boat leapt forward. The bow crashed into the access doors, slamming them open. There was a shudder as it seemed to shake off the impact, then I could feel the acceleration kick in.

We shot out of the boathouse, pointed at the center of the lake, gaining speed at an incredible pace until I slapped the throttles back to idle. We were far enough from shore already to be relatively safe, and I didn't want to go charging around the lake at top speed in the dark.

Behind, the surviving female stood on the dock and screamed at us. Even over the idling engines, I could hear the answering screams from deeper in the woods.

"Well, we're not going back that way," I said to Dog and ruffled his ears.

He leaned sideways and pressed his head into me. Fortunately, he was a dog and didn't understand that I'd forgotten him in the truck when we had to abandon it. He was just happy to see me. After a few moments of making sure I knew he still liked me he walked to the stern of the boat, leaned way out and started drinking from the lake. He drank for a long time before coming back, burping, and lying down next to me between the bucket seats for the driver and passenger.

The boat had powered a couple of hundred yards from the shore and then drifted another fifty or so before bobbing to a stop. The surface of the lake quickly settled and within a couple of minutes it was as smooth as glass and amplifying the reflected moonlight. The dash was backlit with a dim red light, but it still took me a bit of looking to find the fuel gauge. It read just over half full. I hoped it was accurate. I suspected that the two monster engines had a hell of a thirst, and no matter how many gallons that half a tank represented, it would go fast if I was heavy on the throttle.

I dug through the lockers on the boat that were built into the seating, finally coming up with a pair of marine binoculars. They were extraordinarily light; their housing air filled so they would float if dropped overboard. Holding them to my eyes, I scanned a slow 360-degree circle.

I was hoping to spot the cabin cruiser, but it was nowhere to be seen. The dock we had stolen it from still teemed with infected, and the dock that Dog and I had just departed was quickly filling up as more infected arrived, drawn by the sounds of our escape.

I didn't think Rachel would intentionally leave without me. She had no reason to do that. She was smart and practical and realized that we stood a better chance together than apart. I had returned well before the deadline I'd given her as a time to give up on me.

There was no indication that the infected had any way to threaten her while she was sitting on a boat in the middle of the lake. That left one viable option. Other survivors had somehow boarded the boat and taken it and Rachel.

"Fuck me," I muttered under my breath. First, I leave Dog behind in a panic; now Rachel had been taken. I wasn't exactly lighting up the scoreboard with successes today.

I searched the boat again, hoping to find a map or chart of the lake, but no such luck. If Rachel had been taken, which I didn't see any other real possibility, then they were probably still somewhere on the lake. If they had just wanted her, the boat would still be floating at anchor right where I left it. Time for a search.

First things first. I was covered in blood from the infected I had killed, drenched in sweat and smeared with mud and plant stains from my trek to rescue Dog. Removing my boots, socks and weapons, I slipped over the side of the boat into the cool lake water and spent a few minutes rubbing myself as clean as I could.

Feeling refreshed, I climbed back into the boat and pulled socks and boots back on. I was shirtless, and the mosquitoes had found me out on the water and were having quite the feast at my expense. There was nothing I could do except suck it up.

Closing my eyes, I tried to picture the map of the lake I had looked at with Rachel earlier in the day. I remembered the lake was massive, going on for miles and miles as it filled in the low ground in the rolling Georgia countryside.

Multiple little arms sprouted off from the main body of water, and I was going to have to search each and every one of them. Nudging the throttles forward, I spun the wheel and pointed the boat in a southwesterly direction to start my search.

25

It was a slow search. I didn't want to go too fast and waste gas as well as alert Rachel's captors to my approach. Not that the Mercury motors didn't sound like a growl from the hounds of hell even at idle, but the faster I went the more noise they would make.

Two hours later I had lost count of how many coves I had checked. A couple of larger homes had boathouses big enough to conceal the cabin cruiser, and I had cautiously checked them as well. Both were empty.

My stomach was growling. I'd left the boat without eating the meal that Rachel had prepared, and I'd burned a lot of energy. Chastising myself for worrying about my hunger, I pushed on in the dark.

Visions of Rachel at the hands of people like the men I'd killed outside the sporting goods store made the muscles in my jaw ache as I clenched my teeth. Whoever had taken her was not going to have a pleasant time when I found them.

Another hour, and countless coves later, I motored around a sharp bend and immediately slapped the throttles to idle and cut the engines.

On the north shore of the lake, no more than half a mile away, a large house sat back in the trees.

It was lit up like they were having a party. In the light that spilled down to the water, I could see the cabin cruiser tied up at the dock. Next to it were a small bass boat and a sleek ski boat.

Water is an excellent sound reflector and noises will travel long distances across still water. The lake was as calm as a millpond, and I could clearly hear the sound of an engine I guessed to be a generator. There was also loud country music playing along with the laughter of several men.

Raising the binoculars, I scanned the cruiser and other two boats which both appeared to be unoccupied. The dock and lawn were also equally empty. No sentries? Didn't these guys realize what had happened in the world?

I spent another ten minutes watching the house, then took my time scanning the shoreline on either side looking for infected. None to be found. Perhaps the house was just too far off the beaten path. There were no other houses on the shore for as far as I could see with binoculars in each direction. Just thick trees and brush that came all the way to a thin strip of mud that was the shoreline.

Back to the house, I spotted movement on the second-floor balcony that must have had a fantastic view of the lake. An overweight man with long hair walked out through an open set of French doors. He stepped up to the edge and, after a moment of fumbling with his pants, pissed over the rail onto the lawn below. After what seemed like forever, he zipped back up, wiped his hands on the legs of his pants and lit a cigarette before going back inside.

I thought I could identify four different voices yelling and laughing, but between the generator noise and the music, it was hard to tell. There could have been ten men inside, and I was only hearing the ones that were shouting the loudest. I was sure there was plenty of alcohol being consumed and my concern for Rachel ratcheted up to outright worry.

Starting the motors, I had a brief moment of concern that they would hear me, but dismissed it as another burst of laughter floated across the water. Moving the throttles to their first notch, I steered the boat towards the shore. About a quarter of a mile to the right of the house there was a very small indentation in the shoreline where I could anchor the boat out of sight.

Cutting the motors as I approached, the boat's momentum carried it into the cove, which was no more than one hundred feet by fifty. I anchored as close to the center of this as I could, the boat swinging around the anchor point until it settled fully.

I had already reloaded my pistol after blasting my way out of the boathouse, but I checked the loads in each of the magazines anyway. Pistol fully loaded with sixteen rounds and two spare mags of fifteen rounds each. Rifle with a full thirty round mag plus one in the chamber and another nine, full thirty round mags gave me a full military standard load out. I checked the security of my knife and was ready to go.

Taking the key out of the ignition, I hid it under a seat cushion at the bow. No reason to make it too easy for anyone that happened onto the boat while I was gone. I planned to rescue Rachel and recover the cabin cruiser if possible. If not, then we'd have to return to the speed boat. I didn't even contemplate coming back alone. They'd have to kill me to stop me.

I slipped over the side of the boat into the water, which was still over my head. Treading water, I called softly to Dog. He whined, but finally came over the side as well and started paddling. I followed, feet finding the bottom half way to shore. Wading out of the lake, I paused to make sure my weapons were drained of water.

Satisfied with their readiness, I stooped over and grabbed handfuls of mud, which I smeared on all of my exposed skin. I hadn't worried about white skin showing when I was battling infected, but I didn't want to give these guys any more of an advantage than they already had with sheer numbers.

Dog and I headed west towards the house, following the shoreline as we moved. The closer I approached the house, the slower I moved until we melded into the trees. Cutting through the forest at an angle, I intended to bring us to the lawn at the side of the house.

Pausing to listen every few yards, I was glad to note that the tone of the party hadn't changed. My old Army unit's call sign had been Reaper, as in the Grim Reaper. Well, these guys had no idea that death was coming for them.

Reaching the lawn, I dropped to one knee, Dog flattening himself on the ground next to me. His ears were at full attention, his nose twitching as he sampled the air. He stayed silent, and I took that as confirmation of my assessment that there were still no sentries on lookout and no infected in the area.

Across a long stretch of lawn, a large diesel generator purred away. It was obviously built into the house, and I couldn't tell if it was the only source of power or just for emergencies. Next to the generator was a door that I suspected opened into a shop area where maintenance supplies for the house were stored.

The house was two stories with a patio and covering balcony on the lake side that ran the length of the structure. I took a guess that the home was close to six thousand square feet, which meant a lot of rooms to clear once I got inside.

It was relatively dark on my end of the house, and I moved at a quick jog across the open space to the wall. Pausing between the generator and the door, I reached out and tried the knob, not surprised when I found it unlocked.

It turned easily in my hand, and I opened the door a crack, just wide enough to peer inside the room. My guess had been right. A large workshop with an epoxy coated cement floor and walls covered with pegboards that held a vast assortment of tools. No one was inside, and there was no other entrance, so no access to the house from this room.

Creeping along the wall of the house to the front side, the side away from the lake, I peeked around the corner. A sleek Mercedes S-Class sat in a circular driveway made of crushed stone. Surrounding the gleaming car like a pack of hyenas sat six, mud splattered 4x4 trucks. Two of them had Confederate flag license plates on the front, and all of them were obviously brush beaters.

Slipping around the corner, I checked the closest truck and found it unlocked with the windows down. The keys weren't in it, but that didn't matter. I didn't plan to steal it. Dropping to the ground, I slid underneath and risked my flashlight for a moment to locate the correct wire. Using my knife, I disabled the truck's starter. I repeated the process with each of the other trucks.

When done with them I looked at the Mercedes and realized I wasn't going to be crawling under it. Instead, I settled with flattening two of the tires. Now, no one was going anywhere that they didn't walk, unless they were on a boat.

Returning to the side of the house, I made my way to the back and peeked around the corner. Still no sentry and the party sounded like it had shifted into a higher gear. I rounded the corner and crawled to a well-lit window.

Raising my head an inch at a time, I finally got a look inside the house. A large room held three sofas placed along the walls. A billiard table occupied the center, and seven men lounged, watching two others shoot a game of pool. The fat man I'd seen take a piss earlier tried a shot that missed horribly, much to the delight of all the others who hooted and laughed like it was the funniest thing they'd ever seen.

Empty beer cans sat on just about every available horizontal surface, many more dribbling onto the expensive looking carpet. Several empty whiskey bottles lay on the floor, and cigarette butts were everywhere, apparently just crushed out underfoot.

All of the men were armed with holstered pistols, several of them with hunting knives strapped to their muddy boots. None of them looked like they'd seen a shower or a razor in at least a week.

Here were nine drunks, but no Rachel. I dropped back below the window and crawled to the edge of a set of French doors. Peeking around the corner, I looked in at a large kitchen filled with commercial grade appliances and a large oak table in the middle of the room. Two men sat, drinking and smoking. Rachel stood at the stove cooking something while they watched.

She was completely nude. Her back was to me, and I could see angry red handprints on each of her ass cheeks. When she turned to bring the food she was preparing to the table, I could see more marks on her face, neck, thighs and breasts where she had been grabbed, pinched and slapped.

She looked up as she walked across the room, spotting me and almost faltering in her step, but she recovered smoothly enough for the men to not notice. At the table, she shoveled scrambled eggs out of a large cast iron skillet onto the waiting plates and was thanked with another hard slap on the ass. The other man reached up and grabbed her right breast and squeezed it hard enough to make her flinch, but she didn't try to pull away.

Rachel kept her eyes on me while the men groped her, then the breast squeezer dismissed her with another slap on her bare ass that was hard enough to make her stumble. She recovered and quickly moved away to the safety of the stove. The men dug into the eggs, eating like they hadn't had food for days.

I looked at Rachel and used hand signs to tell her I counted eleven men, then raised my eyebrows questioningly. She understood, and without raising her hands, very carefully extended all ten fingers, then two more. Twelve. I had spotted eleven. Where was the twelfth?

I pointed at the room with the pool table and held up nine fingers. Rachel nodded subtly enough to not be noticed. I pointed at the two in the kitchen, then raised my eyebrows again. Rachel shrugged her shoulders no more than a half an inch, but enough for me to tell she was saying she didn't know.

Shit. The odd man out could ruin my day. Surprise and sobriety were on my side. I was confident I could get through the door and take the two in the kitchen with my knife, then the nine with my rifle. The problem was getting blindsided by the missing man while I was finishing off the room full of drunks.

I made a calming motion with my hand to Rachel and moved away from the edge of the door before I was spotted. Dog was next to me, flattened to the ground and as alert as ever. I was glad to have his nose and ears to keep an eye on my back, but I guess even Dog isn't perfect. By the time he growled, it was too late.

"Don't fuckin' move." A male voice with a thick accent said from the darkness at the corner of the house, accompanied by the unmistakable sound of a shotgun being racked.

26

It has always amazed me how the mind speeds up in high stress or high danger situations. I know what it's like in combat, and I've heard professional athletes try to explain the same phenomenon. The body will dump a massive amount of adrenaline into the bloodstream, and the brain immediately goes into hyper speed. Your senses and reactions are so enhanced that everyone and everything else around you is in super slow motion and super HD clarity, your analytical and decision-making processes going into warp drive.

This is an incredible edge in combat, or on the playing field, and not many people can do this. Special Forces operators and pro athletes that play at a high level typically have this ability, and it's what lets us get to where we are in our chosen profession.

A fraction of a second after I heard the voice start to speak, the world around me slowed down. I realized that if I was captured, I'd be dead, and Rachel might as well be. Fighting was the only option that gave us a chance at survival. This thought went through my head and the decision to fight was made in less than the blink of an eye.

My rifle was still slung and would take too long to bring to bear, but my pistol was inches from my hand and ready to go. Launching myself away from the voice with a mighty push of my legs, I drew the pistol as I twisted into a firing position.

Shotguns at close range are devastating weapons. If it was twelve gauge loaded with 00 buckshot, it was essentially the same as firing eight .38 special pistols at the same time, each of the shot pellets being about the same size as a .38 bullet. As I pushed off, my hope was that my assailant didn't really have the shotgun pointed directly at me as most people rely on the intimidation factor rather than expecting to actually have to shoot.

My body reached full extension, and as I twisted, I started firing the pistol at the spot where the voice had come from. After my third shot sounded, the shotgun boomed, and a tongue of flame lit the corner of the porch like a strobe light. I felt something tug my left arm and the left side of my chest, but it didn't hurt so I ignored it.

The flash from the shotgun firing gave me an aiming point, and as I landed on the porch in a fully prone position, I quickly put six more rounds into the spot where I'd seen the flame. I was rewarded with the sound of a body hitting the ground and a shotgun clattering to the wooden surface. Without pausing, I dropped the pistol magazine, popped in a fresh one and holstered it, then swung my rifle up as I leapt to my feet.

The rifle I'd looted from the sporting goods store was most likely illegal as it was a military version of the M4 with a selector setting for Semi Auto and Burst. Semi means for every pull of the trigger, one round, and one round only, will be fired and another loaded into the chamber. Burst will fire three rounds for every pull of the trigger. I thumbed the selector to burst and stepped in front of the window that looked into the room where the men were playing pool.

I couldn't begin to guess how much time had elapsed since I'd fired the first round from the pistol, but it couldn't have been long as the nine men in the room were still basically where they had been, not having reacted to the firefight yet. I was sure the alcohol they had consumed contributed to slowing them down, but I was moving at warp speed and they weren't.

Aiming through the window, I pulled the trigger, and three rounds shattered the glass and punched into the chest of one of the pool players. Before he had time to fall, I adjusted slightly and sent three more rounds into the second player. Now I had their attention.

Shouts and curses rang out as they all started moving. In slow motion, I saw three of them reach for pistols. I targeted them first, putting each down in turn so quickly none of them had time to get their weapons up and into action.

I shot two more as they tried to scramble across the floor and out the door that led to the kitchen. The remaining two were in opposite corners of the room, but I had to swing my rifle to my left when the French doors leading from the kitchen burst open.

One of the men that had been eating rushed outside, pistol up and ready. Before he could spot me, I put a three round burst into his head. I spun back to the rec room, but only one of the men was visible. Three rounds in his back put him down, then I had to move as bullets started punching out through the wall right next to me. Someone was firing blind and hoping for a lucky shot. I didn't know if it was the other man from the kitchen or the last man from the rec room that I'd lost sight of.

I quickly changed the magazine in the rifle and fired five bursts back through the wall towards the most likely location of the shooter. The bullets from inside the house stopped, so I moved to the kitchen doors, nearly shooting Rachel as she stepped into the doorway.

Without a word, I grabbed her arm and pulled her out of the house and past me as I moved into the kitchen. The second man I'd seen eating was lying face down on the floor, the handle of a rather substantial butcher knife sticking out of his back. I made a mental note not to piss Rachel off in the kitchen.

The only man not accounted for was the shooter that I thought I'd gotten when I shot through the wall. I briefly debated the wisdom of just getting out of there, but if he wasn't dead, I didn't want to leave him behind to get pissed off, find some friends and come after us. Pushing ahead I kept the rifle up and ready.

Moving quickly but cautiously, I entered the rec room, scanning with the rifle for any threats. The room was a slaughterhouse. The stench of blood, voided bladders and bowels, and the overlaid haze of burnt gunpowder was a familiar smell that had a strange calming effect on me.

I went to each body, counting corpses and making sure each was dead. When I found the one who was shooting through the wall, I was pleased with my response. I'd fired five bursts, fifteen rounds, back through the wall and I counted thirteen holes in the body.

The adrenaline was quickly draining off, and the post-combat letdown started to set in. With it came the pain. Then I realized I was having a hard time breathing. I stumbled back to the kitchen and out the door to the porch where I would have fallen to the ground if Rachel hadn't rushed forward and wrapped her arms around me for support.

27

Rachel staggered under the sudden weight as John collapsed into her arms. Letting him slip to the porch, she quickly examined him in the light spilling out from the kitchen. Two holes that looked like bullet wounds in his left arm bled freely, but fortunately, neither of them was pulsing blood like an arterial shot would do. Ignoring them for the moment, she checked the wound in his chest.

A couple of inches below his left nipple, it was seeping blood, and when she leaned close, she could hear the whistle of air in and out of the wound. Rachel had done a rotation in the ER at Atlanta's Grady Hospital and knew what a punctured lung sounded like. He needed a modern hospital and a trained surgeon, right now, but all he had was her. A fourth-year med student that supported herself by showing her tits and ass to men.

Never one to panic in a crisis, Rachel jumped to her feet and dashed into the house in search of first aid supplies. Starting in the kitchen, she ransacked every cabinet and drawer without finding anything more substantial than a box of bandages not suitable for anything more severe than a paper cut. She set aside a stack of clean, white kitchen towels and raced to the closest bathroom.

There she found a plastic handled X-acto knife and a small sewing kit. In the next, she found more of what she needed. Rubbing alcohol, gauze pads, medical tape, antibiotic ointment, scissors, and a large vinyl bag with a heavy zipper. Inside the bag, she found syringes with unopened needles, a plastic baggie with a ball of black tar heroin, and a spoon and butane lighter. The spoon was stained from cooking the heroin. Zipping up the bag, Rachel grabbed a towel off a rack, folded everything up in it and ran back to the kitchen.

Grabbing the white towels on her way by she stopped long enough to check on John. He was still bleeding and unconscious, his color not good. Dog sat by his head, furry hip pressed against him as he kept watch.

"Stay with him," Rachel said to Dog, and then sprinted down the lawn to the dock. Dog let out a low whine as if in answer, then went back to watching the area.

Rushing onto the cabin cruiser, Rachel dumped her supplies in the main salon. A few minutes, and a pinched finger, later, she had converted the dining table set up into a large bed. She was still naked as she worked but had more pressing priorities than covering herself. Besides, there was no one to see her other than Dog, and so far he hadn't seemed impressed with what she had on display.

She ran back up the dock and lawn, pounding onto the porch and kneeling next to John. His eyes were open when she looked down at him, and he tried to smile, but it came over as a grimace. Working her arms under his shoulders, Rachel pulled him to her and sat him up, her bare breasts pressed tightly against his face.

"Come on, lazy. I don't stick my tits in men's faces for free. You've got to help me out here. I can't lift you on my own."

John lifted his arms and wrapped them around Rachel's neck, worked his legs under his hips and with her help stood up. He would have crashed back to the porch without her support. Rachel slipped around his body to his right side. Keeping her arms wrapped tightly around him she looked up at his face.

"Can you make it to the boat? It's not far."

"I can make it." John's voice was whispery, and his chest rattled alarmingly when he spoke.

True to his claim, he stepped forward. Rachel moved with him, providing as much support as she could to a man that outweighed her by at least a hundred pounds. The going was slow and had to be painful and exhausting for John, but he didn't complain. They came to a stop when they reached the cabin cruiser, Rachel unsure how to get him across the eighteen inches of open space between the dock and the boat's deck.

John solved the problem by pushing her arms away and stepping across. He staggered when he stepped on the boat, Rachel leaping across to wrap him up again and steady him with her arms. Dog followed a moment later and led the way into the salon where John collapsed onto the bed as soon as he and Rachel reached it.

"I've got some medical supplies," Rachel started digging through the bundle she'd taken from the house.

"No. Get the boat out in the lake. I made a lot of noise, and there may be infected on the way here." John's voice was getting weaker, the chest rattle worsening by the second. His belly looked to be slightly distended, and Rachel was fairly certain he was bleeding internally.

"There's no time. I have to get your bleeding under control, or you won't make it."

Rachel started to reach for the bottle of alcohol, but John grabbed her arm, stopping her.

"If the infected show up, none of us will make it. I'm good for a few minutes. Get us off shore."

His hand slipped off her arm and then his eyes closed as he slipped back into unconsciousness. Rachel let out a deep breath she didn't realize she had been holding. A couple of seconds of indecision, then she leapt up and raced to the bridge to start the engines.

When she got there, she said a few decidedly unladylike words. The keys were not in the ignition. The bastards that had captured her must have taken them when they docked the boat.

Rachel ran back to where John lay unconscious, took the pistol off his hip, told Dog to stay and headed back to the house. She didn't know who had been driving the boat, but she would check pockets until she found the keys.

The first body she came to was the man John had shot as he came out of the kitchen when the fight started. Rachel ran her hands over his body, finding Dodge keys, a can of Skoal snuff, a pocket knife and a battered leather wallet, but nothing else. Moving on, she searched each of the other bodies with similar results. No boat keys.

Standing in the middle of the rec room, Rachel was covered in gore to her elbows and knees, but she ignored it and tried to think of where else the keys could be. She dashed around, checking all the tables, throwing couch cushions aside and going down on her knees to search under the sofas. Nothing.

Returning to the kitchen, she searched the whole room, careful to check the corners and under furniture. Still nothing. Then she remembered the twelfth man. The one John had shot on the porch that led to the all-out firefight.

Dashing outside, she located the body and repeated her search, finding the keys in his left hip pocket. Raising them up to the light, Rachel wanted to shout for joy, but her blood froze when a female infected screamed from the tree line not more than thirty yards away.

Rachel didn't wait to see if there was just the one, or five thousand of the damn things coming. She jumped up, hurdled the small planting bed at the edge of the porch and ran across the lawn as fast as she had ever run. Another scream pushed her faster. She stumbled as her legs had trouble keeping up with her momentum down the sloping lawn, but regained her balance and sprinted the last few feet to the dock.

The cabin cruiser was tied at both bow and stern with heavy nylon ropes wound around iron cleats that were bolted to the dock. Sliding to her knees at the bow line, Rachel quickly unwound it, risking a look over her shoulder while her hands worked the rope.

Three infected females were charging down the lawn, one of them well in the lead and no more than twenty or thirty feet away. The line came free, and Rachel scrambled to the stern line, tearing the skin on her knees and feet on the rough wood. The second line came free as the first infected reached the dock and charged.

Rachel raised the pistol she'd taken off of John and pulled the trigger. The big .45 roared and bucked in her hands, but she missed, and the infected kept coming. Rachel had time for one more shot and took it, missing a second time, then the infected was on her with a flying tackle.

The infected was unbelievably strong. She was a small woman, easily six inches shorter and thirty pounds lighter than Rachel, but she had the strength of a much larger man. Rachel fought hard, struggling to keep the snapping teeth away from her flesh, rolling down the dock with the infected locked onto her. She could feel her strength going, and knew she was about to die, when a nightmare of teeth slammed into the infected and knocked it off of her.

Dog rolled with the infected, flipping back onto his feet and locking his jaws on the back of the female's neck. Gaining his balance, he spread his weight across all four legs and wrenched his big head to the side in a lightning fast and incredibly powerful motion as he bit down. There was a sickening crunch of vertebrae, and the infected went still.

Dog dropped the corpse and moved to stand between Rachel and the other two infected females who had just reached the dock. He was a fearsome sight, hackles raised, head lowered, lips peeled back from bloody teeth as he growled, but the infected have no fear.

Dog crouched, gathering his legs for a leap to battle when there were two quick shots and both females dropped to the dock, dead. Rachel, so certain she was dead just moments before, didn't understand where the shots had come from until Dog whined and she followed his gaze to the boat. John stood in the door to the salon; rifle still pointed at the two females. For a moment, he looked ok, then slid down the doorframe and collapsed onto the deck.

28

The first thing I saw was a furry face and golden brown eyes staring at me. I was on my back, and I hadn't felt this tired since I had gone through the Army's Special Forces selection process. Day after day of running, climbing, shooting, swimming, no sleep, little water and less food. Actually, this was worse.

I tried to sit up, and the pain that lanced through my chest convinced me to stay where I was. Dog whined and looked to the other side of the room where a rustling noise was followed by Rachel leaning over me with a small smile on her face. She was scrubbed clean with her long hair back in a ponytail, but the bruising on her face was a mask of ugly purples, yellows and greens.

"Welcome back," She said. "How do you feel?"

"Like I got hit by a truck," I croaked, realizing how dry my mouth and throat were.

Rachel disappeared for a second then she was back with a red plastic cup. "Water," she said and slipped an arm under my shoulders to help me sit up enough to drink.

The pain was something from another world, but I pushed it down and sipped from the cup. I could feel the coolness of the water all the way down my throat and tried to drink more, but Rachel took the cup away and lowered me back down.

"Not too much, too soon. You don't want to get sick," she said, placing the cup on a table out of my reach.

"Are you OK?" I asked her.

She looked down at me, smiled and shook her head like women do when a man is being a moron.

"Am I OK? Seriously? Are you OK? That's the question. Do you remember what happened?"

I thought for a moment before answering, "I remember finding you, finding the house. There was a firefight. And I remember a guy with a big butcher knife in his back. Was that you?"

Rachel smiled and laid her hand on my arm. "Yes, that was me. Thought I'd help after you started shooting the place up. You killed eleven men saving me, and you got yourself shot in the process. You're lucky I've had some emergency medical training.

"Do you remember saving me a second time? Shooting two infected females on the dock after I got you to the boat?"

I thought about it but couldn't remember anything after checking the rec room and making sure all of Rachel's abductors were dead. That's fairly normal when someone is severely wounded, but it's still rather disconcerting. Actually, it downright sucks. But, on the other hand, it's probably not a bad thing to not remember the pain.

"Nothing. What happened? And how long have I been out?"

Rachel helped me rise up for another drink of water then settled back into a chair, bare feet up on the edge of the mattress. Dog sat next to the bed, chin resting on the edge, staring at me. He was starting to make me feel a little self-conscious.

"Are you sure you're up to it? You don't need to rest?" Rachel asked, pushing a stray strand of hair behind her ear.

"I'm OK for now. Just tell me."

"OK, but you just relax. You've been out for four days, and you still have a lot of healing to do."

"Four days!" I started to rise up, but the pain reminded me to lay still. "Where are we? Are we safe?"

"We're in the middle of the lake, anchored in a hundred and twenty feet of water. We're not showing any lights after dark, and Dog and I are sleeping on deck in case I need to repel boarders." Rachel patted my rifle, which was leaned against a bulkhead next to her.

"Now, if you're done with questions, I'll tell you a bedtime story so you can get back to sleep." Rachel looked at me with her eyebrows raised in a quizzical expression.

"I'm all ears," I said.

"About two hours after you swam away that night, I got tired of sitting on deck waiting for you and went into the salon to get something to eat. I had rummaged around and found a trashy novel in one of the cabins and thought I'd stretch out and read while you were off playing Rambo."

29

Rachel finished her portion of the meal that she had prepared before John went charging off to rescue Dog. Some plastic wrap from the galley covered his plate for later, and she settled down onto a settee to read some trashy romance fantasy novel she'd found while digging through one of the boat's cabins.

The book had been in a nightstand drawer that also held a box of condoms and an oversized vibrator. She'd tried the vibrator and the batteries were still good but put it back with a shake of her head. Self-pleasuring was the last thing she needed to be thinking about right now.

The novel was predictably corny, full of heaving bosoms and tanned, shirtless men, but despite herself, she started getting into the story. She had been reading for about half an hour when a change in the gentle motion of the boat distracted her. It felt like something had bumped the side, but when it didn't repeat, and she didn't hear anything, she went back to the book.

Rachel let out an involuntary scream a few minutes later when a shape appeared in the door from the deck. Her first thought was that John had returned, then she realized it was a stranger standing there staring at her.

"Well, what are you doing out here all by yourself?" The voice was deep and heavy with the type of Georgia accent that you didn't hear in metropolitan Atlanta, rather in the isolated little towns in the north Georgia hills.

Rachel leapt up and tried to reach the pistol in the galley, but she had no chance. The man took two giant strides and backhanded her across the face hard enough to send her spinning to the floor of the salon.

"Now, is that any way to treat company come visiting?" he asked, wrapping her hair up in his grimy hand and yanking her to her feet.

Rachel didn't resist, moving with him and lashing out with her fist. Her target was his testicles, and if she had landed the blow he'd likely have lost one if not both of them, but he saw what she was doing and turned to the side and absorbed the punch on his hip.

"Goddamn it, girl! You've got one hell of a punch," he said, hitting her in the face with a closed fist this time.

Rachel had always heard the expression *seeing stars*, but had never experienced it until now. She was on the edge of consciousness, little pinpricks of light flashing in front of her eyes and her body refusing to answer her brain's commands to keep fighting. Helpless, she felt herself pushed to the floor. Her arms were roughly yanked behind her as he bound her wrists with rope, then her ankles were tied together.

The man left her lying there while he searched the cabin and she got her first good look at him. He was big and heavy, almost as large as John, but instead of heavy muscles he had heavy fat. He hadn't shaved for days and didn't smell like he'd showered recently either. The cloying smell of body odor mixed with tobacco and beer in a rather unpleasant result.

He wore heavy leather boots, stained and fraying jeans and a once white T-shirt that was stretched tight over his bulging stomach. A greasy Atlanta Braves cap covered his head. His hands were large, thick and heavily callused. A hunting knife was strapped to his right boot, and he wore two pistols like an old west gunfighter.

He finished searching the salon and moved on to check the rest of the boat. He made a lot of noise, apparently feeling it necessary to ransack as he searched. A few minutes later he returned and squatted down in front of where Rachel lay on the salon floor.

"Where's the guy, sweet thing?" He asked, reaching out and grabbing Rachel's hair.

"He's dead." Were the first words that popped into her head and she said them. All she could do was hope John would show up and save her, but she didn't want him knowing there was someone coming back.

"Dead. Hmmm. Lot of that going around lately," he muttered. "So it's just you out here all on your own?"

Had she made a mistake? Should she have told him about John and that he was due back soon? Deciding she had to continue the story she'd started, Rachel answered, "Yes. He was killed earlier today at the marina where I stole this boat. He died so I could get away."

"Well, ain't that fucking noble as all hell," he said. "Dumb bastard if you ask me. But he did me a favor. I get me a nice big boat and a good looking woman to go with it. Remind me to say a prayer for him." He said the last with a laugh, released Rachel's hair and stood up.

"Stay put, sweetie. We're going for a little ride."

He left the salon and a few minutes later the big boat's engine rumbled to life. The electric winch for the anchor whined as it retracted, then the note of the engine changed as the boat started to move. Rachel was disoriented after the two blows to the head, but she was pretty sure they were moving away from the marina, deeper into the lake.

She didn't know for sure how big the lake was or how John would find her, but she did know that he would try to find her. Rachel had not led a sheltered life, and she could read men like a book. John was not one that would leave her behind, any more than he'd been willing to sail away and leave Dog to die in the abandoned truck. He would be coming for her.

That thought provided some comfort as they motored farther away from John and Dog. Rachel tested the bonds on her arms and ankles, but she was tied up tight. Too tight. Both her hands and feet were numb from lack of blood circulation. She managed to wriggle around and get into a sitting position so she could look for anything she could use to cut free, but there was nothing in sight.

They kept going for what seemed like hours, but according to the clock in the salon was only slightly more than thirty minutes. Rachel's first indication that they were nearing their destination was when the big boat throttled back to idle. Moments later it thumped against what she assumed was a dock, and there were several rough male voices shouting back and forth. Eventually, the man came back into the salon and squatted down in front of where Rachel was sitting.

"Alright, sweet cheeks. We're getting off the boat and going up the dock to the house. You got two choices, and only two. You can walk, or I can drag your cute ass." He looked at her, seemingly expecting a rebellious answer, but Rachel disappointed him.

"I'll walk," she said, voice tight with anger.

He grinned, revealing a mouthful of teeth that had probably never seen a dentist. "Well, look at you now. Good choice. Maybe I won't have to get as rough with you as I thought."

He drew the knife that was strapped to his boot. It was a wicked looking chromed blade made to resemble the famous Bowie knife. It took some sawing to cut the ropes around her ankles, but they finally fell free. Rachel caught her breath as the blood rushed back into her feet with a storm of pins and needles. Not wanting to show weakness, she forced the pain aside and stood, waiting for the man to tell her where to go.

He walked her out of the salon onto the stern deck. She came to a full stop when she saw the small crowd of men waiting for them on the dock. Several of them started to whistle and shout when they saw her, and Rachel's stomach flip-flopped. Nothing good was going to happen here, she thought as she was shoved from behind.

Stumbling forward, Rachel regained her balance and stepped off the boat onto the dock. Hands were immediately on her, squeezing her ass and breasts, some pinching hard, some just caressing. Rachel stood perfectly still, not responding. The man from the boat stepped onto the dock and started batting hands away before shoving her in the back again.

Rachel was ready this time and didn't stumble as she moved forward with the push. She considered kicking out and running, but there were men on all sides of her. She wouldn't get two steps. Jumping into the lake ran through her head, but with her hands bound behind her back she couldn't swim, and they'd just fish her out and probably punish her for her efforts. Rachel had never been one to give up without a fight, but she was smart enough to know when to fight and when to comply, so she walked docilely with the group to the end of the dock and up a well-tended lawn.

At the top of the slope was a massive house, lit up like there was a party in progress. It was two stories and painted a gleaming white, an oversized porch running the length of the back. A balcony for the second-floor rooms provided a roof over the first-floor porch.

Rachel was herded up the steps and through a set of French doors into a giant kitchen that would have looked right at home in a five-star restaurant. She was pushed, and the whole group wound up in an adjacent room that had several sofas scattered around the walls and an oversized pool table. They all came to a stop. Rachel did a quick head count. Twelve of them surrounded her in a loose circle.

They were all cut from the same mold as the man who had attacked her on the boat. Some smaller and scrawny, some as large as him. None of them looked to place personal hygiene very high on their list of priorities.

The room stank of stale beer and cigarette smoke. The detritus of an ongoing party was scattered everywhere. Cigarette butts and burns marred the carpeting and most of the upholstery. Not a pleasant party Rachel had walked into.

The man from the boat stepped in front of her with the knife in his hand. Rachel didn't shrink back. She wasn't worried about being killed. That wasn't what they wanted her for. He reached out with one big hand and grabbed her right arm, lifting her wrists so he could saw through the ropes binding her.

Moments later the pins and needles pain came. Rachel couldn't stop herself from rubbing her hands together to ease the discomfort. Knife man tossed the cut ropes behind him and raised the knife until the tip came to rest against the soft skin underneath Rachel's jaw.

"Take 'em off," he said, his eyes locked on hers, watching for any sign of defiance.

Rachel held his stare for a few moments before sighing and stepping back from the knife. In one fluid motion, she grasped the hem of her T-shirt and pulled it over her head. She hadn't had a bra since going to work the night before the world ended, so her breasts were bare when the shirt came off. She could hear several of the men catch their breath and others mutter curses of admiration as they got a good look at her in the brightly lit room.

A woman who hadn't worked as a stripper for a living might have been self-conscious to the point of trying to cover her chest with her hands. Rachel understood enough about men like these to know that would just get her hit, and she'd still have to stand there with her tits hanging out.

She looked across the faces in front of her while they all stared at her body, hoping to find a sympathetic face, but failing. There was one man that was staring into her eyes, not at her breasts, with an intensity that turned her blood cold. Rachel tagged him as the one to watch out for.

"Keep going, girl." Knife man grumbled, waving a meaty finger at the baggy sweat shorts Rachel had found on the boat when she cleaned up.

Without comment she hooked her thumbs in the waistband of the shorts and peeled them down to her feet, stepping clear and leaving them lying on the floor. Rachel hadn't been wearing shoes and was now as naked as the day she was born. Knife man stepped close and started caressing a breast, then pinched her nipple hard enough to send a jolt of pain all the way to her toes. Somehow she restrained herself from punching him in the throat, standing there and taking the abuse without showing any discomfort.

After a few more seconds of twisting and pinching, he made a humphing sound deep in his chest and reached for her. With his big hand firmly wrapped around her slender wrist, he led Rachel out of the room, across the kitchen and down a short hall to a small bedroom. Closing the door behind them, he sheathed the knife at his boot and reached for his belt buckle with a smile on his face.

30

"Stop," I said. "I don't need to hear this unless you need to talk about it."

Rachel had been sitting very still with a detached look on her face as she spoke, much like she was telling a story about someone else. In a way, I guess she was. My voice had interrupted her, and she reached up to wipe her eyes, which had grown watery.

"It's OK," she said. "I gave him what he wanted, freely rather than fighting a losing battle. It would have happened one way or another. At the end of the day, it was just sex with someone that I would rather forget."

I looked into her eyes and saw the pain that she was dealing with. There was nothing I could do, and I've finally gotten old enough to know when to leave things alone.

"Besides," she continued. "I took care of him. Remember the guy with the butcher knife in his back?"

I raised my eyebrows and waited. After a minute, she smiled weakly and nodded. Sniffing and wiping her eyes one more time, Rachel stood and picked up my rifle.

"Time to check the area," she said. "The sun will be going down soon, and I want one last scan of the shoreline before it gets too dark."

Rachel left the salon, Dog close on her heels. I could see her through the glass door, standing at the rail with the binoculars to her eyes. Nothing she told me had surprised me. When I saw the group that was holding her, and how they were treating her, I had expected this, but a small part of me had hoped that I had gotten there in time to prevent it.

Another voice in my head reminded me that if I hadn't forgotten Dog in the first place, I would have been on the boat. Rachel never would have been taken. I tried to silence that thought, but it stayed in the back of my head as I drifted back off to sleep.

I woke up sometime the next day, bright morning sunshine flooding the salon. The boat had swung on its anchor. The stern was pointing directly into the rising sun. There was a rustle of sheets next to me, and I looked over to see Rachel sprawled out in bed with me. The bruising on her face was starting to fade, but she could still go out on Halloween without a mask and scare the hell out of the neighborhood kids.

I carefully tested my pain level, and though it felt like the fires of hell ripping through my chest, I managed to swing my legs over the side of the bed and stand up without waking Rachel. I was wearing a ratty pair of boxer shorts that I'd never seen before. I assumed that after treating my injuries, Rachel had cleaned me up and found the underwear that she dressed me in somewhere on the boat.

Taking a tentative step, I shambled to the bathroom, head I suppose I should call it on a boat, pulled myself out of the boxers and peed a bright red stream of urine into the toilet. I flushed and waited for the sound to subside before opening the door so I didn't disturb Rachel. She had probably been on deck all night keeping watch.

I looked at myself in the polished metal mirror mounted over the small sink and was shocked at how bad I looked. Two thick bandages were taped around my left upper arm, and on my body were two more bandages held in place with white medical tape. The first one was a couple of inches directly below my left nipple, and that wound seemed to be the source of the majority of my pain.

The second one was on my left side, a little lower along the rib cage. So I'd taken four of the shotgun pellets. If that shotgun had been loaded with 00 buckshot, I wouldn't be standing here looking at the damage. Must have been birdshot, I mused. I was one lucky son of a bitch.

Exiting the head, I made my way out the salon door and onto the deck. Dog greeted me with a frantic wagging of his tail and a cold nose that managed to slide up my bare leg and end in a very personal location. I rubbed his head and toddled my way to a bench, slowly lowering myself to the cushioned seat. The binoculars were lying next to me, and I picked them up to scan our surroundings while I enjoyed the warmth of the morning sun on my battered body.

I hadn't realized that Rachel had anchored us just a few hundred yards off shore from the house where she had been held captive until I swung the binoculars in that direction. Crows and vultures were feasting on the bodies I had left behind, and a fairly large contingent of infected wandered around the lawn. Most were males, but a few females were in the group.

Several of the females stood on the dock staring at the boat. Whether they knew we were there, or their attention was just drawn to the gleaming white hull, I didn't know, but I was glad they couldn't swim. At least, I hoped they couldn't swim. I hadn't seen any evidence to indicate they could, quite the contrary, but I reminded myself not to assume anything.

I watched the infected for a while, mind wandering. I was feeling horribly guilty over what Rachel had gone through and then it occurred to me that Katie, my wife, might be going through the same thing. Or worse. There's an old saying that goes something like "polite society is just a paper thin veil that masks the true animal nature of man". I had learned the truth of that, years ago in the different third world countries I'd operated in for the Army, but I had never witnessed it in the United States until now.

Sitting there, my mind bounced between worry for Katie and guilt for Rachel. I felt a renewed sense of urgency to get to Arizona, but a degree of despair as well. We had been hiding and fighting for days and were still within a two-hour drive of Atlanta. How the hell were we going to cross the majority of the country?

"Good morning." Rachel's voice startled me, and I almost dropped the binoculars overboard. Recovering my composure, I looked up at her, smiled and returned the greeting.

"Anything worth looking at?" She asked, gesturing towards the shoreline as she came over and sat down next to me.

"The new normal. Bodies on the ground and infected wandering around."

"You're Mr. Sunshine this morning," she teased, then reached out and took my hand and caught my eyes with hers. "If I haven't said it, thank you. Thank you for coming to get me."

The lump of guilt in my throat kept me from speaking, so I just nodded and looked away. I wanted to apologize, explain, and ask for understanding and forgiveness. I wanted her to have never had to experience what had happened, but none of that could be changed, and I wasn't about to dump my emotional needs on Rachel. She had endured enough.

"OK, then. I see you're one of those guys that struggles with gratitude," she smiled to let me know she was kidding. "I'm making some breakfast while you sit here and rest. Any requests?"

I smiled up at her, "Biscuits and gravy, scrambled eggs, thick sliced bacon and hash browns."

"On its way," Rachel replied without missing a beat and walked back into the salon.

A few minutes later she was back, balancing a paper plate on each hand. Retaking her seat next to me she handed over one of the plates, crossed her legs at the knees and balanced her plate on her lap.

"Unfortunately, we were out of biscuits. The gravy was lumpy, the eggs were spoiled, and I forgot bacon and potatoes the last time I went to the store." There was a glint of mischief in Rachel's eye, and the look on my face gave away my thoughts.

"Look," she said, serious again. "It was not a fun experience. They were rough and unpleasant, but after they realized I wasn't going to fight it cooled off their desire to abuse me, and it just became less than consensual sex. I didn't enjoy it, but I survived it and I'm not about to sit in a corner and have a pity party, so knock it the fuck off. OK?"

I looked at her face and realized she was really as OK as anyone could be after such an experience. She was a strong woman and didn't want my sympathy.

"OK," I said with a small grin. "Dead subject. Now, what the hell are you feeding me?"

"Stale bread, stale cheese that I had to cut the mold off of, and an overripe banana that is probably the last one you will ever see, so enjoy it."

After that, we sat in the sun and ate in companionable silence. The bread was hard, the cheese was... well, different, and the banana was so ripe it was almost mush, but I ate every bite. Water drawn from the lake and boiled on the small propane stove in the galley washed it all down, and between the sun and a full belly, I was soon fast asleep.

31

"This is Max broadcasting to tell you the truth about what's going on in the world."

It was eight days later, and we were still anchored in the middle of the lake, resting and healing. I was up on the deck, enjoying some cool evening air when the voice cut through the static of the portable radio. I had taken to keeping the radio turned on and tuned to the frequency that Max used, and was so accustomed to hearing nothing but static, I didn't immediately respond. I quickly scrambled to turn up the volume and shouted for Rachel to come out and listen. Moments later she appeared in the door, finger holding her place in the novel she was still reading.

"There's a lot to tell you, and I'll get through the list in no particular order. First of all, we've had to move camp several times to avoid large herds of infected. I don't know why the infected are herding together, and none of my sources can tell me, but I can say you should avoid the herds at all costs. If they corner you, they won't quit, and they won't leave until you're dead.

"The remnants of the federal government are in an undisclosed secure location. I've got some guesses on where that might be, but I'm not gonna broadcast that info in case there's any bad guys listening. Not that some politicians getting what they deserve wouldn't warm the cockles of my heart, but it would be counter-productive at this point.

"I have confirmation from a government source that the attacks on the US were initiated by the Chinese. They want our land and our natural resources. That's why they haven't sent any more nukes our way. We did hit them with multiple nukes. Most of their major cities and military installations are destroyed, and casualty estimates are in the range of two hundred million dead and another hundred million with lethal doses of radiation. Sounds like a lot, but don't forget that there's over a billion people in China. Even if they lose another half a billion, there's still more of them than there was of us before the attacks.

"Both coasts of the US are either nuclear wastelands or completely overrun with infected. The upper Midwest is in no better shape as well as the gulf coast states. Currently, I'm being told, over two-thirds of the remaining population in the country has been affected by the nerve agent that was released. Apparently for the first forty-eight hours, the chemical was persistent, and if an uninfected person was even touched by an infected that was all it took to infect them as well. I'm also being told that there is a percentage of the population that is immune to the nerve agent. That's about the only good news at this point. The infected are lethal, and will attack and kill any uninfected person they encounter.

"These aren't zombies, folks. They don't have to be shot in the head to die. However, they seem to be able to ignore injuries and pain that would normally put a man down. I've seen infected take multiple bullets to the body and not even break stride until their body finally realized it was dead. Sometimes that can take several minutes. Heart shots and head shots are the only way to ensure an infected goes down quickly.

"Our friends in the UK and Europe, even France if you can believe it, are trying to mobilize military and humanitarian support for us, but the first convoy that headed out into the Atlantic was attacked and sunk by Chinese subs. Britain has threatened China with nuclear retaliation if there is an attack on another British ship. The Chinese have not responded, and it's not clear who's in charge over there at the moment. The Europeans have been bringing in food and medical supplies on cargo planes. With the east coast devastated they're coming farther inland and staging into Nashville and Kansas City. These are the two largest cities left relatively intact, and they're also both on major interstate highway routes and the Army and National Guard are doing all they can to start these supplies moving out to areas where people need help.

"Finally, back to the infected. As I mentioned earlier, we are seeing them congregate in herds for unknown reasons. As of yesterday, there are massive herds moving north away from the gulf coast and west away from the eastern seaboard. The military is making preparations west of the Appalachians and along the southern Tennessee border, to stop the infected from reaching the distribution center in Nashville. So far no herds have been spotted that threaten Kansas City. If you are south of Tennessee and trying to reach Nashville, you need to hurry. The biggest herd is estimated to be three days away from Tennessee, and once it gets there, no one will be able to get through."

There was a pause and rustle of papers. Over the open mic, Max could be heard taking a drink of something then the click and rasp of a Zippo as he lit a cigarette. A long exhale later, and he continued.

"That's it, my friends. Don't quit fighting and for God's sake don't start shooting people because they look Chinese. There's a lot of Asian people in this country who are as patriotic to the US of A as the rest of us. Now if you see an Asian in a uniform you don't recognize, drill the little fucker! Be safe, God Bless, and God Bless America."

32

Rachel and I looked at each other, and her expression mirrored my thoughts. "Oh, shit," I said.

Over the past week, I'd been putting a lot of thought into how we would get to Arizona. I'd stared at maps for hours, made notes, calculated how fast we could move and made lists of equipment we'd need to carry once we left the relative security of the boat.

Rachel had asked to see what I was doing a couple of times, but lost interest quickly and found something else to occupy herself. I was touched by the level of trust she was showing in me. But then, after what we'd been through, if we couldn't trust each other now there was not much point in continuing on together.

Even before hearing Max's broadcast, I had already decided that our best route was to make our way north to Nashville and pick up Interstate 40. I-40 was like the belt of the continental US, running coast to coast right through the middle of the country. As it got closer to the west coast, it dipped down into New Mexico and Arizona and ran within about a hundred and fifty miles of my home where I had a continuing hope that I would find Katie safe and sound and bored out of her mind.

All of our weapons had been disassembled, checked, cleaned and were ready to go. Our packs were ready to grab and go at a moment's notice, and there wasn't anything for us to do to get ready to move except for me to dress. I had been lounging in nothing but boxers while I healed and I wasn't necessarily looking forward to putting pants back on.

Our immediate plan was to use the boat to stay on the lake and river system. We would make our way west to Highway 27, which we would then follow up to Chattanooga. The small city was on the southeastern border of Tennessee, and while it would get us out of Georgia, it was still a long trek west to Nashville, which was pretty much in the middle of the state. The sun was setting, and I didn't want to try to navigate in the dark but wanted to be prepared to leave at first light.

The maps to which I had access were road maps, not navigation maps, and I had no way of knowing if the river we planned to use was large enough to support the big cabin cruiser. We needed a backup plan, and I had just the idea. Starting the engine, I let it idle to warm up while the electric motor whined as the anchor was reeled up from the lake bottom. Ready to go, I bumped the throttle to its first stop and spun the wheel to head for the cove where Dog and I had left the speedboat the night of Rachel's rescue.

The sound of the engine and movement of the boat drew lots of attention from the infected on the shoreline. Their agitation was obvious even without using the binoculars, and screams from the females floated across the water to us. Dog sat near the stern watching them across the water, and I wondered what thoughts were going through his doggie mind.

It only took a few minutes to reach the cove. The speedboat was exactly where I'd left it, bobbing in the water at the end of its anchor rope. Worried about running the larger boat aground, I cut the throttle then reversed for a moment to kill our momentum, coming to a stop a hundred feet or so from the speedboat.

"Where do you think you're going?" Rachel asked when she saw me heading for the stern rail where the small swim platform allowed easy access to the water. I paused and looked up at the flying bridge where she stood with hands on hips.

I started to open my mouth to reply, but she cut me off. "I know. You were going to swim over and get the speedboat. Did it occur to you how many bacteria are in the lake water that will soak into your wounds? I didn't work like a mad woman saving your life to lose you now. Get out of the way."

Rachel had made her speech while climbing down the short ladder to the deck. She pushed past me, pulled her T-shirt over her head, kicked off her boots, stripped her pants off and dove into the lake. She surfaced moments later and started swimming to the speedboat with long, graceful strokes. I shook my head and watched her swim across the darkening water.

Dog was still sitting by the stern rail and started whining when Rachel was half way to the boat. A few seconds later I heard the screams as several females appeared on the muddy shoreline of the small cove.

The wake from the cabin cruiser had caused the speedboat to pivot around its anchor point. I realized that I had left too much slack in the line. The stern of the boat was pointing directly in and was maybe a dozen feet from the shore. I shouted for Rachel to turn back, but she couldn't hear me over her own splashing.

I watched in horror as first one, then another female took a running leap in an attempt to reach the speedboat. Neither made it, both splashing into the lake a couple of feet short, but the cove wasn't deep, and they were both able to stand on the lake bottom and start wading out to meet Rachel at the boat.

Motherfucker! I grabbed my rifle and climbed the ladder to the bridge as fast as my bruised body would allow. On the bridge I dropped to a knee, ignoring the protest from my chest, and rested my arm on the bridge railing as it supported the rifle. We were losing light fast, but the low magnification scope amplified what there was well enough for me to sight my targets.

Just before I fired, I saw that Rachel had reached the bow of the speedboat and was pulling herself along the side rail. She intended to use the swim platform at the stern to climb aboard.

“Rachel! Infected in the water!” I screamed at the top of my voice.

She turned and looked at me, obviously hearing my scream but not understanding the words. She saw me aiming the rifle and understanding dawned on her face. She started to push away from the boat just as a hand broke the surface of the water, grabbed a fistful of her hair and took her under.

I cursed, then reacquired my target and started shooting. The head of the female I had the best line of sight on exploded when the military caliber round punched through, and I shifted aim to another floundering infected. My first shot missed, but my follow on took off the top of her head.

That was all the visible females in the water, and I paused, holding my breath. Finally, with an explosion of water, Rachel and the infected female broke the surface, locked in battle. Rachel had two fists full of her hair so she could keep the snapping jaws away from her face and neck. The infected struggled, clawing and whipping her head side to side in attempts to break Rachel's grip.

I sighted in on Rachel's attacker, taking a deep breath as I tracked its head in the rifle's scope. It was a high-risk shot, but there was nothing else I could do.

As my finger tightened on the trigger, I heard additional splashes and shifted my eyes to see two more females wading through the water towards Rachel. I quickly took each of them out with head shots. By the time I moved aim back to Rachel, she and the infected were submerged again. Maintaining my aim, I waited. And waited. And waited.

I was starting to fear the worst when once again they breached the surface. Rachel still had one fist wrapped in the infected's hair, but her other arm was now locked straight out with her hand gripping its throat. I placed the scope's red dot on the face of the infected, paused a moment to make sure I was adjusting with their motion, then squeezed the trigger as I said a small prayer.

Her head snapped back as the bullet punched through, a spray of blood and brains fanning out across the lake's surface. The infected went limp in Rachel's arms. She shoved the corpse away from her and nearly leapt out of the water into the speedboat's cockpit. The anchor came up quickly with a manual winch, then nothing. I hadn't told Rachel where I had hidden the keys.

In the meantime, more infected had arrived on the shoreline and I quickly picked them off before they could start wading out. Standing up, I grabbed a bench cushion and raised it over my head for Rachel to see. It took a few tries before she got the message and started throwing cushions around until she found the keys.

The speedboat started easily, and less than a minute later she cut the motors as she drifted up to the stern of the cabin cruiser. I met her at the rail and tied the smaller craft off to a cleat so we could tow it with the larger one.

I reached out and helped Rachel cross the open water between the two boats, pulling back a handful of blood. She was missing most of the ring finger on her left hand, and it was bleeding profusely. I grabbed a towel and helped her wrap it up.

"What happened? Did she bite it off?" I asked, leading her into the salon so I could administer some first aid.

I was surprised to hear her laugh in response. "No. Somebody needs to work on their aim."

33

The next morning, I started the engine and raised the anchor as soon as there was enough light to distinguish individual trees along the shoreline. Notching the throttles forward I settled on half power. The instruments on the flying bridge told me we were going fifteen knots, which if my math was correct worked out to about seventeen miles per hour. Exposed as I was to the wind and sounds of the hull slicing through the lake, it felt much faster.

I wasn't a sailor by any means, having driven a boat only a handful of times in my life. Not very comfortable with how fast I could stop the big cruiser or what its turning radius was like, I didn't plan on going any faster than our current speed. Getting there a little slower in one piece beats getting there a little faster in several pieces any day of the week.

We followed the lake for most of the morning. There was the occasional abandoned boat floating at the whim of the wind and currents, but we gave them a wide berth. Twice we saw infected roaming the southern shoreline, but there was no sign of survivors all morning. Shortly before noon, we entered an area of the lake where it spread out. The southern shoreline disappeared over the horizon. I throttled back to idle and pulled out the maps.

We were in the broadest part of the lake, and it was nearly twenty miles wide at this point. We were closer to the northern shore, which was apparently undeveloped. The map offered no clue, but I suspected it was protected land, possibly a state park or wildlife sanctuary. Otherwise, builders would have snatched up the valuable waterfront property and crammed in as many houses as they could.

Over the horizon to the south, the map showed a dense tangle of roads right up to the edge of the water for miles in each direction. A marina was marked as well as an area designated for amphibious aircraft. What I wouldn't give to know how to fly. We'd be to Arizona in a matter of hours, not the weeks that I expected it was going to take.

Rachel joined me on the flying bridge, curious why we had stopped. I showed her the map and traced my finger to the far end of the lake where a river either emptied into or drained from the lake. The map gave no indication, and I wasn't familiar enough with the area to even hazard a guess. I just hoped the river was navigable.

Rachel agreed with me that we didn't want to go anywhere near the southern shore. We not only had to worry about infected, but as we had learned there was a very real threat from survivors as well. I pushed the throttle back to half power and the big boat slowly picked up speed, coming to plane on the surface as we passed through ten knots.

Rachel leaned a hip against the railing and used the binoculars to make a three hundred and sixty degree scan of the lake. We both stayed on the bridge for the next few hours, me driving and Rachel frequently scanning the horizon for other boats.

By mid-afternoon, I was sluggish and sleepy from the sun and wind. I made myself stand to prevent nodding off from the gentle motion of the boat as it motored across the lake. Rachel seemed to have no issue staying alert and was once again holding the binoculars up, resting them on the back of her bandaged hand.

"Got something." She said.

I was instantly alert as those two words triggered a big dump of adrenaline into my system. I looked in the direction Rachel was locked onto, not seeing anything other than water and humidity haze.

"Can't see it. What have you got?" I asked, hand on the throttle in preparation for pushing our speed up.

"Small boat. Looks like three people in it, but I can't tell men from women. I don't think they've seen us. Take a look." Rachel handed over the glasses. I raised them to my face and adjusted the focus for my eyes.

It took some patience and scanning back and forth, but I finally spotted it. It was a small ski boat, probably no more than twenty or twenty-five feet in length. There were three people visible, one driving and two sitting near the stern, but like Rachel I couldn't see any detail other than a human form.

The boat was traveling in the same direction as us, probably about four miles away, moving at a good speed. I agreed with Rachel that it didn't appear they had spotted us. They seemed to be focused on getting from point A to point B and not paying any attention to their surroundings as they transited the lake. I scanned ahead of their direction of travel, seeing nothing except more lake and more haze.

"What do you think?" Rachel asked, watching me scan the lake.

"I think I don't like it," I said. "They could just be survivors heading for the river like us. Or, they could be part of a larger group that's either ahead of us near the river or behind us on the southern shore. Either way, I think we need to exercise some caution here."

Reaching out, I shut down the engine. The depth finder said we had almost two hundred feet of water under us at the moment, and I had no idea if our anchor line was long enough. I flipped the switch anyway. The anchor hit the water with a splash. The nylon line that attached it to the boat made a distinctly serpentine hissing sound as it unrolled and slid through a stainless steel ring set in the rail of the boat's bow.

It seemed to hiss forever, then stopped as suddenly as it had started. I moved the switch to the middle position, which locked the anchor winch. A few moments later the boat came up against the line, stretching it tight and holding us fast to the bottom.

We stayed in that spot for the rest of the afternoon, taking turns on the bridge with the binoculars to keep watch. When it was Rachel's turn to watch, I went below and stretched out in the salon, resting but unable to nap. I planned to wait until dark before resuming our travel. I'd keep the speed down, which would also keep the noise down, and hopefully let us approach the river unseen and unheard.

I didn't know what to think of the boat we'd seen, but if I was of a mind to set up an ambush for unwary travelers I couldn't think of a better place than the natural choke point of the transition from a lake to a river. The lake was great and had provided us with an easy path to cover a lot of miles quickly, but to really make progress we'd have to move on to the river, again assuming it was navigable. It was certainly drawn large enough on the road map I had, but I doubted the cartographer had been particularly concerned with the accuracy of waterways when the map was created.

As the sun slipped below the horizon, I started the engine, waited while the anchor winch did its job, then fed in enough throttle to get us moving. I had taken a compass heading before we dropped anchor and quickly got us moving in the same direction, slowly motoring towards the river.

We sailed with the boat blacked out, the only light showing being the dim, red glow from the instrument panel on the flying bridge. Even though it was dim, I looked for a way to shut them off, coming up empty as apparently the light was on if the engine was on. I checked the panel, thinking to pull the fuse for the instrument lights, but it was poorly marked and I didn't feel like messing around with something I knew little about.

I finally settled for ripping off strips of duct tape and covering each instrument to mask its light. This was a better solution anyway because if I really needed to check something all I had to do was peel back a piece of tape and the gauge would be instantly visible.

Rachel stayed on the bridge with me, again acting as lookout with the binoculars, continually scanning all around us. Neither of us was in a talkative mood and the evening passed in silence.

Finally, shortly after midnight, Rachel lowered the glasses and stepped close to me, speaking in a low voice, “Lights ahead, just a little to the right of our direction of travel. They’re dim, and I can’t see them without the glasses.”

Throttling back to idle, I took the glasses from her and raised them to look in the direction she pointed. Faint spots of light were visible against a darker backdrop. It took me some time to realize that the backdrop was heavy forest, and we had reached the shore where the river cut through into the lake. I guessed the lights were still well over a mile away as they were completely invisible to the naked eye, so I nudged the throttle enough to get us moving forward again.

Taking a moment, I double checked the location and load on our rifles, made sure the extra magazines were loaded and at hand on our vests and pistols had rounds in the chambers and were ready to go. Satisfied we were as prepared as possible, I focused on the darkness ahead, straining to spot the break in the shoreline that would indicate the path to the river.

A few minutes later I lowered our speed to as close to idle as I could get it and still have enough water flow across the rudder to allow me to steer the boat. The term 'steerage way' came to mind, but I wasn't about to try and start talking like a sailor when I didn't have a clue what I was talking about. Peeling the tape off the Indicated Knots gauge I checked our speed, the needle bouncing right around three knots, and then spread the tape back into place.

"What can you see?" I mumbled to Rachel, lips close to her ear. I knew how sound could travel across the water, and I was worried enough about the sound of the engine. I sure didn't want to add in a human voice.

"Same thing," She answered just as quietly. "Dim spots of light. If I had to guess, I'd say they almost look like windows in a house with the curtains closed, but that's just a guess. Oh, and there's a break in the shoreline directly in front of us that I'm pretty sure is the river. It could just be an inlet to a cove, but I don't think so. It looks nice and wide to me. See what you think."

I took the offered binoculars and focused first on the lights, then slightly left to the break in the darkness that Rachel had referred to. She was right about the light looking like house windows, and if this was the river, at least the mouth of it was nice and wide. Of course, we still had the speedboat in tow, which could operate in as little as two feet of water if needed. I hoped we didn't need it.

We kept motoring forward, finally cutting the engines and letting the big boat drift to a stop when I estimated we were about half a mile from the mouth of the river. The spots of light were much more defined through the binoculars now, and it looked like Rachel had called it correctly. They were, without a doubt, windows with curtains pulled over them. We both spent a good amount of time scanning the shore, the opening to the river and the building with the lights, but neither of us spotted any indication of an ambush, and thankfully no infected.

Decision time. Did we try to motor quietly into the river and past the building, risking navigating in the dark in a very large and cumbersome boat? Should we transition to the speed boat and head up river? Was it wise to try and make contact with the people in the building, or should we just pull back out into the lake and wait for daylight to make a run for the river at speed?

Rachel and I discussed and weighed each of the options, finally settling on pulling back and waiting. I was too concerned about taking the boat into the river in the darkness, and neither of us was ready to abandon the big cruiser just yet. Neither were we eager to introduce ourselves to the strangers. Even if they were friendlies, it was almost two o'clock in the morning and not the time of day to make a social call.

As we sat and discussed our options, I noted that we were slowly drifting back towards the open lake, away from the river. Well, that answered that question. We were in a mild current that was resulting from the river emptying into the lake. We rode that current for another hour.

Once we were far enough out into the lake that the lighted windows could only be seen with the binoculars, I dropped the anchor. I sent Rachel below to rest while I settled into the padded captain's chair on the flying bridge to keep watch for a few hours. Dog padded into the salon with Rachel, leaving me to my thoughts in the quiet night.

34

The eastern sky was just starting to lighten when I went below and shook Rachel awake. Her eyes flew open and she sat straight up in bed the second I touched her shoulder, only relaxing when I spoke and she recognized my voice.

"It's going to be dawn soon. Can you take watch and wake me in two hours?"

Rachel nodded, rubbed her eyes, scooted to the edge of the bed and stood. Dog, stretched out on the far side of the mattress, looked up at us without moving and grunted his displeasure at being disturbed before rolling over and ignoring us.

"Anything moving?" Rachel asked, pulling her pants on and picking up her socks and boots off the floor.

"Quiet as a tomb," I said, then grinned in embarrassment at my poor choice of analogies.

Rachel patted me on the chest as she squeezed past, and I fell into the bed, sheets still warm from her body. I twisted the pillows around to get comfortable, pushed Dog's big paws out of my face and closed my eyes. Moments later Rachel was shaking my shoulder.

"It's been two hours." She said.

I opened my eyes and the first thing I saw was Dog's ass aimed directly at my face. Slapping his tail down to cover the view, I sat up, wincing in pain. The good news was my chest only hurt when I moved now, not all the time. The bad news was it still hurt enough to slow me down if I needed to move quickly.

"Still quiet?" I asked, accepting the cup of coffee Rachel pressed into my hand.

"Very. Sun's been up about an hour, but we've got a layer of fog on the lake that's keeping us well hidden. Can't see past the bow, but I've not heard anything so far."

I stood up and sipped from the mug, wincing from the pain in my chest and the bitter coffee. Dog rolled over and laid his head on the pillow I'd just vacated, tail thumping the mattress like a big bass drum. Rachel leaned in and smacked him on the ass until he finally jumped off the bed so she could straighten the covers. While Dog wandered forward to the small deck at the bow to take care of personal business, I did the same in the small head. Finishing the coffee, I made my way out of the salon and up to the flying bridge.

We floated in a world of white cotton. The fog was thick and all enveloping, nothing visible beyond the boat's railing. Leaning out and looking over the side I could make out the steel grey water lapping against the hull, but the sound was muted in the thick fog. Every surface had beaded water on it, and when Rachel climbed the ladder and joined me, I noticed her normally thick hair was damp and plastered to her head.

We sat quiet, listening, but other than the gentle lap of the water all we heard was Dog's nails on the fiberglass deck as he made his way back to the stern.

"When did the fog roll in?" I asked in a quiet voice.

"About half an hour after you woke me. It was clear as a bell when I came up; then it felt like the temperature dropped ten degrees and within fifteen minutes it was like this. This is pretty normal in Georgia for this time of year. In another hour, the sun will have burned it off."

We sat in the fog, talking in low voices, discussing our plan. Neither of us was anxious to make contact with other survivors. We had the supplies we needed for a while, were well armed and still had a good stock of ammunition. There was nothing we could see being gained by taking the risk of approaching more people at this time. For all we knew they could turn out to be even more paranoid than we were and start shooting as soon as they saw us.

With our decision made, we ate a Spartan breakfast, sharing with Dog, and took the opportunity to individually jump into the lake with a bar of soap. Despite the chilly fog, the lake water was warm and refreshing. Rachel had bandaged my wounds with plastic wrap and medical tape before she'd let me get in the water. It felt wonderful to get the last of the blood and grime washed from my body.

The boat did have a small laundry set on board and Rachel had washed and dried a set of clothes for each of us. Before dressing, I rummaged through one of the heads until I found a disposable razor, then sat on the stern rail while Rachel shaved the stubble off my head. I took care of my face, dressed in clean clothes and felt like a new man.

About 8:30, the fog started thinning slightly, then quickly burned off as the sun's light warmed things up. Back on the flying bridge, I scanned with the binoculars and realized that the lights we'd seen the night before hadn't been a building on the shore, but a houseboat tied to the dense trees. The ski boat from yesterday was secured to its rail and there was no sign of movement.

Swinging the glasses a few degrees to the left I was immediately thankful that we had not tried to take the cruiser up the river in the dark. Sitting mostly submerged, and blocking almost half of the river's mouth, was a crashed helicopter that had been invisible in the dark. The nose of the chopper was stuck into the muddy right bank of the river, the body of the aircraft tilted sideways nearly forty degrees and the tail extending out into the channel. The rotor blades were snapped off. It was easy to trace their path of destruction into the trees that lined the shore. I silently handed the binoculars to Rachel. She caught her breath when she saw the downed aircraft.

"Can we get around it?" She asked without lowering the glasses.

"The short answer is, we're going to get around it. Either in this or the speedboat," I answered, looking over my shoulder, trying to identify the low sound I was hearing. Not able to see anything, I reached out for the glasses, rudely taking them from Rachel without asking and using them to scan the open lake to our rear.

Two bass boats with monster outboard engines were coming towards us at what had to be full throttle. Four men were in each boat, and the long, stick looking things in their hands were most certainly rifles. I spun around, started the engine and hit the switch to raise the anchor. Again, it seemed to take forever, but if I started moving forward before it was fully retracted, I could end up driving over my own anchor line and getting it tangled in the boat's propellers.

Rachel had the glasses back and was watching the fast approaching boats. My eyes were glued to the winch, willing it to go faster. When the anchor finally broke the surface of the lake, I slammed the throttle all the way forward. The big boat's engine bellowed. The stern settled for a moment as the props displaced the water directly under it, then we started accelerating. Much too slowly. This wasn't a speed boat, it was a floating luxury home and not made for fast starts.

"Not going to make it!" Rachel shouted over the engine noise.

I looked back and realized she was right. The bass boats were moving at a high rate of speed and would intercept us well before we made the river. I wasn't even sure the river was a good idea at this point. No room to maneuver. No room to turn and fight.

They'd be able to stay on our ass and keep pumping bullets into the boat until they hit something that was either mechanically or biologically vital. Without another thought, I spun the wheel and the cruiser slowly responded to the new course I set towards the middle of the lake.

We kept turning until the bow of the big cruiser was pointed almost directly at the approaching boats. I straightened the wheel and double checked to make sure the throttle was wide open. The duct tape from the night before was still covering the gauges, and I started ripping pieces off, surprised to see our indicated speed as just over twenty-eight knots and slowly climbing. Rachel leaned into me and shouted above the engine noise and slipstream of wind.

“Should we do something to alert the people in the houseboat?”

I shook my head, eyes fixed on the approaching threat. We knew nothing of the dynamic here. The people in the houseboat could be bad guys, and these were the good guys coming to take care of a problem. I wasn’t sure which group, if either, could be trusted. I was more concerned about getting us out of the middle of whatever dispute was going on. The boat was easy to pilot with one hand on the wheel. I had my rifle up and resting on the bridge railing, right hand on the pistol grip and thumb on the safety in case it was needed.

The two boats were now close enough for me to make out more details. One was bright red, the other a color of blue that can only be described as electric. Other than that they were almost identical, both sporting huge Mercury outboard motors that had to be around three hundred horse power each. No wonder they were so fast.

The men riding in the red boat seemed to be fixated on me, the blue boat steering slightly to its right to bypass us and be on a direct course to the houseboat. The red boat made the decision for me when the man in the bow braced himself and pointed a rifle in my direction.

"Drive, and sound the horn!" I shouted to Rachel as I slipped out of the pilot's seat and onto my knee, rifle up and aimed over the bridge rail.

Rachel hit the button for the horn. The blast pierced the morning, carrying for miles across the water. I still didn't know the dynamics here, but if these were good guys approaching they had made a critical mistake by pointing a rifle at me. I hoped the horn would alert the people in the houseboat, and they could keep the blue boat occupied.

Settling into the stock of the rifle, I flipped the selector to burst mode and briefly wished for a heavier caliber machine gun such as a good old fashioned M-60. Oh well, you fight with what you have as I'd been told over and over.

Even at almost thirty knots, the cabin cruiser provided an amazingly smooth and stable ride. The bass boat, on the other hand, was bouncing and jarring around, sensitive to every little ripple on the lake's surface. This was to my advantage as far as a stable aiming platform, but hitting a moving target that is vibrating up and down and side to side at the same time is not child's play. They hadn't fired on us yet, but the threat was clear. I didn't intend to wait to see if I was just misunderstanding some poor souls who only wanted to stop by for tea.

Taking a deep breath and slowly exhaling I tracked the boat, aiming for the man in the bow. As the last of the breath left my lungs, I squeezed the trigger twice, sending six rounds down range. A moment later I was rewarded with an explosion of fiberglass from the bow of the boat, inches from the man holding the rifle that was aimed at us.

He jerked away from the impact point of my bullets and rose up in perfect profile at the very front of the boat, which was getting closer by the second. I quickly sent another three rounds on their way and was gratified to see him pitch over backwards in the boat. Whether hit once, twice or three times didn't matter as he was now out of the fight.

The red boat reacted exactly as I expected. Instead of continuing closer and the remaining men opening up on us, it turned quickly to its right, presenting me with a perfect profile. Ready for the opportunity, I sighted on the big outboard motor, leading it in the scope by what I hoped was the right distance, and started sending three round bursts downrange. The third burst did the trick, the top of the housing shredding into dozens of pieces as thick, black smoke began pouring out of the motor. Propulsion gone, the boat quickly came off plane and settled in the water, momentum carrying it forward a short distance until it fell adrift.

I put six more rounds into the side of the boat, just to keep their heads down, and motioned for Rachel to turn and follow the blue boat. A quick magazine change and I used the binoculars to check on the boat I'd disabled. Two of the men were battling a small fire in the motor while the third watched us through a pair of binoculars. He was a sitting duck and was at least smart enough to not point his rifle in my direction.

The cruiser came about, and I shifted attention to the blue boat. It was sitting still in the water, fifty yards from the houseboat, and all four men aboard were standing, firing their rifles into the side of the craft. They seemed unaware of what had transpired with their buddies. Amateurs.

I stood and leaned into Rachel, telling her to bring us up behind them and cut speed when we were about two hundred yards out, but be ready to throttle up and get us moving. We covered the distance quickly, and I resumed my one knee shooting position at the bridge railing as we came at them. Rachel cut the engine to idle at the right spot and the big boat quickly settled in the water, momentum carrying us forward. At about a hundred and fifty yards, I opened fire, still in burst mode.

The man standing in the stern pitched forward, rifle flying out of his hands and splashing into the lake just before his body hit the water. The two men to the far left were so focused on firing at their target that they didn't notice, but the man closest to him did. He lowered his rifle and stared at the body of his friend in the water and started to turn just as my next three rounds shredded his lower torso. He pitched forward across the pilot's seat and lay still.

The other two men noticed now, turning and gawking at their two dead friends before spinning around in my direction. The man in the bow took the next three rounds to the chest and flipped backwards out of the boat into the water.

The remaining man could have lived if he'd had the sense to put his rifle down, but he raised it and started to aim at the cabin cruiser. Three rounds sped downrange, two slamming into his chest and neck, the third punching through his skull, leaving a faint pink mist in the air for a brief moment before it settled onto the water along with his body.

Another magazine change and I stood and glassed the red boat. They had extinguished the fire and were slowly motoring away from us, a small electric trolling motor their only source of propulsion. I had no idea if the battery powering the motor was capable of getting them to shore and I frankly didn't give a shit. They picked the fight; now they had to live with the results.

"Jesus Christ!" Rachel said, still staring at the four dead men in and around the blue boat.

I just looked at her then turned the glasses back to the houseboat in time to see one of the curtains twitch open, and a pair of binoculars look back at me. Raising my hand in greeting, I kept watching until the curtains were pulled aside and a man waved back. Handing the glasses to Rachel, I told her where to look and after a moment, she waved to the face in the window.

35

The man in the houseboat window turned out to be one of four who were holed up in the small craft. They were the crew of the crashed helicopter, which was an Air Force Pave Hawk, the Air Force variant of the Army's Black Hawk. They weren't in the best of shape, the pilot the worst off with a severe concussion, broken leg, and crushed pelvis.

We had slowly motored in after the firefight, and the cabin cruiser now lay at anchor a hundred feet from the shore the houseboat was tied to. We had crossed the open water in the speedboat, Rachel driving and me standing next to her with my rifle at the ready.

On board the houseboat we were greeted warmly, but with caution. These were Air Force guys, and they were in the Georgia National Guard. They'd been lucky enough to have never been deployed to the Middle East, which answered a lot of my questions about their poor tactical decisions. They introduced themselves and Rachel kneeled down next to the injured pilot, a Captain, who looked too young to be playing pilot, to see what she could do for him.

I stood on the small deck at the stern; rifle slung but hand still on the grip, and started talking with the other three. A very young looking kid wore First Lieutenant's bars and was the only officer other than the pilot. The other two were both enlisted and wore Tech Sergeant's and Senior Airman chevrons. I looked them over as they settled down, the Sergeant by far the old man of the group. He looked to be in his early thirties.

They were haggard and filthy, their flight suits smeared with mud, blood and other things I didn't want to think about, faces unshaven and gaunt. The Airman had a dirty bandage wrapped around his head and the Lieutenant had a crude splint on his left wrist and bruising across his face. The kind of bruising that comes from getting punched in the nose. Or hitting your face on a control panel when your helicopter crashes. Each of them carried an Air Force issue side arm, but they didn't have any other weapons.

"I'm John," I introduced myself. "That's Rachel in there with your Captain. She's had medical training and will do what she can for him." I nodded towards the interior of the boat.

"Thank you, Sir. I'm Lieutenant David Anderson, Georgia Air National Guard. This is Tech Sergeant Blake and Senior Airman Mayo. We just want to thank you for helping us out. I thought for sure those guys were going to kill us." I acknowledged his thanks with a nod and looked over at Sergeant Blake when he lit up a cigarette.

"Think I could bum one of those, Sarge?" I asked, mouth already watering at the thought of a smoke. I'd been without since the morning the world fell apart and probably should have stayed quit, but all things considered, I'd probably die of a thousand different things before a cigarette killed me. Blake smiled and handed me the pack and a battered Zippo.

Lighting the cigarette, I inhaled deeply, blew the smoke out with a satisfied smile and handed the pack and lighter back. The head rush hit a moment later, and I took another long, satisfying drag off the cigarette. Fuck the Surgeon General. He was probably dead anyway.

"Thank you. That's a damn good smoke." I said to Blake. "Now, I have some questions, and I'm sure you do too, but first I want to make something clear. Nothing personal, but we've not exactly had the best of experiences with survivors, and it appears you haven't either. That said, I don't want there to be any misunderstandings between us. I see each of you with a sidearm. That's fine, but those pistols stay holstered until further notice. Am I clear on that?"

To drive home my point, I flicked the rifle's safety lever off with my thumb. The click was clearly audible, and three sets of eyes got very large. I looked at each of them in turn and didn't see anything that concerned me at the moment.

“We understand,” the Lieutenant spoke up. “We aren’t looking for any trouble, just trying to survive.”

“Fair enough,” I said, clicking the lever back into the SAFE position.

Rachel came out the back door and paused, picking up on the tension of the moment, then walked over to me and took the cigarette out of my hand. She took a long drag, closed her eyes and held it for a moment before smiling and exhaling through her nose.

“God, that’s good,” She said. “I’m going to run back and get some supplies. He’s in bad shape. There’s not much more I can do with what we have than make him comfortable. I’ve got the stuff I found in that house that should help him.” Rachel was referring to the heroin she’d found in the house she’d been held captive in.

“OK. Take Mayo here with you,” I answered, gesturing to the young Airman. “Airman, when you get to that boat you will go straight to the flying bridge. There’s a pair of binoculars up there, and you will use them to keep watch. If you see anything approaching, another boat, infected, whatever, you sound that horn. Understood?” I held his eyes with mine, waiting for an answer.

"Yes, sir." He replied and got to his feet to climb into the speedboat with Rachel.

"Oh, and Airman," I stopped him. "There's a nasty tempered dog on that boat. He'll let you on the bridge as long as Rachel here is with you, but... if you try to leave the bridge without one of us on the boat, he'll likely bite your balls off and have them for breakfast."

Mayo's eyes went wide. He looked back and forth between his Lieutenant, Rachel and me. When no one smiled, he got the message. "Yes, sir. Got it."

He scrambled into the speedboat with Rachel already at the wheel, untied the line holding it to the houseboat, and they were gone.

"He's a good kid," Blake said. "He won't mess with anything."

I grinned and looked over my shoulder and watched Rachel maneuver the speedboat to the stern of the cruiser where Mayo grabbed a line out of the water and tied the two boats together. Dog stood at the stern rail, tail down and ears up. Mayo didn't make another move until Rachel boarded the boat and motioned him to follow.

"So gentlemen. How did you wind up in this little corner of paradise?" I asked.

36

Lieutenant David Anderson hung up the phone, grumbling to himself at the emergency call in. Three months out of college, he was honoring his commitment to the National Guard in exchange for four years of tuition having been paid in full. He didn't mind the National Guard, especially since things were winding down in Iraq and Afghanistan and it was very unlikely that he'd get deployed. However, he had just walked in the door of his cramped apartment and had planned to grab a shower before meeting Melanie for a drink.

Melanie was a student at Georgia Tech, in her senior year, and was the most beautiful girl Anderson had ever seen. Tall, with a runner's body and long blonde hair, he was still amazed that she had ever agreed to go out with him two weeks ago. This was now their third date, and he was hoping he was reading the signs right, and she would be coming home with him tonight.

"Damn call-ups," he fumed, almost throwing his cell phone against the wall. Instead, he calmed himself and called Melanie and canceled their date. To his surprise, she asked him if he would call her as soon as he was free so they could go have their drink. He agreed and, mood lightened, set about gathering what he needed to take to the Guard base.

An hour later he sat in a briefing room with Captain Gerry Helm, the pilot of the Pave Hawk to which Anderson was assigned. Their crew chief, Tech Sergeant Blake, and a young Senior Airman named Mayo sat in the row of chairs behind them. At the back of the room were four men wearing a mishmash of civilian and military issue clothing. All had thick beards, three with long hair to their shoulders and the fourth with a shaved head.

Anderson didn't need to be told they were Special Forces operators. No one other than SF walked around any military installation looking like a dirtbag, or as Captain Helm put it, 'Rejects from the Hell's Angels'. He had seen SF Operators before but never worked with them. They were almost a mythical creature to someone like him, and a thrill of excitement ran through him at the thought of adding an SF operation to his military resume. He snapped out of his reverie when Captain Helm shot to his feet and yelled, "Attention!"

He was on his feet, ramrod straight in the blink of an eye, as were Blake and Mayo. From the back of the room, he could hear shuffling about and chairs being repositioned as the SF guys got to their feet in their own sweet time. Anderson kept his eyes straight ahead, focused on the US flag standing at the front of the room. In his peripheral vision, he could see Colonel Hamm, his air wing commander, accompanied by an Army Colonel, stride into the room and take up position between the US and Air Force flags.

"As you were," Colonel Hamm rumbled in a baritone voice that always made Anderson think of a gravel crusher. Hamm was an early middle-aged black man who in his prime had been a star linebacker for Air Force, and he still had the thick chest and arms from the football days of his youth. As large and intimidating as he was, he didn't compare to the Army Colonel standing next to him.

The man was a shade over six feet tall and obviously spent a great deal of time in the gym. His shoulders and back strained the ACU blouse he wore, and his biceps threatened to rip through the sleeves. He was one of the ugliest human beings that Anderson had ever seen and not anyone he'd want to have pissed off at him.

After the men had settled into their seats, Hamm spoke briefly. "Gentlemen, this is a classified top-secret briefing for an equally classified operation. It is not to be discussed with anyone not present in this room. Clear?"

The four Air Force personnel immediately answered with an affirmative, but the back of the room was silent. The SF guys didn't do anything that wasn't classified at least top secret, and this was old hat to them. Anderson wasn't even sure they were paying attention, but he wasn't about to turn around to find out. Hamm glared at the back of the room for a moment, then introduced the Army Colonel.

"With me is Colonel Flowers from Army Special Operations. This mission shall be under his operational control, and he will brief you on what you need to know."

Hamm stepped aside, but the larger Flowers didn't feel the need to move from where he already stood. Flowers? Anderson suspected it had been a very long time, if ever, since anyone had made a crack about the Colonel's name.

Looking at him standing with his feet wide apart and hands clasped behind his back, Anderson felt a shiver of uncertainty as the man looked at each of the Air Force personnel in turn before speaking.

"Thank you, Colonel Hamm." His voice was nearly a falsetto, almost an amusing counterpoint to Colonel Hamm. Almost.

"Gentlemen, we have received intelligence that the United States is in imminent danger of attack. Not overseas, but CONUS (Continental United States). I am not at liberty to discuss the details of that intelligence with you, and beginning now you are in blackout status. No communication with any persons not directly involved in this mission. Am I clear?"

A chorus of "Sir!" sounded from the back of the room, but Captain Helm was the only man in the front row to acknowledge the order. Flowers' head swiveled to Anderson, then Blake and Mayo.

"Gentlemen? Did I mumble?" His expression never changed, but the tone of his voice was chilling.

"No sir. I mean, yes sir, the order is clear!" Anderson stumbled over his words. Blake and Mayo also acknowledged the order.

"Good. Now, your mission is simple." He was clearly addressing the flight crew.

"You are to depart this installation at 2300 hours with the team in the back of the room with you. You will have a full load out of war shot for this mission. Your call sign will be Cadillac Two Seven. Your destination is the CDC, the Center for Disease Control, in metro Atlanta. Colonel Hamm tells me your flight time should be fifteen minutes from wheels up to touchdown. Pilots, the briefing packet under your chairs contains your flight plan, radio freqs and designations, and destination landing details. Once on target, you will stand by while my team retrieves a passenger.

"Once they are inserted you will remain on station and will defend the aircraft from any and all personnel who may try to approach. Your ROE (Rules of Engagement) are as follows. Absolutely NO personnel, civilian or military, may approach or board the aircraft. Deadly force is authorized. Am I clear?"

This time, the flight crew spoke as one with a firm, "Yes, Sir!" Years of training was all that kept them from giving any other answer.

Use of deadly force within the continental US was unheard of outside the personnel that secured nuclear weapons or sensitive installations. Deadly force to prevent someone from wandering up to an Air Force helicopter was beyond exceptional.

"Upon the return of the team with your passenger," Colonel Flowers continued, "you shall disembark the CDC and make all possible speed to Fort Campbell, Kentucky. You will be met approximately half way by an escort flight of Apaches, designated as Whiskey Flight.

"Also, in your briefing packets is a photo of the passenger you will be picking up. If my team is occupied providing rear cover and he arrives at the aircraft unescorted, you shall provide protection for him, bring him aboard and depart immediately. The team is expendable. He is not. You are not to wait for them, or any member of the team, once your passenger is onboard your aircraft. Questions?"

Anderson had about a thousand questions but kept his mouth shut. Anything operational should come from Captain Helm, and most of Anderson's questions had little to do directly with the operation.

Right on cue, Captain Helm spoke up, "Sir, should we expect resistance at the target?"

"Captain, you should expect resistance. You need to be prepared for possible panic from the civilian employees, and cannot hesitate to do what is necessary to complete your mission."

Flowers stared at Helm for a moment, then moved his gaze across the rest of the men in the room, satisfying himself that his message had gotten across.

When no one else spoke up, he looked over at Colonel Hamm, who had an expression on his face like he'd just sucked on a lemon. Stepping forward, he dismissed the assembled men.

Captain Helm shot to his feet, calling the room to attention as the two officers walked out the door. A moment later Flowers stuck his head back in and motioned for the SF team to follow him. They quickly exited the room, leaving the four-man Air Force flight crew alone.

“What the fuck, sir?” Blake asked with a look of incredulity on his face.

“You heard what I heard, Tech Sergeant. This is all way off the reservation for me, but our orders are pretty clear.” Helm flipped open the briefing packet and thumbed through until he found the glossy photo of their passenger.

The man in the photo was in his mid-fifties with thick, graying hair, bushy eyebrows, and a drinker’s nose. Anderson thought he kind of looked like his uncle. Helm stared at the photo for a few minutes then handed it to Blake.

“Tech Sergeant, I want you on the door gun this flight. Here’s our passenger. No one other than him or the SF team boards the aircraft. You good with that?”

Blake stared at the photo in his hand, Mayo peering over his shoulder to get a good look.

“Sergeant Blake?” Helm prompted after a few moments of silence.

“Yes, sir. No problem.” Blake finally looked up and answered.

“Good. Let’s get our bird pre-flighted and make sure the ordnance monkeys don’t forget to give us bullets.” Helm stood and led the crew from the briefing room.

Just over an hour later, Captain Helm pulled back on the collective and the Pave Hawk jumped into the dark Georgia sky. Anderson kept a hand on the controls, ready to take command if needed as Helm spun them around and transitioned to forward flight on a direct course to the CDC.

In back, Blake sat in the open door of the helicopter, strapped in and ready on the machine gun that hung from a complicated sling system. Mayo, strapped in to the side, sat ready to provide support to the gunner as needed. The four SF Operators were settled in canvas web slings that hung from the walls of the helicopter.

They were heavily armed, and despite the expected short duration of the mission, each carried a large amount of spare ammunition. They weren't big talkers. The only words came from the team leader when he boarded the aircraft and asked for a headset so he was on the internal intercom while they were in flight. Pave Hawks make all the racket in the world, and the only way to communicate was over a headset.

The flight to the CDC was fast and uneventful, almost enjoyable as the soft, warm air of the evening flowed through the helicopter's door and the lights of Atlanta spread out beneath them.

When they reached the CDC, Anderson identified the helicopter pad for Helm, IR strobes embedded in the rooftop landing pad flashing brightly in his night vision goggles. He then kept watch for other aircraft as they quickly descended and touched down.

The SF team was out the door before the rotors could spin down, running towards a metal door that led into the building. They moved in a diamond formation, each of the men with their weapons raised as they scanned their individual areas of responsibility.

"Cadillac Two Seven, Alpha Team moving. See you in a few," the team leader radioed over a secure commlink to Helm and Anderson.

"Copy, Alpha Team. Luck." Helm responded, then turned around in his seat. "Mayo, grab an M4 and some extra magazines and take up watch at our nose. I don't want anyone coming in from our blind side. Remember your ROE, Senior Airman."

"Yes, sir." Mayo sounded a little shaky but did as ordered. When he was in position, he plugged his headset into an externally mounted jack on the front of the helicopter so he could stay in communication with the flight crew.

The rotor spun slowly overhead, the engines at idle while they waited. Helm would normally shut down the engines to save fuel. A Pave Hawk is a very thirsty bird, but he wanted to be ready to lift off the moment the SF team returned with their passenger.

It didn't take long for the first signs of trouble to start. Mayo came on the intercom with a report of gunfire from the south.

"Could it be the SF guys, Mayo?" Helm asked.

"Negative sir, I don't think so. They were carrying sound suppressed weapons, and besides, this sounds like pistol fire with the occasional shotgun." The stress in Mayo's voice was evident, but Anderson knew he'd grown up in the gang infested streets of South Atlanta and would know the difference in sound between a pistol and a rifle.

"Lieutenant, take a look. Mayo, stay on your position." Helm ordered.

Anderson gave a thumbs up as he pulled off his headset and released the flight harness that held him into the seat. Exiting the cockpit, he trotted around the nose of the Pave Hawk and stopped next to Mayo to ask where he was hearing the shots, but didn't need to as he heard them for himself. Jogging ahead, he reached the edge of the roof and knelt at the low parapet to look over.

At first, he thought he was looking at a small riot in the street below. Three police cars, roof lights strobing red and blue across the surrounding buildings, were sitting at haphazard angles in the middle of a large intersection. Five uniformed officers faced a large crowd of people who were advancing on them. Several bodies lay on the pavement, already being trampled by the advancing crowd.

As Anderson watched, a slight figure that looked like a woman suddenly raced forward from the edge of the crowd, quickly followed by two more. All five officers opened fire, two of the women dropping to the street but the third made a mighty leap, landed on the hood of one of the patrol cars then launched herself at one of the officers. They went down in a tangle and started fighting until another officer cracked her over the head with a baton. She went limp and was pushed aside.

The officer who had used the baton turned his attention back to the rioters, engaging another runner before she could reach the hood of his car. As Anderson watched, the officer who had fought with the woman slowly got to his feet, stumbling like he was injured. Then, to his horror, the cop lunged forward and appeared to sink his teeth into the other officer's neck.

They fought for a few seconds before falling to the ground, the first officer's jaws still locked onto his prey. The other three officers stared, distracted for a minute, and paid the price. Five more women raced forward and quickly dragged them down. The screams were clear on the night air, and soon the crowd of rioters reached the struggling officers and fell on them like a pack of hyenas.

"What the fuck is going on?" Anderson asked himself as he backed away from the edge of the roof, turned and sprinted back to the idling Pave Hawk. He ran past Mayo, ignoring him, and skidded around the nose of the chopper. Yanking the door open he fumbled his headset on and relayed what he'd seen to Captain Helm.

"What?" A shocked Helm asked.

"Exactly what I said, Captain. I've never seen anything like it except in movies. It was just like a scene out of 28 Days Later."

Helm might not have believed Anderson if it weren't for how obviously shaken the young Lieutenant was. He hadn't known Anderson for long, but from what he'd seen the younger man was steady and level headed and didn't seem to have a tendency to want to exaggerate or play jokes. Making a decision, he pushed the button for the secure comm channel.

"Alpha Team, Cadillac Two Seven," he broadcast.

"Go Two Seven," the answer came back almost immediately, the SF team leader barely speaking loud enough to be heard.

"Alpha, be advised we have a civilian riot in progress in the street to the south of the LZ. Local law enforcement has engaged, and shots are being fired." How the hell could he tell someone over the radio that the zombies were here?

"Acknowledged, Two Seven. Keep a sharp eye Captain. We've located package and am en route to you. Seven mikes (minutes) out."

Helm had intentionally left the radio feed switched to the intercom so the whole flight crew could listen in. They exchanged nervous glances as Anderson set a countdown timer on the Pave Hawk's console to seven minutes, glancing at the center mounted chronometer display and noting the time was 2340.

While he was looking at the display, a bright red LED started pulsing in the center of the panel. An emergency indicator telling the pilot to switch to a specific encrypted military channel. Helm rotated the dial on the radio and entered the passcode of the day when asked. A click followed by a hiss, not unlike a fax machine connecting, then a clear voice was speaking in all their headsets.

"...Condition one. Bugs Bunny. All units set Condition one." The short message started repeating, and all the blood drained from Helm's face.

"What's Bugs Bunny?" Anderson asked, almost afraid of the answer. Helm looked like he was about to go into shock and didn't react to Anderson's question. "Captain Helm, what's Bugs Bunny?" Anderson asked again, louder.

Helm regained a degree of composure and looked over at him with the most haunted eyes Anderson had ever seen up to that point.

"A nuclear weapon has been detonated in an American city." He finally answered.

The crew was stunned into silence, listening to the pre-recorded message repeat. Finally, Helm reached forward and silenced the radio, switching back to the secure comm frequency for the SF Team. Pressing the button, he spoke in a calmer voice than Anderson expected,

"Alpha Team, Cadillac Two Seven."

"Alpha, go." The stress was audible in the SF team leader's voice. Anderson was sure he could hear the sound of suppressed weapons fire over the open circuit.

"Alpha Team, we have received Bugs Bunny. I repeat, we have received Bugs Bunny."

There was no reply for a few heartbeats, then, "Alpha acknowledges Bugs Bunny. Out." The voice was as calm and cold as ever, and this time, Anderson was certain he'd heard a suppressed rifle firing on full automatic.

Anderson climbed all the way back into the cockpit and strapped in, ready to go as soon as the team returned. Out the windshield he could see Mayo looking around nervously, fingering the fire selector on the M4 rifle in his hands. He turned to see Blake scanning the roof, back and forth, the door gun traversing with him as he scanned. He turned back and started scanning the instruments, making sure the helicopter was ready to go when they were.

"Contact," Blake announced over the intercom.

Anderson and Helm spun around in time to see a small crowd of white-coated civilians coming onto the roof through the metal door the SF team had used to access the building. They spotted the helicopter and the man sitting in the door and started a shambling, shuffling walk forward. Two women in the group, one of them blonde with long hair, screamed and ran towards them.

"Sir?" Blake shouted over the intercom.

"Fire Sergeant. Remember your ROE." Helm answered instantly.

The heavy machine gun spoke in short controlled bursts. The M240 is a belt fed weapon and fires a NATO designated round that is 7.62 mm. At any range out to a thousand yards it is lethal, but at less than two hundred feet it is absolutely devastating to the human body. The two women fell to the roof as they were shredded by Blake's fire.

The group of men behind them didn't pause or disperse, just kept on coming. Blake feathered the trigger and wreaked the same devastation on them. As Blake fired, Helm got back on the radio and notified Alpha Team that they were repelling attackers. More people came out of the door, meeting the same fate as the first group as Blake cut them down.

"Contact." Mayo's voice came over the intercom.

At the far side of the roof, another door swung open. A small group stumbled out, several white-shirted security guards leading the way, followed by workers wearing lab coats. As soon as they saw the helicopter and Mayo aiming a rifle at them, they stopped. One of the guards pushed back through the crowd and slammed the door, bracing his shoulders against it and digging his heels into the surface of the roof.

"Sir?" Mayo asked.

"ROE has not changed, Airman. If they try to approach, you will open fire." Helm's voice was amazingly steady.

"Yes, sir." Mayo's voice, however, betrayed his doubt in their orders, but he held the rifle steady, finger on the trigger.

One of the guards stepped forward a couple of steps, then stopped and cupped his hands around his mouth. He obviously was shouting to them, but neither Helm nor Anderson could hear him from inside the Pave Hawk over the idling of engines.

"What's he saying, Mayo?" Anderson asked over the intercom.

"Sir, he's asking for help. Says 'they're coming', whatever the hell that means."

Helm and Anderson exchanged a worried look.

"Stay frosty, Mayo," Anderson said while Helm called Alpha Team.

"Two Seven, acknowledge hostiles and civilians on roof. I have two men down, and package is wounded. We're at your location in thirty seconds." More gunfire in the background, this time, pistol fire that wasn't suppressed. Had they run out of rifle ammo?

Helm made sure Blake knew the SF team was about to exit the door when Mayo fired a burst at the crowd he was watching. One of the guards had started walking towards the helicopter, and Mayo shot him in the chest.

The man with his back against the door shouted something, and the remaining guards drew their pistols and began firing at the helicopter. The impacts of the bullets were audible, even over the idling engines. Mayo opened up with the M4.

Two of the guards went down, but two more continued firing. Mayo had to do a quick magazine change and before he could bring the rifle back to bear, the guard holding the door flew forward as it burst open and a large crowd of people flooded onto the roof. They immediately attacked those who were already there. Mayo stared in mute shock as blood and gore began staining all the white clothing.

Blake resumed firing as more hostiles stumbled out of the other door. Anderson unhooked the flight harness again and scrambled into the back where he extracted the last M4 from the weapons locker, grabbed the last two magazines and jumped out to go support Mayo. His feet had just hit the roof when he spotted Alpha Team leader emerge from the inside of the building amidst a crowd that was trying to grab him and drag him down. He had a firm grip on the arm of the man Anderson had seen in the photo and was pulling him along as he kicked people out of his way and fired his pistol into the surrounding bodies.

Blake had stopped firing for fear of hitting friendlies, and Anderson shouldered the M4 rifle and started to run towards Alpha Team. He wasn't halfway there when, with no apparent warning, the man they'd been sent to evacuate turned and bit into Alpha leader's neck. There was a spray of arterial blood then both collapsed under the weight of the crowd as it surged inward.

Anderson stopped and started backing up, turning and running when a woman detached herself from the crowd and charged him with a blood chilling scream. Her face was smeared bright red, stains down the front of her once pristine lab coat. Anderson dodged out of Blake's sight line, and the Tech Sergeant chopped her down with a brief press of the trigger.

Back at the helicopter, Helm was frantically pointing at Mayo as Anderson ran up. Mayo had stepped away from the helicopter to fire at the hostiles and had inadvertently unplugged from the intercom. Helm had no way to tell him the mission was a bust and to get his ass back inside the Pave Hawk. Anderson ran to him, grabbed him by the shoulder and pulled him with him as he ran back to the side door.

Helm had throttled up the engines, and the rotor was spinning just below take off speed. Blake was still pouring controlled fire into the approaching crowd. Anderson was shocked to see Alpha leader, throat gashed open, stand up and stumble forward with the rest of the hostiles. Anderson dove through the side door a split second behind Mayo and slapped Helm on the shoulder.

The Pave Hawk leapt into the air, gaining fifty feet of altitude in seconds before Helm settled it into a stable hover. Mayo strapped himself into the door gunner support position. Anderson climbed forward and resumed his seat, clicking the flight harness into place. With his crew safely on board, Helm pointed the nose towards their home base and fed power to the engines.

37

I had kept a vigilant watch on the tree line, frequently checking on the young Airman I'd sent to the cabin cruiser while the Lieutenant had told his story. Rachel had returned quickly with the small, zippered package. She disappeared inside for a few minutes then joined us in the open air to hear the story.

She had placed herself on the rail next to me, so close that her shoulder and hip were touching mine. This was the first and only 'intimate' contact we'd had, and I knew she was sending a subtle message to these men that she was not available. I noticed both of them noticing, their eyes quickly sliding off of Rachel and focusing on me. Choosing to use me in her deception didn't bother me at all.

"So how did you wind up here?" Rachel asked.

"We were on our way back to our base. Captain Helm got on the radio to let our CO know that the SF team and our passenger hadn't made it and that we were returning. We were told that our base was under attack by rioters, a fence had already fallen, and the administrative and support staff were all that was left on the base and were being evacuated. We were told to continue on to

Fort Campbell in Kentucky, even though we didn't have our passenger.

"We changed to the new heading, and just a few minutes later we started getting an over temp warning from the rotor shaft. Sometimes those warnings are false alarms, so we continued on when it didn't climb anymore. We made it out over this lake when the temp suddenly shot up. Captain Helm aimed for the shore, but before he could set us down the shaft seized. We spun in where you see the helicopter now. Captain Helm was trapped, and it took us hours to bend and pry enough of the metal out of the way so we could get him out."

"Where did the houseboat and ski boat come from?" I asked, enjoying my cigarette and checking on Mayo. He stood with his back to me; binoculars raised to his eyes as he scanned the open water.

"They were here just like you see them now. There was no one here when we crashed, and no one has returned. We've got no idea where they went or what happened to them."

I had a pretty good idea what happened to them. "So you've been here since you crashed? We saw you yesterday coming back from the south in the ski boat. Did you do something to stir up our friends, or were they just dropping in to say hello?"

"We were running low on supplies and hadn't heard any news, so we headed across the lake. There was a big marina and a bunch of stores we saw the night we flew over."

Lieutenant Anderson talked for another fifteen minutes, telling us about finding an armed camp at the marina, huddled behind hastily erected barricades. They had traded one of their M4 rifles for food and were making their way back to their boat when they were jumped by two men who wanted their packs full of food and their other rifle.

They had fought back, killing one of the men but losing their rifle and half the food in the scramble to get away as more men started chasing them. They had made it to the boat and thought they'd made it back across the lake without anyone knowing where they had gone.

"OK, so now you know our story. How about telling us how you wound up here?"

I agreed in exchange for another smoke. Blake handed me the pack and lighter with a smirk and Rachel stole a cigarette from me as I lit up and started telling an abbreviated version of our story.

As I spoke, their expressions went from cautious optimism to depression. They knew a lot of the shit that had happened to the US; knew about the nukes and had seen the infected firsthand, but they didn't realize the infection was so widespread. When I was finished, both men were wide-eyed.

"It's amazing you've survived," Blake spoke up. I had glossed over several details, especially where Rachel's abduction was concerned. "You had to be Army or Corps, am I right?"

"Army," I answered with a grin. "A long time ago in a galaxy far, far away." I got blank looks from everyone, Rachel included. None of these people had ever seen Star Wars? Really?

"So, Lieutenant, you're a pilot?" I asked.

"Rotor wing qualified, yes sir." He answered, a puzzled look on his face.

"Well, the map I have says there's an amphibious plane facility to the south of us. If we can find a plane do you think you could fly us out of here?"

Anderson stood up, the first sign of a smile on his dirty face, "I sure as hell can. I was flying single and twin engine light planes when I was still in high school. Never done a take-off or landing on water, but I've read about it. It shouldn't be a problem, just need more room to get into the air than a normal runway." His excitement was infectious, and Blake got to his feet also.

"Don't get too excited," I warned. "I haven't seen a plane, just a reference on a map."

"It's worth checking out," Blake said.

"I agree," Anderson chimed in. "But where would we go?"

I told them about Max and the report I'd heard that Nashville was safe, at least for the moment.

"Hell, yeah!" Anderson was excited. "Nashville is maybe an hour away in a light plane, and it's only another half hour to Fort Campbell."

"OK," I said. "Tell me about everything you saw on your excursion south."

They filled me in, and we pulled out the maps and identified that the seaplane facility was far enough away from the marina that they might not have seen it if they weren't looking for it. They were pretty sure it was outside the barricades the survivors had erected, so we would likely have to deal with hordes of infected to get a plane.

We talked over the maps for most of an hour then started working on a plan to get a plane. Rachel checked in on Captain Helm, who was out cold with a weak dose of heroin in his veins to relieve the pain of his injuries, then took Mayo's place on watch aboard the cabin cruiser.

Mayo and Blake went swimming, recovering the M240 door gun from the crashed Pave Hawk and three OD green cans of ammo belts. We were pleased to see the cans had remained dry inside when Blake opened them on the deck of the houseboat.

Blake sent Mayo back into the water to scavenge tools and parts while he stripped the machine gun down for a thorough cleaning and oiling. While we didn't have any gun oil, we did have a can of WD-40 that I had found in the cruiser. Not perfect, but you make do with what you have. At least, it would provide enough lubrication to keep the gun from seizing up at the wrong time. I hoped.

Mayo kept surfacing next to us, bringing back tools, a large assortment of thin walled aluminum tubing and a good length of flex hose. Blake would stop cleaning the gun every time Mayo made a delivery, checking the items and giving him instructions on what else to look for. I had to give the young Airman credit. He never once complained or argued, just kept going back under and finding what Blake asked for.

Machine gun cleaned and reassembled, Blake set it aside and started working on the speedboat that Rachel and I had ridden over to them. First, he used the flex-hosing to extend the exhaust pipes down over the stern of the boat and into the water, securing them to the hull of the boat with metal straps and screws. He accomplished this with a lot of splashing and cursing, but when he had me start the engine after his modifications I was amazed at how quiet it was.

Next, he set to work with several lengths of the aluminum tubing and a large steel plate. He mounted the plate to the deck of the speedboat in the bow, between two thickly padded benches that lined each side all the way to the pointed nose of the boat. Plate firmly bolted to the deck, he and Mayo started attaching the tubing, spread at the bottom but meeting about four feet up from the deck and forming a crude teepee shape. They punched holes through the aluminum with a hand drill and gallons of sweat in the hot Georgia sun, then bolted the whole assembly together and to the plate.

Blake spent another two hours working on a piece of metal that he finally attached to the top of the teepee, then hoisted the M240 onto the makeshift pintle he had created, securing it with two nuts threaded onto a thick bolt and tightened against each other. This arrangement would allow the machine gun to move freely, but not come off the pintle without the nuts first being removed. Work completed, he dove into the water to wash off the sweat.

"Outstanding work, Tech Sergeant." I stuck out a hand and helped him climb back aboard the speedboat.

"Thank you, sir." He grinned and wiped water out of his eyes.

"One thing guys," I said. "Please stop siring me. I was a Master Sergeant, not an officer."

Anderson looked as surprised as a virgin on his wedding night. Blake let out a short bark of laughter. I had not bothered to correct their assumption earlier that I had been an officer when I was in the Army, but I just couldn't take all the "Sirs" anymore.

Anderson had shown himself to be one of those rare officers that actually listened to his more experienced men, so I didn't think I was going to have a problem with him trying to assume command. If I did, I'd deal with it. We were about to try and penetrate a hostile facility and make off with an airplane. This was my world, and I'd done something very similar before, minus hordes of infected that wanted to eat me.

"All right, let's get something to eat and then get some rest," I said, watching Anderson out of the corner of my eye to see if he was going to have a problem with me still giving orders. When he didn't make a peep, I continued. "We'll take two-hour watches, and I'll take first watch. We'll review the plan at 0100 hours and launch at 0130. Everyone good with that?"

Heads nodded all the way around, and Blake gave me a nod and a wink to let me know he was happy to have me in command.

An hour later I sat on the flying bridge of the cruiser, halfway through my watch, eating the Spartan meal that Rachel had brought up. She sat next to me, sipping from a bottle of water.

"Think we can pull this off?" She asked, stretching her long legs out and propping her feet up on the bridge railing.

"I think we've got a good shot at it," I answered around a mouthful of pork and beans. "However, we don't know how many infected are going to be waiting for us. The planes might not be fueled with no way to gas them up. There might not even be any planes there. We're going in with no intelligence, which is never a good thing, but it's the best we can do.

"Ideally, I'd take a quiet ride down there tonight to scope things out and delay the operation until tomorrow night. But, with the herd moving north that Max talked about, I don't think we have time. It's probably tonight or never."

Rachel finished her bottle of water and looked up at me.

"Well, you'd better not fuck it up," she grinned to let me know she was just yanking my chain.

A moment later she stood up to go check on Captain Helm before her watch started. The newly quieted speedboat started and before it reached the houseboat only a hundred feet away, I could no longer hear the exhaust.

38

I woke up at midnight, still tired and groggy, initially not remembering where I was. Looking over at the woman sleeping next to me, it took a moment for my mind to remember why I was seeing someone other than Katie. Then everything clicked back into place. I let out a quiet sigh and careful to not disturb Rachel, I climbed out of the bed. She had taken to sleeping with me ever since I had rescued her. There wasn't any cuddling or spooning. In fact, we never touched, but every time I woke up, there she was on the far side of the bed.

Standing, I stretched, and Dog jumped off the foot of the bed where he'd been curled into a surprisingly small ball for an animal his size. I made my way out of the salon and to the stern rail where I pissed over the side into the lake while Dog watched. Zipped up, I checked the flying bridge, glad to see Mayo on watch. He wore one of the sets of night vision goggles from the Pave Hawk and looked like an alien out of a low budget Sci-Fi flick from the 60s.

Climbing the short ladder, I joined him, wanting a cigarette but resisting. The flame from a lighter would destroy my night vision and could be seen for miles, standing out like a beacon to any hostiles. Mayo nodded when I slipped into the seat next to his but didn't seem to feel the need to talk.

The night was warm with a slight breeze, small wavelets marching across the lake's surface to softly slap against the cruiser's hull. The sound almost mesmerizing. Clouds obscured the moon, and it was nice and dark. Another reason to move tonight. We had two more sets of NVGs from the Pave Hawk and the darker the night, the more of an advantage we would have.

Less than a minute later I heard an engine start and settle to an almost inaudible rumble. I turned and peered through the darkness to where the speedboat was tied to the houseboat, but couldn't see anything. Mayo had turned as well to look and reported that Blake and the LT were on their way over before resuming his scan of the open lake.

It only took a moment for them to cross the short amount of open water and I felt a slight bump as they nosed up to the cruiser's stern and tied off. The engine cut off and first Anderson then Blake climbed over the rail. Slapping Mayo on the back I went below to greet them.

We met on the deck, and Rachel stepped into the doorway, yawning and rubbing the sleep from her eyes. It was too early to think about launching, so we made some coffee and sat out in the darkness and talked.

Anderson spoke about his family, glad that his parents were already gone and weren't having to live through the hell of the aftermath of the attacks. He had a sister who had moved to France the previous year to pursue her dream of becoming a painter, and he assumed she was OK since there was no word that Europe had been attacked.

We had already learned that Mayo was from Atlanta, having joined the Air Force to escape abject poverty with no opportunities. His mother was his only family, and he was sure she was either one of the infected or had died when Atlanta had burned.

When asked by Rachel, Blake told us he was from a big family in Brooklyn. That killed the conversation, and we sat sipping bitter coffee in silence for a bit. Tired of waiting, I decided that there was no reason we couldn't jump off a little earlier than planned. It was after 0030, 12:30 AM civilian time, and I called Mayo down to the deck so we could go over the rough and simple plan I had made.

We would all be on the cruiser, at first, heading south towards the marina with a slight bearing to the west to hopefully bring us close to the amphibious air service noted on the map. When we were about three miles from the shore, the cruiser would cut engines and go silent.

Anderson, Blake and I would move to the speedboat, Mayo and Rachel turning the cruiser around and returning to where we were currently anchored. I had originally wanted to take the speedboat the whole way, but Blake warned that the jury-rigged exhaust suppressors would only hold up for so long at any speed over about ten knots.

For the trip south he would loosen the retaining straps that were attached to the hull and pull the ends of the flex hose out of the water so the cruiser could tow the speedboat at a faster pace. The cruiser was a luxury boat and the people that could afford it didn't want to listen to a loud engine, so it was well muffled and relatively quiet at any speed under full throttle.

Once on the speedboat the three of us would make a low-speed run into the shore to look for a plane that could fly all of us out of there. Each of us would have NVGs, Blake manning the machine gun, me piloting the boat and Anderson along for the ride until we acquired a plane for him to fly. I didn't like leaving Rachel and Mayo without NVGs but didn't see a viable alternative. We needed them for combat, or hopefully to avoid combat, and all they had to do was pilot the big cruiser back across the lake and drop anchor.

With everyone acknowledging they were ready, I suited up in my tactical gear while Blake leaned over the stern of the speedboat and worked the flex hose exhaust tubes up out of the water. Climbing back aboard, he gave a thumbs up, stepped into the salon for a moment and returned with two lit cigarettes cupped in the palm of his hand.

Handing one to me, he met my eyes and gave me a nod, letting me know he was ready to go into battle with me. I glanced around the deck to make sure we were ready to go then climbed the ladder to the flying bridge, started the engine and hit the switch to raise the anchor.

The instrument panel gauges were covered with duct tape again and the night was dark as I spun the wheel to point us to the south and slowly fed in throttle. The big boat started moving, the speedboat in tow at the end of its tether and I kept advancing the throttle until a peek under the duct tape at the gauge showed we were making about eighteen knots. Rachel stood next to me on the bridge using a set of borrowed NVGs to scan the horizon for any threats. She hadn't said much since we woke up and was still uncharacteristically quiet.

"What's on your mind?" I asked, taking the last drag of the cigarette and crushing it out below the instrument panel where the faint light from the burning tobacco wouldn't be visible to anyone scanning the lake. She didn't say anything for a moment, then pushed the goggles up onto the top of her head and looked at me.

"Just remembering the last time you left me alone on the boat. No biggie. I've got Mayo and Dog this time so everything will be fine." I was trying to find the right thing to say, but she continued before I could speak.

"I'm worried you won't be coming back. You barely survived saving me, and I know you're still not close to a hundred percent. Not sure I want to try to survive this on my own." I didn't know what to say to that, so I settled for reaching out and taking her hand in mine. We stayed like that, holding hands, until I cut the throttles when the cruiser's navigation system showed we were three miles off the shore.

On the shore to our left was the camp Anderson had described, brightly lit and shining across the water. I raised the binoculars and took a look. Apparently the lights were a beacon for the infected, which pushed up against the barricades in throngs too large to even begin to count.

The walls protecting the camp looked to be made of boat trailers turned on their sides with steel plates welded to them and stacked two and three trailer widths high. On the inside of each trailer, a steel strut had been welded at a forty-five-degree angle from the higher edge of the trailer to the ground where it provided bracing against the constant push of the infected.

Makeshift watchtowers had been built, and I could hear the occasional report of a rifle as some sentry shot an infected. I was too far away to tell, but my guess was they were having to watch for and shoot the much more agile females when one would find a way to start climbing the outside of the barricade.

Still using the binoculars, I scanned the shore to the west, but it was too dark to make out any details, and the NVGs weren't any good at this distance. We'd have to get in close to the shore and hope the map wasn't wrong or just grossly out of date. I started to climb down the ladder, but Rachel stopped me with a hand on my arm. I met her eyes, smiled more jauntily than I felt, and quickly made my way down to the deck.

Blake was already in the speedboat, reconnecting the flex hoses and Anderson was nervously checking and re-checking his pistol's load. Mayo stood at the bottom of the ladder, waiting for me to clear the bridge. Stopping in front of him, I looked him in the eye.

"I'll keep her safe," he said.

I nodded, clapped him on the shoulder and herded Anderson into the speedboat. Blake had the exhaust back in place. As I settled into the driver's seat, he leaned over the bow rail and released the line tethering us to the cruiser. Reaching up, he pulled the charging lever on the machine gun, gave me a wicked grin and sat down. Anderson settled into the seat next to me, and I hit the boat's starter.

Rachel had followed me down to the cruiser's deck and with a wave, gave a push to get us clear of the larger boat. Returning the wave, I gave the motor a couple notches of throttle and headed to shore. Behind, I heard the cruiser's motor start.

I kept our speed down to just under ten knots until we were a mile from shore, then dropped us down to five knots to reduce our noise as much as possible. Next to me Anderson continually scanned the shore with a pair of binoculars that had come from the houseboat, looking for a seaplane depot. Half a mile from shore I cut the throttle back to idle and the boat slowed to only a couple of knots.

I was steering us parallel to the shore, heading away from the barricaded compound to give Anderson a good look when I heard the boat motor behind us. Looking over my shoulder, the NVGs let me clearly see a small boat heading out of the marina and in our general direction. Three men were on board, one driving and the other two sitting in the bow with rifles held pointing skyward.

They were still a good distance away, but the military grade NVGs allowed me to make out that they were also wearing night vision. I had no way of knowing if they'd managed to get their hands on some government issue hardware or if they were using the much lower resolution units that can be purchased at any sporting goods store. If they had military units, then they would spot us any moment. Otherwise, we were well outside their range.

Anderson suddenly sat up straighter and stared through the binoculars at the shore, then pointed excitedly.

"There," he said. "I can see a large hangar with a concrete apron that runs right down into the lake. That has to be it."

"Can you see any planes?" I asked, keeping my eyes on the approaching boat.

"No, but they could very well be in the hangar. If I had a hangar available, I wouldn't leave a plane sitting out in the weather."

I pushed my NVGs up onto my head and took the binoculars from him, looking where he pointed. He was right. A large hangar sat about fifty yards back from the edge of the lake with a concrete apron that ran from the hangar all the way down to the water. There was a large sign over the doors, but it was too dark to make out the lettering.

The place appeared to be deserted with no sign of survivors or infected. Making my decision, I bumped the throttle forward and pointed us at a small dock that jutted out into the lake at the edge of the apron.

"We've got a problem," Blake called out from the front of the boat. "The noise they're making is attracting infected, and they're bringing them right down the shore with them." He gestured at the boat that had appeared behind us.

I looked at the boat coming our way, its exhaust loud, then checked the shoreline to see dozens of infected stumbling along as they stared out across the water at the source of the noise. At their current rate, they'd be at the hangar just a few minutes after we arrived. Not good.

I had no idea how long it would take us to break into the hangar and get a plane ready to go. Anderson was confident that any plane we found would be fueled and ready to fly, but I didn't want to count on it. Shit!

Keeping the throttle where it was, I spun the wheel and pointed us out to the open lake. I didn't know if these guys were a patrol or just some assholes who decided to take a late night joy ride, but the last thing we needed was them bringing a pack of infected down on our heads while we were trying to get a plane in the air. This is what happens when you don't have time to do reconnaissance and gather intelligence.

We had just settled on a new course that would take us away from the shoreline when the sound of another motor roared from the direction of the marina. All of us looked to our right and saw a bass boat – what was it with these guys and bass boats? – quickly gaining speed and heading directly towards us. Three armed men accompanied the driver. One of them raised a giant spotlight and turned it on, swinging it in our direction. They'd spotted us from shore. Someone had some military issue hardware. Well, so did we.

"Light 'em up, Tech Sergeant," I said, spinning the wheel and accelerating to put the new boat directly in front of us.

Blake stood up, grasped the machine gun with both hands, swung it a little up and to the left to adjust and squeezed the trigger. The gun started hammering, and Blake adjusted fire as red tracers lanced out and splashed into the water to the boat's right. There were shouts of panic and the driver turned the wheel to try and avoid the incoming fire, but Blake adjusted with him and shredded the boat and the four men aboard.

We were all deafened after the hammering fire from the M240. I watched in silence as Blake's chest disintegrated in a spray of blood and his body pitched over the side into the water. The other boat had someone who could shoot!

I slammed the throttles to their stops, not worried about noise discipline any longer, pointed at the wheel and scrambled forward to man the machine gun as Anderson slipped into the seat I had just vacated. Standing behind the machine gun, I flexed my knees to absorb the motion of the boat and swung the barrel onto target as I pulled the trigger. The gun started hammering out rounds, and I used the tracers to walk my fire up and into their boat.

The heavy, high-velocity slugs destroyed everything they hit. Fiberglass, aluminum, flesh, bone; it didn't matter. They punched through everything, and I kept the fire up for a couple of seconds to make sure everyone in the boat was down for the count. One of the tracer rounds found the gas tank and the boat exploded in a bright flash and ear shattering boom. A few moments later flaming debris started raining down onto the water.

Letting off the trigger the barrel smoked heavily, the wind of our passage quickly cooling the weapon back down. I scanned around and didn't see any other threats, then looked for and spotted Blake's corpse floating in our wake. I motioned Anderson to slow down and come about, and moments later we slid up next to Blake, engines idling.

Unclipping a boat hook from the side rail I snagged the body, pulled it close and grabbed the NVGs off Blake's head. Tossing them into the boat, I let the body slip away and re-clipped the boat hook. I don't like leaving a fallen comrade behind, but trying to recover Blake's body and take it with us would almost undoubtedly cause our mission to fail, and failure would mean death for all of us at this point.

Anderson had pushed his NVGs up on his head and stared at me with eyes as big as saucers. I grabbed his shoulders and moved him to the passenger seat, jumping behind the wheel. We'd just alerted all the people in the camp as well as every infected for miles around to our presence, and we still had to steal a plane. Jamming the throttles forward I steered around the flaming wreckage of the other boat and aimed for the concrete apron.

The speedboat covered the water at a fast clip as we made a beeline for the seaplane hangar. As we approached, I could see infected swarming down the shoreline, still a good distance from the hangar, but closer than I was comfortable with. I shouted to Anderson to be heard above the roar of the engine and the wind whipping past our faces.

"I'm going to pull right up to that small dock. You get the hangar open and find us a ride. I'll hold off the infected."

"How do I get in if the hangar's locked?" He shouted back.

"You have a pistol. Shoot the lock off if you have to. Watch your back, too. There might be infected inside."

Anderson nodded he understood and a moment later I cut the throttle as we roared up to the dock. The boat settled and slammed hard into the wood, snapping off the stainless steel railing that ran along the top of the bow rail.

Anderson was out in a flash, up on the dock and running for the hangar. I checked the area through the NVGs and didn't see any infected yet, but I could hear the screams from females coming our way.

Checking on his progress, I saw Anderson reach the hangar and tug on a man-door that was set into the larger rolling doors. It didn't budge, and he didn't waste any time, stepping back, drawing his nine mm pistol and firing several rounds into the knob and deadbolt. Grabbing the door, he yanked and it flew open.

He disappeared inside, and I had to turn my attention back to the business at hand as female infected appeared around a building a couple of hundred yards down the shore. I also noted the noise of several boat motors, but they sounded to still be a fair distance away.

Tilting the machine gun on its pintle, I fired four very short bursts and was rewarded with all of the females in view falling to the ground, legs and bodies destroyed. I shifted attention to the lake and spotted three small boats heading my way, each packed with men.

They were still too far away to effectively engage with the machine gun, but it wouldn't be long before I would need to deal with them. More infected started appearing. I waited briefly, giving them time to cluster together as they tended to do, then opened fire again and took out eight of them as the machine gun ran dry.

Tossing the empty ammo can overboard, I opened the next one in line, grabbed the end of the ammo belt and fed it into the gun. While I had been distracted doing this, another dozen infected came into sight. I cut them down before swiveling the gun towards the lake and sending some tracer fire towards the fast approaching boats.

I've been shot at in the dark by machine guns with tracers, and I'm not ashamed to admit it is downright terrifying. If you've had any exposure to weapons at all, you know what a single bullet can do to you, and the thought of hundreds of them coming your way in the span of a few seconds will make even the bravest soul dive for cover. So it was with the boats, each driver executing a fast turn to try and put a big cushion between them and me.

Glancing over my shoulder at the hangar, I was frustrated to not see the big doors rolling open yet. I had to trust Anderson to do his job, and I had to do mine. Three more bursts from the machine gun took down another ten infected; then another burst out into the lake to keep the boats a respectful distance away.

I moved my attention back to the shore and had to fire more bursts to cut down the next pack of females who ran screaming towards me, then paused and stared as a solid mass of infected appeared downrange. At the same time, bullets started smacking into the dock in front of me, a few of them also finding the speedboat, splintering the fiberglass hull where they struck.

Swinging back to the lake, I pulled the trigger and walked the stream of bullets into the closest boat. Men dove overboard as their boat started coming apart, then I found the gas tank and another explosion lit the night.

The bullets coming my way stopped as the remaining boats moved farther out into the lake and I swung back to the infected and started laying down fire. Infected fell before the withering fire from the machine gun, then it went silent, another belt used up. Cursing, I fumbled the empty case out of the way, opened the last remaining can and fed the final belt into the gun.

"Move your ass, Anderson!" I screamed over my shoulder, hoping he would hear me inside the large hangar.

Mowing down more infected, it was obvious I didn't have enough ammunition to hold my position much longer. I was maintaining fire discipline, using very short bursts and risked a glance out at the lake to make sure the boats weren't creeping back into shore.

They were keeping their distance, but I knew as soon as I ran out of ammo they would make a dash forward and light me up. Just as I hit a green tracer, telling me I was halfway through my last belt of ammo, I heard a metallic squeal as Anderson pushed open the hangar doors.

"Let's go!" He shouted, shoving one of the doors the last few feet before running back to get the second one open.

More infected were showing up by the second. Hundreds of them were now shambling my way. A large group diverted towards Anderson, having been attracted by his shout and the squeal of the hangar doors opening. Two packs of females sprinted out ahead of the main group, one towards Anderson and the other towards me.

With less than half a belt of ammo left I swung the machine gun and mowed down the pack approaching Anderson. Switching to my rifle, I started firing on the pack running straight at me to conserve the last of the heavier ammo.

In three round burst mode, I burned through a full magazine, slapped in a fresh one and used most of it to neutralize the females. As I brought down the last one, bullets started smacking into the dock a few feet from me. I looked out at the lake in time to see the muzzle flash from the shooter that was hoping for a lucky shot.

I had to decide between the shooter in the boat and the herd of infected that was almost to the edge of the concrete apron. I didn't have enough ammo left for the machine gun to engage both.

My decision was made for me when I heard first one then a second airplane engine sputter to life. Anderson had gotten a plane started and was taxiing out of the hangar, propellers spinning up and engines roaring. He'd found a fairly large twin engine plane with big floats. Underneath each float were two sets of wheels so the plane could take off, land and taxi on a paved surface.

As the plane fully emerged from the hangar, a bullet sparked off the concrete too close to it for my comfort. Slinging my rifle, I swiveled the machine gun out to the lake and pressed the trigger, using the tracer rounds to walk the stream of lead up and into the boat. Perhaps they thought they were out of range at close to eight hundred yards, but the M240 chewed up the boat and the men in it then ran dry.

One of the lessons the Army hammers into you during training is that you never leave a functioning weapon behind on the battlefield unless you're willing to have your enemy recover the weapon and use it against you. Even though I was out of ammo didn't mean there wasn't someone in their camp that had some or knew where to get some.

Grabbing a thick cloth I'd brought for this purpose, I wrapped it around the sizzling hot barrel, pushed the release and twisted ninety degrees. The barrel came free from the machine gun's receiver, and I threw it as far out into the lake as I could. Not the best way to dispose of it, but it was too hot to put in my pack, and I still had infected to fight before I could catch my flight.

Climbing onto the dock, I started firing at the front ranks of the herd as I moved towards the concrete ramp where it met the water's edge. Every time I pulled the trigger, an infected fell down dead, but there were already more infected in sight than I had bullets. My goal was to drop the front ranks, so those behind them stumbled and tripped over their bodies, slowing the herd enough for us to escape.

The plane's engines revved as Anderson headed for the water, but the infected were approaching too quickly for me to stop shooting. If they cut off the open ramp, we were screwed. The propellers, spinning at thousands of revolutions per minute, would shatter upon impact with an infected. The human body has a lot of very hard bone in it, and unlike in the movies, propellers don't dice up the bad guy to end the fight then keep on spinning like nothing happened.

I ran across the ramp, directly towards the herd, waving Anderson to the water behind me. Firing as I ran, the infected kept dropping, but there were too many of them, and they were within twenty yards of me as the plane passed behind.

Dropping two more shambling males with the last rounds in my magazine, I let the rifle drop on its sling, turned and ran for the airplane as the front of the floats hit the water. I never saw the female that tackled me from behind as I reached the plane.

We went down hard, my hands reaching out and grabbing one of the struts that connected the plane to the float. She started to slide down my legs but was able to wrap her arms around my ankles and hold on as the plane dragged us out into the lake. The pain from the wounds in my chest and left arm was like a searing hot bolt of lightning, but I managed to hold on as Anderson leaned across the cockpit and popped the door open for me.

The plane was moving at taxi speed, about eight knots, and my legs and the female holding on were in the water, putting more drag on my battered body than I could withstand. Taking a deep breath in preparation for going under, I let go of the strut. Already fifty feet off shore, we were in deeper water, and both of us went down, the female taking advantage of the change to start trying to claw her way up my body.

Kicking, I felt my heavy boots connect, but the water slowed and softened the blows to the point they were ineffective against the raging woman. Still kicking to try and break free, I fumbled on my chest for the Ka-Bar knife, hand finally grasping the hilt and yanking the wicked blade out of its sheath.

The infected had not only managed to hang on but had worked her way up to my waist. My heavy clothing and equipment were all that was protecting me from her repeated attempts to bite. Reaching down with my weakened left hand, I grabbed a handful of hair and held her head back as I stabbed the knife into her throat, twisting and cutting until she went limp and slid off my body.

Kicking her corpse away, I started to try to swim to the surface. But, in the dark water, I was disoriented and didn't know which way was up. My lungs were on fire and screaming for me to take a breath, but I calmed my mind for a moment and exhaled a small amount of air.

I was surprised when the bubbles tracked across my chin then down my body as they headed for the surface. I was upside down and had almost started swimming deeper.

Switching directions, I kicked hard for the surface. Breaking through, I exhaled and gulped in air. Looking around frantically for the plane, I spotted it another three hundred feet off shore. Anderson saw me in his NVGs and revved the engines to come to me. I grabbed a handle on the float as the plane slid by and scrambled up out of the water then into the cabin. I flopped across the row of seats behind the pilot after slamming the door behind me.

"Go!" I shouted, but Anderson was already turning the plane towards open water and had pushed the throttles to the firewall.

The plane responded sluggishly at first but quickly gained speed as the floats came up out of the water and skimmed the surface. Quicker than I expected the vibration from contact with the lake ceased and Anderson pulled back hard on the stick, gaining altitude and turning as sharply as he could.

There was a metallic ping, followed by the sound of rushing air, as a bullet hole appeared in the floor of the plane only inches from my head. A matching hole was in the roof where the bullet exited. Anderson kept us turning and dropped altitude until we were barely skimming the surface of the lake. His evasive maneuvering must have worked because we didn't take any more bullets that I could see.

39

The flight back to pick up Rachel, Mayo, Helm and Dog only took a few minutes. Anderson never got us more than fifty feet in the air. Landing on the water was smoother than I expected, the plane decelerating quickly when the floats hit the surface. We taxied to the cabin cruiser, sitting dark where Mayo had anchored.

Anderson cut the engines and let our momentum take us the rest of the way until the floats bumped the back of the boat. NVGs on, I could see Rachel standing in the doorway to the salon, Dog at her side, watching as Mayo scrambled over the stern rail and made a line fast to each of the plane's front struts.

"Nice flying."

I slapped Anderson on the shoulder, happy to have survived another fight and ready to get loaded up and back in the air.

"Thanks, but I need some help here," Anderson answered, pain obvious in his voice.

I looked at him through the NVGs but didn't see anything wrong. Pulling them off, I reached up and snapped on an overhead map light and immediately saw the blood staining the arm of his flight suit around a large, ragged tear in the fabric.

"Fucking infected was in the damn plane. I opened the door and reached in to check the instruments and he bit me, right through the flight suit."

I leaned over and popped the door open and yelled for Rachel. She stuck her head in the door, saw Anderson's injury and shouted for Mayo to grab the first aid kit out of the salon. Climbing into the plane, Rachel elbowed me out of the way so she could check Anderson. I made myself useful by taking the first aid kit from Mayo and handing it to her before exiting the plane.

"Where's Tech Sergeant Blake?" Mayo asked, peering around me into the plane.

"I'm sorry," I said. "He didn't make it. We got into a firefight with the people from the camp and he took a bullet."

Mayo nodded his understanding and lowered himself to a seat on one of the benches lining the cruiser's stern deck. I sat down across from him and absently scratched Dog's ears while waiting for Rachel to finish treating Anderson. A few minutes later they climbed out of the plane, Anderson's flight suit cut away from his lower arm, which was heavily bandaged.

"How is he?" I asked Rachel.

"The bite was deep," she answered, sitting down next to me. "I'm pretty sure there's nerve damage, and he lost a surprising amount of blood considering no arteries were involved. Infection is the biggest concern right now."

"Infection? You mean..."

"No," She cut me off. "Not that kind of infection. He would already have turned if that were the case. Just the good old fashioned kind. The infection rate for bites from a human are normally in the seventy percent range, but considering these things are eating anything and everything... Well, God only knows what kind of bacteria are swimming around in their mouths."

"Can he still fly?"

"Yes, I can fly," Anderson spoke up before Rachel could answer me. "I can get us out of here. No problem. Just some numbness in my arm and hand but that won't stop me from flying."

"Alright. Let's get loaded up and get the hell out of here before any more assholes from the camp show up."

We all stood. Rachel and Anderson started gathering all the gear in the cabin cruiser while Mayo and I took their ski boat to collect Helm from the houseboat. Helm was a big man, about the same size as me. It took everything both of us had to carry him from his bunk to the small boat, then once we were back to the plane, up and into the cabin. When we finally got him situated and strapped in we were both drenched with sweat. Rachel checked him over and said he was as ready to go as he'd ever be.

Untying the lines holding us to the cruiser, I called for Dog. He leapt into the cabin and settled down next to Rachel in the second row of seats, Anderson and Mayo occupying the pilot and co-pilot positions. I held onto a wing strut and, with one foot on a float, pushed the plane away from the boat and climbed into the cabin to settle in next to Dog and Rachel.

Anderson started the engines and let them idle for a few minutes as the plane drifted a safe distance from the anchored boat, then added some power and lined us up with the open lake. "Everyone ready?" He asked, eyes scanning the gauges.

"Let's get the hell out of here," I answered, looking out the window at the cabin cruiser that had been my home and safe haven for what seemed like months but was less than two weeks.

"Here we go," Anderson said and shoved the throttles forward. The plane responded and quickly gained speed, lifting smoothly off the water and rapidly gaining altitude.

We were all quiet, each lost in our own private thoughts as the plane continued to climb and turn towards the north. I looked around at the world below us as we gained altitude. To the southeast, there was an angry red glow that had to be the remnants of the fire that had consumed Atlanta.

Closer to us, and very visible, were the bright lights of the camp on the south shore of the lake, but other than that one location there was not a single electric light to be seen in any direction. The world was as dark as it had been a thousand years ago. As we made our way north there was the occasional campfire visible below, but so few for how many people had lived in the area.

We had been in the air about half an hour when Anderson started looking around outside the plane, then adjusted some knobs on the console and spoke into the headset microphone hanging in front of his mouth. He carried on a conversation for a few minutes, then made a slight adjustment to our heading.

Rachel poked me in the arm and pointed out the window on her side of the plane. Hanging slightly behind and above us was another aircraft, only visible when its anti-collision lights flashed.

"We've got an escort," Anderson said loud enough for all of us to hear. "There's a pair of F-

16s out there, one on our left wing and I'm guessing the second is on our six (directly behind us) to make sure we don't do anything stupid."

"Do we need to be worried?" I asked, leaning forward and getting a grunt from Dog as I disturbed his sleep.

"I don't think so," he answered. "I've given them a brief version of who we are and where we're headed. They're re-routing us, won't allow us into Nashville. Makes sense with everything that's going on. Guess we should be glad they asked questions before firing a missile up our ass."

"So where are we going?"

"Arnold Air Force Base. It's about eighty miles southeast of Nashville. We should be there in about another 20 minutes."

I didn't have a warm fuzzy about being diverted to an Air Force base, but I could understand why the military didn't want us flying into Nashville. Just because we said we were red-blooded Americans didn't mean we weren't really Chinese agents loaded down with either a nuclear bomb or more nerve agent. We'd just have to deal with the military bureaucracy when we landed.

Fifteen minutes later we started descending. I peered ahead out of the windshield but saw no lights. It took me a moment to remember that all US Military installations had to be on a war footing, and that meant blackout conditions at night. Not that it mattered as everything functioned off of GPS these days, but there was still no reason to light up your base like a Christmas tree and make it even easier for the bad guys.

As we continued to descend, Anderson maintained a conversation with who I assumed was an air traffic controller on the ground. Soon, directly in front of us and a couple of miles ahead, runway lights came on, unmistakable against the dark terrain. Anderson brought us down smoothly, the fighter jets roaring overhead as we touched the tarmac, slowing quickly and turning left onto the first taxiway we encountered. Waiting for us was a Hummer with a flashing orange light on the roof and a large illuminated sign on the back that simply read 'FOLLOW ME'.

I could make out the dim outlines of dozens of fighter jets as we followed the guide down a taxiway that paralleled a row of hangars that were all closed up tightly and completely dark. Ahead was a gap in the row of jets and the Hummer turned into it, proceeding through the doors of a massive hangar that was completely dark inside.

Anderson had turned off the plane's landing lights when we started following the guide. The Hummer was running with just parking lights and the orange beacon on the roof. When we pulled into the hangar the driver shut off his lights, and Anderson cut the engines, leaving the propellers to spin down in the dark hangar.

From behind I heard the rumble of the big metal doors closing, ending with a dull boom as they met in the middle of the opening. Immediately, lights hanging from the ceiling flickered into dim existence, quickly brightening as they warmed up. Another Hummer waited for us. This one marked Security Forces in bold black lettering on a white background, which was the Air Force version of Military Police.

Why they had to call them something different I never understood. But ever since breaking off from the Army and becoming its own branch of the military right after WWII, the Air Force had worked hard to distinguish itself from the Army much like an ungrateful child. Beside the Hummer, sat an Air Force ambulance, two corpsmen standing in front of it with a gurney at the ready. Anderson must have told them to be waiting to take Captain Helm to the base hospital.

A young Captain stood next to the Hummer while a Staff Sergeant and Senior Airman carrying M4 rifles stood to his side waiting for us. We popped the doors and climbed out, Dog jumping down and coming over to stand between Rachel and me as the corpsmen wheeled the gurney up to the plane and climbed aboard to check on their patient.

Mayo held back by the plane as Anderson approached the MP Captain – I know, Security Forces, but I wasn't about to think of him as SF which meant something entirely different in the Army – came to attention and saluted. The Captain returned the salute, and they talked for a few minutes with frequent glances in my direction.

Anderson led the Captain over, the two MPs following, and introduced him as Captain Roach. At one point I would have had to salute the kid, but now I wasn't in the military chain of command and could act like a civilian and get away with a simple handshake. We all watched as the corpsmen carefully lifted Helm out of the aircraft.

He was strapped to a backboard, and they expertly maneuvered him through the door and onto the gurney. They wasted no time in getting him into the ambulance. Driving to the back of the hangar, they passed through a door just large enough for the vehicle to fit. It closed quickly behind them.

"Folks," Roach said, addressing Rachel and me both. "Welcome to Arnold Air Force Base. And thank you for assisting Lieutenant Anderson. We appreciate your patriotism."

He appreciated our patriotism? Seriously? Who the hell talks like that?

"We've got accommodations for you, hot showers, food and clean clothes. The intelligence staff wants to speak with you first; then we'll get you settled. I do need you to surrender your weapons to my men before we go any farther. Civilians aren't allowed to carry firearms on base."

Roach turned slightly at the waist and motioned the two MPs – oops, Security Forces members – forward with a little wave of his hand.

"Not going to happen," I said. My rifle was slung across my chest, and my right hand was resting on the pistol grip, index finger adjacent to the trigger guard and thumb on the fire selector switch, which was currently on SAFE.

The two MPs stopped, and the Airman started to raise his M4 in my direction, but I was faster on the draw, getting my rifle up and sighted on him before he knew what was happening. His eyes opened wide in fear, and he froze in place.

"Son, you do not want to find out what will happen if you point a weapon at me," I said, stepping to the side to put some distance between Rachel and me in case bullets did start coming my way. The Staff Sergeant started to slide off to the side but froze when Dog stepped forward with a low warning growl and Rachel drew her pistol, keeping the muzzle in the low ready position.

"Enough," Anderson said, stepping forward and placing himself directly in front of my rifle. "No one is going to shoot anyone, and everyone is going to keep their weapons. Let's relax."

"You're out of line, Lieutenant," Roach said, but he didn't step into the line of fire. "These civilians will surrender their weapons, and if you interfere any further, I'll have you brought up on charges for insubordination."

Anderson looked at Roach with his mouth open in shock. I didn't blame him. I had encountered officers like Captain Roach in my day and knew we were dealing with someone who would resort to us actually shooting at each other in order to save face. However, I didn't care.

In a normal world, I would have willingly surrendered my weapons to them. But this wasn't a normal world, and being unarmed could very well be the difference between life and death, even in the middle of an Air Force base.

"Lower your goddamn weapons and stand down!" A commanding voice rang out from the shadows in the back of the hangar.

Heavy footsteps came forward, and a large man wearing an Army uniform and a Colonel's eagle stepped into the light. All of the Air Force personnel snapped to attention, and I slowly lowered my rifle and motioned Rachel to holster her pistol. The Colonel walked right up in front of me and looked me in the eye for a long moment. The name tape on his uniform blouse read Crawford and he wore Airborne and Special Forces tabs as well.

"Captain, you and your men are dismissed. Leave your vehicle." The Colonel remained facing me and didn't see the look of disdain he received from Captain Roach, and a second later the look of hatred I received.

"Yes, sir!" Roach snapped out and turned to depart with his men.

"Thank you for your hospitality, Captain." I was surprised to hear the barb come from Rachel, and wasn't surprised to hear the rebuke she received from the Colonel.

"Knock that shit off, ma'am." He barked, still maintaining eye contact with me. He stood rock still until we heard a door slam at the back of the hangar, then relaxed and extended his hand to me.

"Jack Crawford," He said. I liked him immediately. A full bird Colonel that can introduce himself without feeling the need to include his rank was my kind of officer.

"John Chase," I said, taking the offered hand. "Thank you for that."

He waved it away and stepped over to introduce himself to Rachel and even bent to give Dog an ear scratch after getting an approving sniff of the back of his hand. Noticing Anderson and Mayo for seemingly the first time he told them to stand easy – meaning they could relax as much as possible with a Colonel in their presence – then pulled out a pack of cigarettes and offered them around before lighting up. I was the only taker, and cigarettes burning we wandered over to the Hummer where he leaned on the front fender as we talked.

Colonel Crawford commanded the 5th Special Operations Group (SOG) based at Fort Campbell, Kentucky. Most of his operators were deployed when the attacks came and were now on hold where they were until the remnants of the government decided how best to punish our attackers. He happened to be transiting through Arnold AFB on a flight from a secure government facility when he heard about our inbound flight. Curiosity got the best of him, and he came to see whom we were.

I told him my story or, at least, the highlights.

"When did you serve?" He asked. Not, 'did you serve'. Even now I guess I wore the look that was obvious to another soldier. I told him and gave the generic answer when asked about my MOS – Military Occupational Specialty – of 11B or infantryman.

Technically that was true as I had started out as an infantryman before applying and being accepted first into Ranger School then progressing from there. My clothing covered tattoos that would have answered his questions in more detail, but I felt OK giving the answer. I didn't know why I wanted to stay under the military's radar, but something was telling me to play it low key.

He was also curious about Rachel, but I evaded the questions as best I could, not wanting to go into the details of what she had been through. Standing close to us, listening, Rachel got the idea. Stepping forward, she linked her arm through mine.

"Put it this way, Colonel. We've been together since we met at his hotel in Atlanta." She gave a coy smile, leaned her head onto my shoulder and let him draw whatever conclusion he wanted. I could see the wheels turning behind his eyes, but he apparently decided to let it go for now.

"OK then," he pushed off from the fender and stood up straight. "We should get you checked in with the intel guys so you can get them taken care of, then get some chow and some rest. Hop in." He gestured at the Security Forces Hummer with his thumb, waved Anderson and Mayo over and climbed behind the wheel.

40

Colonel Crawford drove straight to a large building on the far side of the base, parking in a spot reserved for a Major somebody. The four-story building was substantial looking, as most structures on military installations are. It was built of all red brick with a concrete porch running the full width of the front. Heavy, Roman style columns painted a gleaming white supported the four-story high roof that extended out over the porch. All the windows were dark, and as we got closer, it was obvious they were covered on the inside with blackout curtains.

Two Air Force MPs – oops – stood on either side of the front entrance. They snapped to attention when the Colonel was close enough for them to see his uniform in the dark, then one of them stiffly reached out and held the door open for us.

Crawford strode into the dark vestibule either like he owned the place or he was attacking it, I wasn't quite sure which. He waited for all of us to enter the building and the door to close behind us, then brushed aside the blackout curtain and led us down a brightly lit hall.

He stopped at an unmarked door that was closed and locked, knocked loudly and stood waiting. The impatience oozed out of him and as soon as the door started to open he pushed through, waving for us to follow. The room was actually a series of large rooms connected together and was well staffed even at this hour.

Anderson and Mayo were met by an Air Force Master Sergeant, who led them down a long hall that opened up to our left. He placed each of them in separate rooms that opened off the hall then returned to gather us. Rather than straight to an interview room, he led us to his desk where we were each asked to place our right hand on a palm reader that sat on the edge of the desk and was connected to his PC via a long USB cable.

Rachel went first, the device scanning her hand and fingerprints in only a few seconds, then it was my turn. With a sigh, I rested my right hand on the backlit glass plate, and the machine flashed green when it had read my identity. Crawford stood behind us, waiting patiently now, as the Intel clerk stared at his monitor waiting for the results.

"Ms. Miles, welcome to Arnold Air Force Base," he said when the system returned data on her scan.

I wondered how many databases the military was tied into now. Probably everything.

"Thank you."

Rachel gave him her best smile, and he blushed slightly before focusing back on his monitor. Almost two full minutes later he blinked in surprise and looked up.

"Colonel, his data is classified above my clearance. You'll need to enter your credentials." He stood up, gave me a questioning look and moved far enough away that he couldn't see the monitor.

Crawford came around and sat in the empty chair, looked away in thought for half a second then typed in what I assumed was a user ID and password. He then stood and turned the palm reader towards him, placed his right hand on it and hit a button on the keyboard with his left index finger.

When the light glowed green, he sat back down and stared at the monitor. And stared some more, then scrolled with the mouse and stared some more. Apparently satisfied with the results he clicked the mouse a few times and nodded to the clerk who returned to his desk.

"Ranger, Green Beret, assigned to Operational Detachment Delta. Saw action in Afghanistan, East Germany, Honduras and Nicaragua with a whole string of missions that are classified even higher than my clearance. Infantry my ass. I didn't think so," he grumbled.

I could only offer a sheepish grin in response.

“You’re Delta Force?” The clerk blurted out, then slammed his mouth shut and busied himself with his computer when Crawford gave him a look that could freeze iron.

“I hope you’re still going to be able to grin after I tell you this,” Crawford smiled. “The President has ordered the recall of all former military personnel, with no exceptions granted. Welcome back to the US Army, Master Sergeant.”

What a bag of dicks!

Continue the adventure with Crucifixion: V Plague Book 2, available now from Amazon!

Made in the USA
Middletown, DE
28 August 2024

59947900R00208